A fire was growing inside Lilah. It burned and burned. The only way to get rid of it was to light something else up—Jules. She'd incinerate her. When she was done with Jules, Carter would see that he'd been wrong to have ever been charmed by the girl. He'd remember that *forever* meant forever. He'd understand that Lilah was where his heart belonged.

WIC KED GAM ES

a novel by

SEAN OLIN

KATHERINE TEGEN BOOKS
An Imprint of HarperCollins Publishers

Katherine Tegen Books is an imprint of HarperCollins Publishers.

Wicked Games

Library of Congress Control Number: 2014933030
ISBN 978-0-06-219238-7

Typography by Carla Weise
15 16 17 18 19 PC/RRDH   10 9 8 7 6 5 4 3 2 1
❖
First paperback edition, 2015

PROLOGUE

On their third date, way back in freshman year, Carter Moore and Lilah Bell spent the evening at Harpoon Haven, the small amusement park that Dream Point had erected near the beach ten years earlier to entice tourists away from Miami. They ate cotton candy until their tongues turned blue. They rode the Ferris wheel and did the bumper cars three times in a row. Carter popped five balloons at one of the dart games and won Lilah a stuffed lion that was so large, she had to carry it with two hands.

When ten p.m. hit and their curfews drew near, neither of them wanted the date to end. They wandered the promenade that wove between the palm trees and across the plush green lawn along the edge of Dream Point's sparkling white beach.

"Full moon tonight," said Carter. "It's beautiful. The way the moonlight glimmers off the sand. We don't get this sort of thing in Savannah."

Carter had only just moved to town for the start of the school year. There'd been something preppy about him, but a hip preppiness—it was a style choice, not a symptom of uptightness. He wore khakis and gingham shirts, and he parted his shaggy, not-quite-short brown hair on the side—so different from the surfer dudes and football players and fashion-obsessed Cubans who made up the majority of Christopher Columbus High School's population.

"Well, you've only been here for a month," Lilah responded. "When you've lived here your whole life, you start to take all this beauty for granted. You need someone else to remind you to see it."

"I mean, look at how high the waves are coming in tonight. And how much power they seem to have. That's because of the moon. When it's a full moon the tide's just so much stronger."

Lilah readjusted the stuffed lion in her arms. She really could see the beauty in Dream Point tonight. It was like the old town she'd known her entire life had been transformed into the most magical place on earth. "I wish I could see this town through your eyes all the time," she said. "The way you talk about it, everything's just so much more alive. Maybe it's 'cause you're into nature and science and stuff."

Carter gazed at the beach for a moment, and Lilah wondered what he was seeing—something much more nuanced than the simple lapping of the waves against the beach that she saw, she was sure. She sensed a deep seriousness moving behind his clear, hazel eyes.

"I'll make a deal with you," he said finally. "When I notice things, I'll point them out for you. I'll help you remember the beauty. Cool?"

"Absolutely," said Lilah. She felt like she was seeing some special secret place in him, like he was showing a tiny bit of the sensitive, attentive person hidden beneath his tan skin. She felt very lucky in that moment and she wondered what she could do to prove she was worth the attention he was showing her. Then she had an inspiration.

"Let's go down to the water," she said.

"I thought the beach closed at eight."

"So?"

"Won't we get in trouble?"

"You worried? It's not like they enforce that rule," said Lilah.

Carter ran his hand through his sandy hair and grimaced nervously.

"Okay," she said, "how 'bout if I dare you?"

Before Carter could either reject or accept the challenge, she threw the lion into his arms and quickly pulled her wavy light-brown hair up in a ponytail.

"Race!" she said, and then she took off, her flip-flops clacking along the concrete of the promenade, the knee-length purple jersey dress she wore flapping behind her.

He chased after her, holding the lion with two hands above his head and trying to make up distance, but she was an athlete, a swimmer—she'd been on the team since sixth grade—and even in her flip-flops she could pack a lot of speed in her powerful legs. They made their way down onto the beach, churning up cascades of sand under their feet. There was no way Carter could catch up. Lilah was just too fast. And he was wearing boat shoes and long pants, not the sort of thing for sprinting.

Turning around, Lilah ran backward. She slowed her pace until Carter came within a few yards of her, and then she matched his speed, teasing him, just out of his reach.

"Come on, slowpoke," she said. "You gonna let a girl beat you?" She couldn't remember the last time she'd felt so free, and she couldn't hide the grin that spread across her face.

Finally, Carter threw the lion in her direction, and she instinctively stopped and reached out to catch it.

In that instant, he was able to leap and wrap his arms around her waist. They both fell to the sand, laughing, as the lion tumbled away from them.

"God, that was fun," said Carter, between heavy pants.

"So much fun," she said. "See, that's what I can do. If you keep reminding me that there's beauty in the world, I'll keep daring you to go out into it and be a little wild."

"Deal," he said.

He was lying on top of her, his chin on her breastbone, and for a brief moment, their stares lingered in each other's eyes. Then he rolled off her and gazed up at the sky, and she wondered why he hadn't kissed her then. Maybe he was shy, less sure of himself than she'd thought.

Eventually, they gathered themselves and stood up. Carter dumped the sand out of his boat shoes. He shook out the short-sleeve green linen shirt he was wearing and did a little wiggly dance trying to get the sand out of his tan pants. Lilah found her flip-flops where they'd scattered, and she brushed off the lion. They walked back to the manicured grass that buffered the beach from Shore Road and began heading the long way back along the promenade toward the center of town.

"So, I guess that's it," she said. "Time to go home."

"Oh, I don't know," Carter said, smiling at her softly. He checked the time on his Gucci watch. "We've already blown our curfew. What's the worst that could happen?"

"Let's sit for a while, then."

They found a bench and Lilah set the lion down and they watched the tide roll in, talking through the night.

He told her about Savannah, Georgia, where he'd lived before his parents divorced and he and his mother had moved to Dream Point. He talked about rap music—Lil Wayne, Outkast, Jay-Z, and Snoop—and the variations in the sound and style and attitude toward the world depending on which region of the country the artist came from. Lilah could hear his deep, overriding passion for the music in the force and timbre of his voice. She could see it in the way his whole body got involved as he illustrated the difference between an East Coast beat and a West Coast beat and a Chicago beat and a Dirty Southern beat.

And he listened, too, as Lilah told him about her friends from the swim team—Kaily and Margarita and Teresa—and how terribly, terribly much winning meant to her. She talked about her parents and how weirdly awkward and formal they were.

"They're like people from an alien ancient culture where high tea and the church coffee hour are the center of life," she said. "I mean, they get dressed up to go to the mall. And my mother. You've never seen anybody so anxious. You can see it in her eyes. They dart all over the place, everywhere except at the thing she's supposed to be paying attention to. She's so worried about what people think. And she does it to me, too. It's unbearable sometimes. She's just so high-strung."

"That must put a whole lot of pressure on you," Carter said.

Lilah's hand had been resting on the bench between them, and he reached out and placed two fingers over her thumb, testing to see if she'd accept the comfort he was offering her. When she did and he knew it was okay, he went ahead and held her hand.

They let the silence and the salty sea air wash over them. There was something so comfortable about it. Lilah felt like she'd been holding his hand her whole life and had only just now realized it.

The next five minutes felt like they lasted forever. Their heads stutter-stepped inch by inch toward each other. They slowly stopped watching the ocean and began to watch the deep seas in each other's eyes. Then their faces were touching, just barely, and then they were kissing, arms wrapped around each other, pressing the emotions that had been building up inside themselves onto each other's bodies.

"I've been wanting to do that all night," he told her. His face had gone deep red.

Leaning in close, Lilah whispered, "Me too." She nuzzled her smooth cheek against his, just for a second, and he felt the ticklish sensation on his skin work its way all the way down into his stomach.

They laced their fingers together and gazed into each other's eyes again, and then they both chuckled, embarrassed.

There were things Lilah was afraid to say to Carter, small admissions about her insecurity. She still marveled at the fact that he'd asked her out—she didn't think of herself as the prettiest or most popular girl in school. She had freckles and plain brown eyes, and she could never seem to get her wavy not-quite-blond hair to go in the direction she wanted it to.

"Why me?" she said suddenly, not meaning for the words to come out of her mouth.

He thought for a moment before letting himself speak. "You've got a spark in you. Like a drive, you know what I mean? Like the way you convinced me to break the rules and run out onto the beach tonight. I'm always so worried about doing the right thing that I wouldn't have dared do that without you." He thought for another moment, taking in the smooth skin of her cheek and the sleek swimmer's body she hid under her loose jersey dress, and then he let himself say it: "And you're crazy hot and you don't even know it."

Embarrassed, she grimaced ironically. She looked away, then back to him.

"You know, every girl in school is curious about you," she said.

He blushed. "Really?"

"Yeah."

"I find that hard to believe."

"It's true, though," she said. "You're different from the other boys in Dream Point. You're, like, a gentleman." Then she felt a kind of shame, like she'd spilled an important secret and if he knew there were options, he'd lose interest in her and find some flighty, sexy other girl to spend his time with.

"Well, they can't have me," he said.

"You mean that?"

"Yeah. Here. I'll prove it." He took a Swiss Army knife out of his pocket and started carving in the bench between them. He shielded what he was doing with his left hand.

"Breaking the rules again," teased Lilah as she watched him work.

Looking up and smiling in her direction, Carter said, "Yeah, well, I'm learning."

When he was done carving, he revealed what he'd written:

CARTER + LILAH

"That's a promise," he said.

"You sure?"

"I'm sure."

The serious expression on his face was so intense that she had to believe him.

"Okay," she said. She dug her iPhone out of her purse and snapped a photo of the graffiti. "But I warn you, I'm going to hold you to that."

PART
one

1

"Are you sure you're okay?" said Carter.

"Yeah. I said before, I'm fine. Everything's fine," Lilah responded, tucking her crossed arms more tightly across her body.

It was the first Saturday in March of the last semester of their senior year, and they were cruising in Carter's black BMW convertible up Magnolia Boulevard toward his friend Jeff's luxurious Spanish-style mansion on the north side of town, for what promised to be an epic, "What happens at Jeff's house, stays at Jeff's house" party.

"You don't seem okay." Carter waited for Lilah to say something in response, but she just stared up at the tops of the palm trees streaming past one by one, and rolled her eyes. "If you don't want to go, it's okay. I can take you back home and go by myself. I won't be mad."

"I want to go. Look. I got dressed up and everything."

She was wearing a white halter-top sundress with small, red embroidered flowers along the hem and a pair of thin-strapped sandals. She looked elegant, but anxiously so, like she'd worked too hard to give this appearance. Carter knew she'd be the most dressed-up person at the party. He himself was proudly wearing the gray T-shirt festooned with the blue-and-red UPenn shield that he'd bought on his campus visit last fall.

"You sure? 'Cause you're acting sort of like you don't want to go."

"I want to go and I don't want to go. Don't you ever feel that way?"

Carter didn't push it.

He kept his hand on Lilah's leg, twirling his finger on the smooth skin of her knee. He could feel the tension in the muscles as he rested his palm on her thigh. They hit the red light at Pelican, and as Carter rolled to a stop, Lilah peeled his fingers off her skin and emphatically placed his hand on his own lap. She seemed, if anything, to be becoming more resentful and nervous by the second.

"Are you ever going to tell me what's going on with you?" he said.

"There's nothing going on," she said with a clipped voice.

"But there is. You've been acting weird ever since your parents took us to dinner to celebrate us getting into UPenn."

"I haven't been acting weird."

"Really? Lately it seems like absolutely everything makes you angry. And like you don't want to talk to me anymore."

"We're talking right now."

"You know what I mean. It worries me when you try to shut me out."

Lilah spun in her seat and leaned forward against the seat belt. Her face was red with rage, an angriness heating up in her freckles. "God! Carter! So I don't want to go to a stupid party with your bozo friends. Is that a capital crime?"

Carter took a deep breath and held it for a moment to keep himself calm.

"It won't just be them. Everybody'll be there. The whole school, probably. That's not the point, anyway. I'm trying to say, I'd hate for what happened last time to happen again."

"It won't," said Lilah, spitting the words out with a great deal of spite. She hated herself when she was like this, hated especially that she couldn't control it. She turned again, this time to face the window. She sunk low in her seat and stared at herself in the passenger-side mirror.

The light turned and Carter drove on. He tried to concentrate on the warm wind whipping across his face, but he couldn't stop thinking that her behavior now reminded him of junior year. For a few weeks then, Lilah had stopped sleeping. She'd had a particularly tough swim meet against a girl named Melissa on the team from Coral Gables. Melissa had beaten Lilah badly, worse than she'd ever been beaten before, and as she stewed over her loss, Lilah had flickered with a rage Carter had never seen in her before. Over the following two weeks she couldn't talk about anything—not a single thing—except this Melissa girl and how she must be doing steroids. In her manic exhaustion, she searched down the phone numbers not only of Melissa but also of the Coral Gables coach and the principal of the school. She'd called them so many times that they'd reported her to Coach Randolph and Lilah had been kicked off the team.

"I mean," he said to her as they reached the dead end where Magnolia ran into the beach and turned onto Shore Drive, "you haven't gone off your meds or whatever, have you?" he asked quietly.

Lilah's face fell in disbelief. "Are you really asking me that?"

"Like I said, I'm worried about you," Carter said.

"Well, don't. I can take care of myself."

It occurred to Carter that she hadn't answered his question. "But have you?" he said.

Lilah didn't answer. In fact, Lilah didn't say a word to Carter for the rest of the ride to Jeff's place.

They made their way up Shore Drive past the neon-lit entrances to the glitzy hotels and on to the north side of town, where the beachside mansions and the weathered gates leading to their private beaches paraded past.

When they pulled into Jeff's circular, crushed-shell driveway, they had to navigate around the tangle of everybody else's cars, and then seeing that all the good spots were already taken, they looped back out and parked a ways away down the sand-strewn street.

"We're here," said Carter.

"Looks like it," Lilah responded sarcastically.

They sat there, neither of them moving for a moment.

"So, listen," Carter said. "Before we go in, I want to say—" She was fiddling with the red plastic bracelet she'd been wearing every day since she'd gotten her job as a lifeguard last summer. "Will you look at me a sec?"

She did, and Carter caught her chocolate eyes and held them. She seemed so fragile, so scared, in that moment in the car. He took both her hands in his and held them out in front of himself.

"The girls from the swim team might be here, and—"

Lilah's head bobbed forward and she covered her face with her hands, but Carter pressed on.

"—I know you think they hate you, but really, they don't. I promise you. Just . . . try to relax and let yourself have a good time. And if you can't, then let me know it's too much for you and we'll leave."

"Okay," said Lilah, glancing back up at him with a sharp glare. "Are we gonna go in, or what?"

"Yeah. Let's go in." Carter carefully tucked a loose strand of wavy light-brown hair behind her ear. He cracked a sad grin. "This is going to be fun. You'll see."

2

Inside Jeff's house, the party was blazing at full speed. The music—Nelly and Mac Miller and Nas—blasted from the surround speakers mounted in the corners of the cavernous, arch-ceilinged main room, and the whole senior class seemed to have already arrived. People Carter and Lilah recognized and people they didn't raced barefoot around the swimming pool, pushing one another in, swatting at one another with neon-colored pool noodles.

She squeezed his arm, hoping he'd notice her insecurity and buck her up again like he'd done in the car, but he was preoccupied with searching the faces in the crowd, looking for Jeff, probably.

"I'm gonna go find the drinks table," she said.

"Lilah," he said, the concern for her showing all over his face, "you know you can't mix—"

"I'll have a Diet Coke, Carter. Stop monitoring me already."

The worry on his face relaxed. "You're right," he said. "Sorry."

"You want something?" she asked.

"Yeah, sure."

"Where will you be?"

"I don't know—" Carter was up on his tiptoes, ducking his head back and forth to see over the crowd. "Oh, wait, there he is."

He pointed across the house and out the window, to the backyard patio where Jeff was stationed with a bunch of other guys. He was wearing a pair of gargantuan red sunglasses—each lens must have been six inches tall—and doing some sort of goofy dance that had the other guys hunched over with laughter.

"I'll be out there," Carter said.

Before she could say, "Okay, I'll meet you in a minute," he was gone from her side, down the marble steps and ducking around people on his way toward the sliding glass door that would lead him outside to his comedian friend.

Lilah made her way into the massive open-plan living room. As she headed toward the kitchen island where the drinks were set up, she saw that a Ping-Pong table had been erected in the corner of the cavernous space, and Kaily and Teresa, her old swim-team friends, were playing a girls versus boys doubles match against two guys from the football team who'd carved their uniform numbers into the sides of their faux hawks.

Her heart sank.

Before she could duck and hide her face with her hair, Teresa saw her. "He-e-ey!" she shouted, her almond-colored face breaking into a smile. She pointed her Ping-Pong paddle out toward Lilah like a gun. "Look who's decided to grace us with her presence."

Kaily looked, too. "*L* to the *ah*," she said. "Where've you been? Get yourself over here, girl! We need help whipping these guys' asses!"

Lilah waved. She forced herself to smile. Part of her felt the urge to take Kaily up on the offer.

One of the football guys, number sixty-four, beat his paddle rapidly against the table and said, "Come on. It's your serve. Are we playing, or what?"

Kaily unleashed her long red hair from its hair band and bent forward to throw it in a wave over her head before rebanding it loosely behind her back again.

"Oh, are we ever playing," said Teresa. She held the ball up and readied herself to serve. "Zero-six," she said.

And just like that, both she and Teresa forgot about Lilah. *Figures.* Lilah knew that they didn't really want her to join them. They'd been inseparable when they'd all been relay partners together, but they'd barely spoken to or even texted with her in over a year, not since she'd been kicked off the team and gotten so depressed.

Feeling slighted and a little bit humiliated, Lilah slunk over to the drinks table.

She still wasn't up for this, she realized. She felt totally trapped. And despite Carter's many reassurances that he wouldn't be upset if she wanted to stay home, she knew—she just knew—that he would be. She wanted to please him, but the more she tried to do so, the more she resented the effort it took. What if this was the night when everything fell apart for good? She couldn't bear the thought. But she couldn't get rid of it, either.

Squeezing through the throng, she pushed herself to the front of the line.

She knew what she was going to do, even if she wouldn't admit it to herself. She was going to get drunk. If the alcohol mixed wrong with her antidepressants, well, she just didn't care. Not tonight.

Jeff had really stocked up for this party. There were two kegs of beer and a whole mess of bottles of vodka, rum, gin, and bourbon, along with any mixer she could have possibly wanted. There was even a bottle of Moët champagne.

She poured herself a Captain Morgan and Coke and poked a straw into the cup. Then, knowing she'd need even more fortification, she splashed an extra dose of rum into her cup.

Carter would want beer. He wasn't a big drinker, and one beer, hidden inside a red cup, could last him for hours.

She staked out a place in the scrum that had formed around the kegs, and waited for Paco Bermudez, a cool kid who was already making money spinning records sometimes and who dressed just a little more fashionably than anyone else in the senior class—tonight he was wearing a Gucci fedora and a pair of clear Ray-Bans—to finish pumping the foam out.

While she waited, she sipped at her drink, sucking it through the straw. Then, still waiting, she realized that her drink was gone, and she wasn't feeling any different, so she ducked out of line and poured herself another.

By the time she'd managed to get Carter his beer, her second drink was almost gone as well.

Finally, a slight buzz had kicked in. But looking around the room, she saw all these people, her classmates, kids from all walks of life—from the lowliest stoners in their torn army jackets and heavy-metal T-shirts to the slickest, most glamorous, Prada-wearing divas in school—having fun together like they actually liked one another. It was all too unbearable. Especially Kaily and Teresa over there, flailing after the Ping-Pong ball as it soared past their paddles, pretending that they didn't know how to play in order to impress a couple of linebackers.

She pushed past Paco Bermudez and squeezed back up to the drinks table, refreshing her rum and Coke one more time.

A drink in each hand, she slid the screen door open with her foot and stepped out onto the patio to deliver Carter's beer to him. She had to watch out for flying beach balls and diving revelers as she walked past the pool, and each time she stopped, she took the opportunity to gulp down another swig of her drink. Part of her worried that by the time she got to Carter, her cup would be empty again. And then what? She'd be left with her worries and nothing to knock them out.

So she took another swig of rum and Coke. She couldn't get drunk fast enough. It was the only way she knew how to escape the feeling that everyone here was laughing at her behind her back.

When she arrived at his circle of friends, Carter held out his arm, beckoning her to his side and inviting her into the group. She handed him his beer.

"Mmm. Warm beer. My favorite," he said to her, putting his cup to his lips. She knew he wasn't criticizing her—he was just trying to be funny, or cute or something. But she couldn't help but feel like he should have just said thank you.

His core group was all there. Jeff, of course, and Andy

and Carlos and Reed. They were a multicultural group. Carlos was Cuban, Andy was African American (his mother was white and his father was black), and Reed's real name was Ranjit—they called him Reed because he was so skinny. What bound them together was their sense of humor, goofball stuff—they loved Seth Rogen especially—and the fact that they were slightly smarter than their classmates.

"You doing okay?" he whispered to her, ducking his head toward hers for some small semblance of privacy.

She shrugged and adjusted the dress strap around her neck. "We're here," she said. "So . . . whatever."

Carter smelled the alcohol on her breath—she could tell by the sour face he made, the sharp look of disappointment in his eyes—but he didn't say anything about it. Instead, the two of them turned their attention back to the guys.

Jeff was a great mimic, and Lilah recognized that right now he was doing his Paco Bermudez imitation—thus the oversized glasses. He arched his back so he looked like he was sitting in a convertible, slowly bobbed his head, looking from side to side, and mumbled with a slight Latin accent, "Yeah, man. Yeah, man. Killer beat, man. Yo, that's how we do. Yeah, man."

Even though Carlos and Andy chuckled, Reed knocked the giant sunglasses off Jeff's nose and frowned. "That shit is so stale, dude. You need to broaden your range."

Carter leaned in and whispered in Lilah's ear. "Aren't you going to miss this?"

"Yeah," she said, trying to be cheerful. In truth, she looked forward to the day when Jeff made good on his promise to move to LA and try his luck in the film industry; then she and Carter could be alone, building a life together without the constant distraction of Jeff gobbling up all of Carter's attention.

She went to gulp down some more of her drink and discovered that it was empty again.

Carter, who was always conscious, carefully attentive of Lilah at his side, watching her out of the corner of his eye even when he seemed to be giving all his attention to something else, noticed that she stabbed her cheek with the straw before finding her lips.

"Do Rollo," said Andy, egging Jeff on. Rollo was the captain of the wrestling team, a legend around school for his excessive appetite and his exceedingly small brain.

"Me Rollo," said Jeff. "Me eat. Me eat you." He held his arms out Frankenstein-style and went toward Lilah with them, but then seeing that she wasn't into the game, he stopped and said, "Man, you know? Sometimes I wonder. How's Rollo ever going to survive once he's got to be out there in the real world?"

Lilah didn't hang around to hear the answer to the question. "I'm going for a refill," she said.

"You sure?" Carter said. "It's going to be a long night."

"Yes, I'm sure. Anyway, you're the one who told me to have fun and relax. That's what I'm doing."

"It's just—"

"What?"

"Nothing," Carter said. "Go ahead, get your drink."

"Thanks, I will." Lilah could feel her face turning red.

Reed, who was quieter than the rest of the guys and always attentive to the subtleties of what was going on around him, looked at her with his wide, dark eyes, confused. Jeff, seeing Reed look, started gawking at her, too.

"That's right, drink up, dude," said Andy, always ready to lighten the mood, even if he did so in all the wrong ways. "Par-tay! Par-tay! Par-tay!" To prove his point, he tipped his red cup to his mouth and guzzled his beer, spilling half of it down the sides of his chubby cheeks.

God. It made her want to die. And though she knew he hadn't really done anything wrong, she couldn't help blaming her boyfriend. "You know, we can't all be perfect like you, Carter."

"Come on, Lilah," he responded. "I didn't—"

But she'd already stalked off for more rum and Coke, determined this time to get the balance right—ninety-nine percent rum, and a splash of soda.

3

Twenty minutes later, Carter and the guys were still hanging around on the deck and Lilah still wasn't back. Though the party continued to swirl crazily around them, they'd moved into a lower key, sitting on the cushioned wooden platforms of the chaise lounges and feeling the sea breeze on their sweaty heads as they compared notes about their college-admissions statuses.

"Looks like I'm down to my safety school," said Andy with a sigh. "Tallahassee, here I come."

Jeff smirked and leaned back onto an elbow. "Tallahassee's not so bad. Maybe you'll come home next summer with a mullet."

"At least I get to major in alligator wrangling, like

28

I've always wanted to," said Andy, trying to laugh off his disappointment.

"Jeff can come out from UCLA. And I'll drive down from Duke," Reed said. "We'll film you getting your arm bitten off. We'll be like the next wave of *Jackass*."

"Ha." Jeff slapped the cushion next to him and fell over himself laughing. "The United Colors of *Jackass*," he said.

Carter tracked all this with half an ear. Mostly he was wondering where Lilah had gone, and fighting the urge to go find her. He sat slightly apart from the guys, his chin on his forearm on the deck railing, gazing at the water. It was calm out there tonight.

Noticing Carter's mood, and wanting to bring him into the group, Jeff asked, "What role would Carter play?"

Carter smiled out of the side of his mouth. He ran his hand through his sandy hair and pulled his attention back to his friends. "I'd be the one who scientifically explained to you all the possible ways the alligator could kill you. Just so you'd know."

"They couldn't kill me," said Andy, grabbing his belly with two hands and shaking the rolls he trapped there. "It takes a whole lot more than the razor-sharp teeth of an alligator to get through all this."

Everyone laughed, and then one of those natural pauses in the conversation fell over them. They listened to the *thwack*s of pool noodles on bare skin and watched the bikini-clad girls in the pool, doing battle with one another from the shoulders of Rollo and his wrestling buddies.

Reed was looking around, taking everything in as usual, his head bobbing on his thin neck like it did. Gradually, his attention settled somewhere up high above them. His wide eyes widened even further. Touching Carter's elbow, he whispered, "Don't look now, but you might want to check out what's happening up there."

When he looked up, Carter couldn't believe what he saw. There was Lilah, scrambling clumsily on her hands and knees over the curved terra-cotta shingles of the steeply angled roof, her white sundress streaked in places with thick, black grease. She appeared to be trying to raise herself up to stand from a sitting position, but Carter could see that she was too drunk to do this with any confidence.

"Jesus," he said. He stood up and studied the stucco walls of the house, searching for a climbing path to the roof.

"Jeff, you seeing this?" asked Reed. "You might have a liability issue on your hands."

Jeff and Andy both saw it now. They all stood up. They all craned their necks to stare at Lilah, three stories up on the roof.

"How'd she even get up there?" asked Carter. He

had both hands on the top of his head, holding his hair back as he tried to figure out what to do.

"There's a ladder built into the wall around the side," said Jeff.

Lilah had now managed to get herself into a standing position. Her sandals swung from one hooked finger, sometimes slapping into her thigh. She gazed out over the deck, swaying drunkenly as she surveyed the scene down there: the chicken fights in the pool; the clusters of people in the corners of the deck; the wet, tattooed guys in their knee-length, tropical-print swimsuits ducking in and out of the pool house. And of course, Carter and his friends, staring up at her as though they really cared. As though Carter really cared, she thought.

Her body tilted to the right until she lost her balance and lurched. She caught herself before she fell, but just barely.

Carter shouted up to her. "Lilah! Sit down."

"No," she shouted back.

"You have to, Lilah," he said. "You're going to fall."

"I'm not gonna fall," she said defiantly. "You don't know. You don't know anything."

She stumbled again and took two stagger steps toward the edge of the roof before catching herself.

People were noticing. The kids in the pool had stopped their game. The girls had slid down from the shoulders of the guys and they were all staring up at her now.

"I'm gonna find a way up there, Lilah," said Carter. "Just . . . sit. Okay? I'll come help you down." He turned to Jeff and whispered, "She's totally bombed. Where's that ladder?"

Jeff pointed to the alley between the pool house and the main house. "Around that corner."

"I like it up here," said Lilah. "I don't want to come down." She tried to do a little twirl to prove her point, but she stumbled again, two more feet closer to the edge.

The people inside had started streaming out the sliding glass doors and congregating below her on the deck. She could sense that she'd become the center of attention. She didn't care.

"Please, Lilah. Sit down. I'll be there in two minutes."

"I don't have to do anything!" she shouted. "You don't own me, Carter!"

He pushed his way through the throng of sweaty people gathered on the deck. They made a path for him. He was part of the show now.

"Just wait right there," he called.

"Quit telling me what to do!" Lilah screamed.

Then, as though to make her point more dramatically, she reeled the sandals over her head and whipped them as hard as she could at him. They flew together toward the edge of the roof, one losing momentum almost immediately and plopping down to the rain gutter, the other soaring out toward the mass of people gathered below her on the deck before falling with a splash into the pool. The sound made her smile.

She peered over the edge.

"You have to scoot up away from the edge, Lilah." Carter was pleading with her now.

"I said, stop telling me what to do!" she screeched.

And then she reared up and leaped off the edge of the roof. Arms flailing at her sides, legs pinwheeling below her, her skirt billowing out around her, she flew through the air and landed in the pool with a splash that cascaded onto the deck and drenched the three rows of people standing there.

People gasped. People clapped.

For a second people gawked at her floating there, waiting to see if she was okay.

She raised her head and shook her hair out. She looked at the clear black sky and laughed, and then she started sidestroking toward the shallow end of the pool.

When she reached the ladder, Carter was right there to help pull her out.

"Come on, Lilah," he said, reaching out a hand for her to pull herself up with. "Let's get you home."

She scowled at him. "Just leave me alone."

When he tried to take her hand, she slapped him away, so he stepped back and let her pull herself up out of the pool. Not knowing what else to do, he fished her sandal, which had migrated toward the diving board, out of the water.

She grabbed it from him and staggered away through the crowd.

He took a step after her, ready to do what it took to calm her down and get her into the car and home, but a hand on his shoulder stopped him.

It was Kaily, Lilah's old friend from the swim team.

"Don't," she said. "It'll just make it worse. Me and Teresa were about to take off, anyway. We'll get her home."

"You sure?" he said.

"Yeah. You hang out. Have fun."

Before he could protest, she was on her way, following after Lilah around the side of the house.

Whether or not he wanted to admit it to himself, it was the first time he breathed all night.

4

Reeling from everything that had just happened, Carter needed some space to think.

He snuck through Jeff's parents' coral, Mexican-themed bedroom and slipped out onto their private deck off the side of the house. It was smaller than the back patio, just big enough for a Jacuzzi and a small glass table with a shade umbrella over it. The deck was on the second floor, but there was a staircase leading down from it to the grassy path that opened out into Jeff's family's private plot of beach. It was peaceful out there. The sounds of the party were distant and muted.

Sitting at the table, breathing in the warm sea air, Carter stared at the waves lapping against the sand, at the half moon in the sky and the constellations around it, and tried to imagine a future for himself with Lilah. He couldn't do it. Not tonight. This made him sad. It made him angry, too, but he tried not to think about this side of his emotions.

"Whatcha thinking about?" said a voice behind him.

He turned to see who was there. It was a girl named Jules Turnbull. She was leaning against the railing of the deck, holding a lit cigarette between her long, elegant fingers. The red skirt she wore hugged her hips, exposing the smooth skin of her abdomen, and her long black hair hung loose down her back.

"Oh, you know," he said. "Lilah and . . . matters of life and death."

"Yeah," said Jules. "That was pretty intense. It was admirable, though, how you tried to help her. I don't know if I could have done that. It takes so much patience when someone's screaming at you like that."

"I guess . . . ," he said. He stared at his faded, green, old-school sneaker, for a second and then looked up at her. "It doesn't feel admirable right now. It feels pretty hopeless."

He didn't know Jules that well. They ran in different circles. Her friends were artsy theater people and they kept mostly to themselves, spending their time in rehearsals. He'd seen her onstage when he and Lilah had gone to see the fall musical—they'd done *Camelot* and she'd played Guinevere—and he remembered thinking that she had a nice singing voice.

"You're an actress, right?" Carter said, to change the subject.

"Yeah," she said.

"And your name is Jules. I saw the show last fall. You were great."

Jules blushed and scrunched up her nose. "Oh," she said. Then, "I mean, thanks. Sorry. I'm still learning how to accept compliments."

In the awkward silence that followed, Carter couldn't help but notice how pretty Jules was. She had large, unusually expressive almond-shaped eyes that were a deep shade of greenish blue, and there was something striking about the shape of her face, something both soft and angular all at once. In the flowing red Mexican skirt that she wore low on her hips so the top of her bikini bottoms peeked out, she had an elegance, it seemed to Carter—a grace. He could imagine her dancing slowly, by herself.

"UPenn," she said, pointing to his T-shirt, across which a big, bold, thunderstruck blue-and-red *P* was festooned.

"Yeah. How did you know?"

"My acceptance letter came two weeks ago," she said.

"You're kidding. Mine too. Maybe I'll get to see you act again, up there."

"I'll make sure to invite you." She flashed a smile and Carter was struck again by how beautiful she was. How had he missed all this before? Or maybe, more urgently, was it okay that he was noticing it now?

Carter stood up and gazed out at the sea for a moment, leaning over the railing, careful not to invade Jules's space, or study her too obviously. A warm breeze lilted through the salty air. The music of the waves rocked gently beyond the dunes. A lone pelican glided low and dark over the water. A nervous tension coiled in Carter's heart.

"Look," he said, pointing at a bird flying low over the water. "A pelican."

She edged up to the railing next to him, and joined him in gazing out at it.

"Nice," she said.

They watched it fly for a while.

"I love nights like this," said Jules. "It's like everything's alive and at peace with the world somehow, and you just want to stay there and hold on to that moment for as long as you can. You know what I mean?"

"Totally," said Carter. But he didn't, really—not tonight. It was hard to find peace after everything Lilah had just done.

She pointed at the pelican, which had made its way south along the shore without a single flap of its wings and was now directly across from them. Carter noticed that she'd painted her fingernails a nice shade of bright yellow. He couldn't help comparing it to Lilah's haphazard attempts at giving herself manicures. Lilah went for the ruby reds, and she had a habit of biting her nails when she was nervous, and picking at the polish until there were nothing more than a few chips scattered like tea leaves above her cuticles.

"Where do you think it's going?" Jules said.

Carter wondered. "Maybe into the Everglades? Maybe it's out hunting, trying to scrape up enough fish to feed its five insatiable chicks?"

"I don't know," Jules said. "I think it's more adventurous than that. I think it's a loner and it's restless. It's got it in its head that there's more to see in the world than the other boring pelicans think there is, and it's decided to take a risk and soar out to sea. It's getting ready to hopscotch over the keys and find a rocky island out in the Caribbean where no other pelican has ever gone."

The vision made Carter smile. "You know what?" he said. "I think you're right."

He relaxed a tick. He couldn't help it. She was so comfortable with herself—you could see it in her posture, in her easy conversation, in the way she was able to look at the things outside herself without worrying about how they related to her—that she put him at ease.

He let himself look at her. She had a mass of string bracelets in every conceivable color tied around her right wrist, and she was wearing a tight white tank top that rode up above her belly button.

His phone—which he kept at all times on vibrate—buzzed in the cargo pocket of his shorts. Two short bursts. A text. Maybe the guys trying to find out where he'd disappeared to.

He did a quick check. It was Lilah. "WHYD U MAKE ME GO TO THAT PARTY?" it said.

Carter put the phone back in his pocket without replying.

"Everything okay?" asked Jules.

"Yeah," he said. "As okay as it can be, anyway." Before she could ask more, he said, "So, UPenn. It's crazy that we're both going there next year. It's not the sort of place many kids from Chris Columbus apply to."

"Yeah. It takes a certain kind of dork to risk venturing up into the snowy north for something as unimportant as an education."

He laughed. "I know what you mean. Who'd want to do that?"

"Well, you for one."

"And you for two."

His phone buzzed again. Another text. It had to be Lilah. He could feel her anxiety teleporting itself into the phone. "IM SORRY, IM SUCH A MESS," it said.

He was too exasperated with Lilah to get into an extended texting session with her. Instead, he focused his attention on Jules. "So, if you're going to college next year and I'm going to college next year, then we're obviously both seniors, which is weird," he said. "I never really see you at the parties or anything."

"I keep a low profile," she said. "Junior CIA. The goal is, I see you and you don't see me . . . until it's too late!"

"CIA, huh. So, spy, what dirt have you uncovered about me?"

Jules tapped her lip with one finger. "Well," she said. And to Carter's shock and amazement, she ran down a list of facts about him. His four-year relationship with Lilah, of course. But also, his taste in clothes—button-down shirts in bright, colorful checkerboard patterns and baggy chinos worn over an ever-changing collection of kicks. He used to be on the track team—the 400-meter dash—and his best time was 1.03 minutes, back in freshman year in a race that he'd won. She knew about his love for science and that last year he and Andy had tried to cultivate a coral bed in one of the aquariums in Mr. Wittier's biology lab.

Another *buzz-buzz. Jesus, Lilah!* It was like she was trying to make what had happened tonight his fault. But it wasn't his fault. He'd done the best he could.

Forcing Lilah out of his mind, he said to Jules, "Wow, that's a lot. You've been doing your job well. But now that I know who you are, I mean, you're compromised, aren't you? What's to stop me from telling the whole world?"

She raised one eyebrow and nodded her head know-ingly.

"Uh-oh," he said.

"Yeah, you guessed it. Now I'm going to have to kill you."

"Can I plead for my life?"

"Sure. But it's not going to help. Protocol and all that," she said.

He straightened his shoulders. "Okay, I'm ready. Take your best shot."

Jules mimed cocking the bolt on a sniper rifle. She aimed at Carter's heart. She made two short, sharp whistling sounds. "*Twhoo-twhoo.*" Then by way of expla-nation, she said, "We use silencers."

Carter put his hands to his heart and made his best I'm-dying face, reeling backward like he'd just been shot. He fell into one of the ornate wrought-iron deck chairs that circled the table.

His phone buzzed again. Not the short double buzz of a text, but the sustained vibration of an incoming call. He'd known this would come eventually, but that didn't make him any less annoyed.

"Sorry, hold on," he said.

He pulled out his phone and stabbed at the button along its side, holding it down until the phone was off. Then he couldn't help but let out a small exhale of frus-tration. He cocked back and mock-threw the phone out toward the beach before shoving it back into his pocket.

"What was that?" said Jules.

"Lilah." Though he tried to sound cool about it, Carter could hear the annoyance infiltrating his voice. For a second, he imagined her, stewing in her room at home, trying and trying to call him. Something inside of him—some buzzing feeling—collapsed in on itself. The difference between the drama with Lilah and this nice, light flirtation with Jules was too much for him. He couldn't do it anymore, he realized. He was too exhausted by the vigilance it took to hide the cracks in his supposed perfect, loving relationship while so much of it was crumbling around him.

"I'm sorry," he said, taking his phone out again. "It's just . . . she's going to keep calling." He rubbed his eyes. "It's frustrating," he said. "It's exhausting."

Jules wasn't stupid. She could see the change taking place inside Carter—the sad expression wresting control of his face, the way he ran his fingers through his flop of sandy hair, holding them there at the top of his head like he was trying to stop his brain from exploding.

"There's no need to be sorry," she said, taking a seat in the chair next to his.

She gazed at him, attentive but calm, and let his mood float in the silence between them.

"You want to talk about it?" she said.

Carter took a deep breath, and though he'd never

dared to put his fears into words before, he let it all pour out. Everything. How he wasn't sure anymore if his relationship with Lilah was going to work, and all the ways this terrified him. Who was he without Lilah? He didn't know. He was afraid of what life without her would look like, but he didn't know how to be with her anymore. It was horrible. He could barely remember what had made their relationship so beautiful before, and the little glimpses he did catch filled him with sadness because he couldn't find a way to get that beauty back.

"I've tried so hard, for so long now," he said, "but things just keep getting worse between us. No matter how hard I work to keep her together, she continues to fall apart. And now she doesn't even trust me. I mean, look at what happened tonight. It's like she's punishing me for caring about her. And the worst part is that just *thinking* these things feels like a betrayal."

"But sometimes, no matter how hard you try, things just don't work out," Jules said. "You're not always in control of everything, no matter how much you want to be. Something I learned from doing the I Ching with my mother. Chance sneaks in and changes everything, no matter how prepared you thought you were."

"I know that. I've even tried to tell Lilah something like that. She's so anxious, though. She needs me so much." He furrowed his eyebrows. "And she holds on so tightly that she doesn't realize she's . . . killing us."

Jules felt for him. She understood his fear. Walking away from love was hard—even if the love was bad.

"I don't want to hurt her," he said.

She was impressed, actually, that he was working so hard to understand and grapple with his emotions. It proved the suspicion that she'd always held about him. He had an unusual amount of integrity. He was a nice guy, a kind guy, mature beyond his years. The kind of guy she'd always secretly wanted to date, if only the gulf between guys like him and the new-agey, beachy stoner culture her mother had raised her in hadn't seemed so huge. Any other guy in school would have thrown Lilah overboard a long time ago, without even thinking about how she'd feel. Either that or he'd have been oblivious to his girlfriend's hopes and dreams, too busy partying and posturing for his friends to realize how much trouble his relationship was in.

That's what Todd, her ex-boyfriend, had been like, so busy playing beach volleyball and smoking pot with his buddies that he hadn't even noticed when Jules began to wonder if maybe there was more to life than bumming around the beach and listening to The String Cheese Incident all day. They'd dated for two years, and even though she'd known she had to do it, she'd put off breaking up with him for months.

After four years together, it must be that much harder. She wished there was something she could do to ease

Carter toward the realization that, no matter how protective of Lilah's feelings he might be, eventually, he was going to have to admit to his own feelings and take care of himself. She knew better than to push him, though. He'd figure it out in his own time.

"So if you can't control the future," she said, "and you can't change the past, I wonder if maybe sometimes the best thing to do in the present is to throw your hands up and say, You know what, my fate's going to take me wherever it takes me and there's nothing I can do about it."

"You have to have some sort of plan, though," he said.

"Yeah, of course. But like you just said, if you try to control everything all the time, then you end up totally paralyzed."

He hunched forward in his seat, listening, intrigued.

"I mean, look at it this way. We're at a party. There's a reason we came to this party, right? We want to have a couple drinks. We want to have some fun. Talk to some people. Maybe dance a little. Flirt a little. There's nothing wrong with having a little bit of fun."

"Okay," he said. "Sure. Fun is good."

"And if Lilah is going to assume that you're here for some sort of nefarious purpose, there's nothing you can do about it. Just like I can't do anything about what Todd, my ex, might think. So best to let it go, no? You can only be you. No matter how much you might want to be the person they think you should be, you can't change who you are. It's up to them to accept you. Meanwhile, you just do what you do and let it work itself out. Or that's what I'm trying to do, anyway."

"You're right," he said. "What's the worst that could happen?"

Gazing out at the beach, he seemed to be taking this question seriously. She watched as he considered the possibilities. When he looked at her again, there was a hint of mischief in his eyes.

Which made it impossible for her to resist. "What do you say to a walk on the beach?" she said.

5

Carter and Jules picked through the beach grass, along the path, over the dunes, and down toward Jeff's family's private beach. They walked single file at first. Then when they exited the narrow path, they allowed themselves to walk side by side—conscious of the boundaries of each other's personal space, careful not to get too close, not to touch each other, even incidentally.

They carried their shoes in their hands, dangling them, swinging them beside themselves, and the sand felt cool and soothing beneath their feet. They made their way to the upper edge of the tide's reach and let the water wash past them.

A poignant silence floated between them: the sense

that they were together, feeling the same breeze, hearing the same rustling of the grass in the dunes, watching the same waves breaking in front of them, the same foamy water licking at their toes.

Carter nabbed a stick and flicked it into the water.

Jules poked at a bubbling hole in the wet sand where a crab was digging below the surface.

They gazed out at the sea. The lights of Miami glowed red to the north. The dark outlines of the keys loomed in the distance to the south.

They were both separately, silently thinking the same thoughts. That it was nice being out here under the stars. Peaceful. There was no one else on earth but them. Like all their problems were far, far away.

"You cold?" Carter asked.

Jules shook her head. She smiled.

"You gonna go in?" Jules said.

"Are you?"

She made a face. "I will if you do."

"I don't have my trunks," he said.

She laughed—one sharp *haw*—and then she said, "Silly boy. There's no one here. You don't need trunks."

"Ha," Carter said. Then he saw she was serious, and he couldn't help grinning. "Really?"

"Swimsuits just get in the way," she said. "Isn't it better to be unconstricted? To feel the water sliding on your skin?"

Behind them, the deck of Jeff's house seemed far away, and with it all Carter's worries about Lilah. It was dark now, abandoned. The party had dwindled. The only light came from the window of the rec room, and this was dim—probably Jeff and one or two of the guys watching *Anchorman* for the three hundredth time on the large-screen plasma mounted on the wall in there.

"I dare you," she said.

Carter grinned. "Well, if you dare me, then—"

"I double dare you."

Screw it. Carter dropped his shoes and stripped off his shorts and T-shirt. He hopped out of his boxers. He ran into the waves and dove under. He felt like he was at the top of a roller coaster. The car he was in had just tipped and it was about to race down the ramp toward the loop-di-loop, and his heart was leaping up into his throat.

Crouching to keep himself hidden in the water, he turned back and waved. Jules was laughing so hard that she'd doubled over. Her long, dark hair dangled almost to the ground. When she flipped herself back upright and pulled the hair away, he saw that she had an expression of absolute joy on her face.

He watched as she stepped out of her skirt and pulled her tank top over her head, folding each article of clothing carefully and placing it all in a neat pile.

God, she was beautiful.

When she went to unhook her bikini top, Carter

politely looked away. He pretended to be suddenly fascinated by something floating in the water. When he heard her splashing toward him, he glanced up at her and caught a glimpse of her tan lines before she dove under.

She resurfaced in front of him, still giggling. "See?" she said. "Don't you feel free?"

"Free as a bird," he said. "Absolutely."

They grinned at each other. They floated on their backs, staring up at the stars. They each in their own way were surprised by what was happening. And though they didn't speak of it, they both maintained the illusion that what they were doing now was entirely innocent, that it could stay that way, if they were careful, and they'd get through this night having done nothing more than take a swim together.

There was something so liberating about it, though. Carter had almost forgotten it was possible to feel like this.

Suddenly, out of nowhere, he splashed water at Jules and ducked under and swam away.

When he resurfaced, he saw that she had an expression of mock shock on her face. "You know that means war," she said.

They danced around each other, edging gradually closer and closer to each other, and then she sent a wallop of water in his direction. He slapped one back at her.

Splash, splash, splash. They created a tsunami between them.

And then, the game got riskier. It accelerated. Someone had to win. Carter dove under and took her legs out from under her, flipping her. She spun and grabbed at his arm. They were, all of a sudden, grappling with each other, wrestling in the water. Touching. For the first time they were touching.

He felt like he was melting inside. Every time he went to push her under one more time, he lingered a little bit longer by her side, soaking in the slippery warmth of her skin. And he sensed she was doing the same thing when she went to take him down.

She bopped up right in front of him and somehow, he had his arms wrapped around her. He didn't even realize how it had happened. He was holding her now. He could feel the dimples at the base of her back. She had her arms around him, too, her finger tracing lightly up and down his spine.

And then it was too late. Neither of them was quite sure who started it—maybe both of them did, maybe it just happened, but they were kissing now. Grazing lips. Playfully rubbing their noses against each other.

It felt so good. Their hands slipping around on each other's soft skin. Something wild and beautiful was passing between them. Neither of them wanted to be the one to tame it.

Jules forced herself to pull back.

"If I let you keep kissing me, you're going to end up hating me," she said.

"I won't."

"You will. You'll blame me for whatever happens with Lilah. I don't want to be that girl."

"You won't be," he said. "I promise."

He kissed her again, this time harder, more deeply. He wanted to feel every inch of her skin, to get inside her skin, to shrink the distance between them until they melded into one person. He couldn't stop. He couldn't remember ever desiring Lilah like he desired Jules right now, right here.

They stared into each other's eyes for a moment, each searching for an explanation to the mysterious emotions that had been unleashed in them.

And when they kissed again, whatever lines they'd been worried about crossing had been washed away by the tide. They couldn't ignore what their bodies were telling them. She could feel his excitement pressing against her abdomen. Cupping the backs of Jules's thighs with both of his hands, Carter lifted her halfway out of the water and pulled her tight to him. She wrapped her legs around his waist and they drank each other in.

6

The next morning, when the sun came streaming in through the ocean-facing glass wall of Jeff's pool house, Carter woke up in a sweat. It was six a.m. The wind chime mounted above the sliding door was tinkling, and he was lying under a pale green sheet on the pool house's futon, which had been pulled flat into bed mode.

He was naked, and next to him, Jules was naked, too—beautifully, lusciously naked. Seeing her there, her lips slightly open, her breasts rising and falling with each breath, a hook of tenderness tugged at his heart.

For a while he watched her sleep. He studied the way that the light played on her skin. She had a small tattoo of a dove on her shoulder. He hadn't noticed it before. He lightly caressed her arm with his knuckle.

"Mmm." She stirred. She turned onto her side and smiled at him without opening her eyes. "Hi."

When she finally opened her eyes, she didn't say anything. She just gazed at him, a pure, simple tenderness softening her face.

He leaned in to kiss her, brought his lips close to hers, but just before they touched, his mind clouded with thoughts of Lilah. Somehow, kissing Jules in the light of day felt very different from kissing her under the moonlight. It was like Lilah was watching them this time.

Pulling away, he sat up and blinked in the golden light of the sunrise as it streamed in through the glass wall of the pool house. He held the bridge of his nose between two fingers and squeezed his eyes shut, trying to get his head around what he'd done. He'd never once cheated on Lilah before, and though he didn't regret what had happened with Jules, it worried him that he didn't know what it meant.

Gradually, though, she registered his anxiety. She pulled the sheet up to cover her chest. She leaned up on her elbows and studied the tension constricting the muscles of his tan back.

"We should get up. We need to get out of here," he said in a voice pinched with worry.

Tugging lightly on his hand, she coaxed it away from

his face and got him to look at her. They locked eyes briefly, and in his hazel irises, she could see the worries he'd shared with her the night before, while they'd been sitting on that porch, pressing their way back into his thoughts. She held his hand softly in her two hands, took it between her palms, and brought it to her mouth, kissing the meaty pad of his thumb.

"You're thinking about what you're going to tell Lilah," she said.

"Yeah. I'm sorry. I can't help it."

"It's okay. I don't expect you to all of a sudden be my boyfriend. I understand. You've been with her forever. I don't want to be the girl who broke up the class couple."

She meant this as a mild kind of joke, to put him at ease, but Carter flinched when she said it. "What do you mean?" he said.

Reluctantly, she let go of his hand. "Just let me know when you're ready," she said. "Maybe you never will be. I don't know. It's the chance we take. Like the I Ching, remember?"

"I'm sorry," he said. "I've created a total mess, I know."

"It takes two," she said.

He'd tensed up—listening to something outside.

There was someone moving around by the pool. The rustles and metallic clankings of cans in a trash bag. They couldn't see who it was—the pool-side wall of the house wasn't made of glass like the ocean-side wall.

Before either of them had time to gather themselves, the doorknob turned and the door flew open. There was Jeff, hiding behind a pair of Ray-Bans, his short hair matted with bedhead. He was shirtless, barefoot, wearing only a bright yellow swimsuit festooned with blue palm trees.

Jules was up and slammed shut into the bathroom with her clothes before he could say, "Oh! Shit!"

Jeff's trash bag full of empty beer cans fell to the floor. He lifted his Ray-Bans onto his forehead, and his bloodshot eyes bugged out of his head as he stared at Carter in disbelief.

"Wow," he said. "I didn't think you had it in you."

7

After Jules left, Carter sat with Jeff by the edge of
the pool, dangling his legs in the cool, clear water.

"But, man. Lilah. She's totally wound up already.
Can you imagine how she's going to react to this?"
Carter asked. Part of him thought that the best thing to
do at this particular moment would be to drown himself
in the chlorinated water—at least then he wouldn't have
to face her.

"Just don't tell her," Jeff said. "I sure as hell am not
going to say anything."

Carter shook his head wearily. He resisted the urge
to unload the secrets only he and Lilah knew about the
depths of her depression after the swim-team blowup.

Instead he cupped a handful of water and splashed it on his face, hoping this might help him think more clearly. "It's not that simple," he said.

"You're eighteen years old, dude. These are your best years. You're smart. You're good-looking. Chicks are gonna be into you. And you know, that's a good thing." He punched Carter lightly on the arm. "I gotta hand it to you, though, bro. That Jules is way above your weight class. If I hadn't seen it with my own two eyes, I'd never believe you could bag someone like that. You know what I mean? Hot chicks are my thing. You're the old married guy. But, yo, I guess not so much, huh?"

This was just like Jeff. He could be so crude sometimes. And even though Carter knew his friend was trying to be funny—playing his part as the freewheeling hedonist he thought he should be, and talking tough in a way he would never dare to act—he wasn't in the mood for jokes right this moment.

"Come on, man," he said. "I'm trying to be serious."

Jeff sized him up for a few seconds, studied the misery clouding his face. "Okay, being serious," he said. "Whatever happens, you're going to live. I mean, you know that, right? Either you'll stay with Lilah and try to forget about last night, or you'll finally leave her and then you'll be a free man. You want to know what I really think?"

Carter shrugged. "Sure."

"I think maybe this could be a wake-up call for you. I've always thought you could do better than Lilah, if you weren't so scared of trying."

"I take it back," Carter said. "I don't think I do want to hear what you think."

"I'm serious, dude. Sometimes I wonder if you even still like her. It's not like the two of you are feeding your larger lives . . . you know what I mean? Except for last night—and look at how that worked out. When was the last time the two of you hung out in public together? Sometimes it seems like you're just still with her because you've been dating her so long you don't know how to do anything else."

"That's not fair," said Carter. He was wishing he'd asked someone else for advice, but there was no one he trusted more than he trusted Jeff. And since Jeff had walked in on the scene of the crime . . .

"Whatever. I'm not trying to be a dick, Carter. I'm just saying."

Carter slipped his hand into the water and waggled it around.

"Anyway, it doesn't matter," said Jeff. "What we really should be talking about is your cover story."

Jeff slid into the pool and swam out a couple yards. He doused his sunglasses and then put them on. Treading water, he turned to Carter and said, "The best lies are ones that keep close to the truth, so really, it's simple.

After Kaily and Teresa took Lilah home, you hung out with me and the guys. This actually happened—for a minute or two, anyway. If she double-checks with Reed or Andy or Carlos, they'll back you up without even realizing that they're supporting your alibi. So, you had a few beers. The guys left. Then you had a few more. And you figured you were too drunk to risk driving home. Cool?"

"Sure."

"You and I stayed up watching old episodes of *Futurama* on Hulu. Piece of cake."

Jeff was right. It was that simple. The complicated stuff was all inside Carter's heart. He closed his eyes and felt the morning sun, warm on the backs of his eyelids. He was suddenly exhausted. He'd been up with Jules until four, at least. He'd barely slept at all the night before.

"Whaddya say, bro?"

Carter reluctantly nodded. "Sounds like a plan," he said quietly.

"All right, cool," said Jeff. Then, splashing a plume of water at Carter, he said, "I gotta say, though, man—you're one lucky dog."

Slowly lifting himself from the edge of the pool, Carter wandered back into the pool house and laid down on the unmade futon. He could smell Jules's scent on the sheets—peaches and rosewater. He remembered his face buried in her hair the night before, breathing her in, gulping down these smells. Images from their hookup flooded his head—his hands running up her smooth legs, the devilishly playful expression on her face as they'd chased each other up the beach toward Jeff's house, and then the warmth of her skin when he'd covered her body with his own. An enticing, lingering memory of the night before.

Was it possible that Jeff knew what he was talking about? That the problem wasn't with what he'd done the night before, but with the fact that his love for Lilah was disappearing? And then what? What would happen to Lilah if he up and left her?

The possibility disturbed him. He imagined her spiraling into a depression like she had after the swim-team fiasco. Hurting herself, maybe seriously. It made him sick to his stomach.

In a sudden panic, he leaped up and stripped the bed, crumpling the sheets into a ball and stuffing them deep in the hamper in the bathroom.

Back on the futon, he closed his eyes and tried to calm himself. If he could just somehow get back to sleep, maybe he'd wake up in a world where he wouldn't have to worry about any of this.

8

In the three and a half years they'd been together, Carter had never once neglected Lilah's calls. Never once failed to return a text.

If only she hadn't gotten drunk, if only she'd tried a little harder to enjoy Jeff's party and not made such a spectacle of herself. She should have remembered how fragile things were in their relationship. She should have been more careful, more attentive, less selfish. She should have put Carter's needs before her own.

She regretted every single thing she'd done, and her regret made her hate herself, and her self-hatred filled her with an uncontrollable need to hear Carter tell her that everything was okay.

Now he'd gone AWOL. And it was all her fault.

At eight thirty a.m., unable to stand it any longer, she called the landline at his house. Maybe his mother would be able to get him on the line. And then Lilah could say she was sorry, and everything would be okay again. She could hear her heart beating in her throat as the phone rang and rang.

Finally, Carter's mother answered, and the sound of the sweet Georgia drawl she'd picked up while they'd lived in Savannah almost broke Lilah in half. "Hi, Mrs. Moore. Is Carter there? Can I talk to him?" It took all of her self-control to squeeze the words out.

"Oh, Lilah, no. He's at Jeff's house," Mrs. Moore said.

Lilah refused to believe that this could be true. "Are you sure?" she said.

"Sure as the sunrise."

"So . . . he's okay?"

"He seemed fine when he called to say he was sleeping over," said Mrs. Moore. "Are *you* okay, honey?"

Lilah definitely wasn't okay, but she didn't want to make the mess she'd created any bigger. "Yeah. I'm . . . I'm okay," she said. "Just, he's not answering his phone."

"You know Carter," his mom responded. "It's Saturday. He's not going to be awake till noon."

"He didn't answer last night, either, though. I called him, like . . ." Afraid she'd said too much already, and not wanting Carter's mom to think she was crazy, Lilah stopped herself. "I called him. And I sent him some texts. He's, like, disappeared."

"I'm sure his phone just died," said Carter's mom. "You sure you're all right, sweetie? You sound a little—"

"I'm sorry, Mrs. Moore. I've got to go. Thanks!"

Lilah hung up before Carter's mom could probe any further.

In a daze, she stared at the pink walls of her room, at the line of intertwined roses her father had painted along the baseboards, at the white dresser and the white bedside table and the white carpeting on the floor. She studied the poster of Allison Schmitt—an action shot of Allison bobbing out of the water, with her arm stretched in front of her as she won her gold medal in London— that she hadn't had the nerve to take down after her own dreams of Olympic competition had combusted.

Then, finally, her eyes drifted to the huge, round mirror above the antique cherrywood dressing table she'd inherited from her grandmother. Among the photos she'd taped there was one she especially cherished. CARTER + LILAH carved into that bench. "Forever," he'd said.

But did *forever* really mean forever? Maybe not, after what Lilah had done last night. She couldn't help but wonder if he'd taken the first steps toward leaving her—if he'd hooked up with some other girl after she'd left, it would explain why he hadn't been answering his phone. The old familiar hurt tickled the edges of her heart, that dark hopelessness she sometimes felt when she was alone, the flip side of her manic behavior the night before. She felt herself moving across the room, sitting on the stool in front of the mirror. Staring at that photo like she was in a trance.

Her hand reached down and opened the bottom drawer of the dressing table. She rummaged through the old lipsticks and mascara cases there, digging around until she found what she was looking for. There it was: the tiny cartridge of razor blades she'd managed to keep hidden from her mother.

As her fingers touched them, she shuddered, horrified at herself.

"Stop it," she told herself. "Don't do it."

She threw the cartridge back into the drawer and slammed it shut.

Throwing on a pair of baggy gray sweatpants and a black sports bra, she slammed out of her room and stomped down the stairs and through the bright sunlit kitchen of her house.

"Mom, I'm taking your car," she called out.

Then, before her parents had time to surface from wherever they were and interrogate her, she grabbed the key to her mom's Dodge Caravan off the hook by the garage door and headed to Jeff's house in search of Carter.

9

Jules took her time walking home.

She lived on the southern side of town, in a neighborhood called the Slats because all the houses there were the same gray clapboards, perched on stilts, lined up tight next to one another. It was a three-mile walk from the ritzy opulence of Jeff's neighborhood, but today Jules didn't mind.

She swung her sandals in her hand and brazenly trespassed through the five or six private beaches between Jeff's house and the hotels, watching the perfect rows of red and blue umbrellas lined up above the sun-bleached chaise lounges grow incrementally closer. She waved at the strangers parked under these umbrellas—the few who were out at this early hour. She tracked the waves as they tumbled and crashed. She watched the early-morning surfers catching waves, the seagulls hopping along the shore, and a few bright-eyed families setting up their chairs on the glimmering white public beach.

She couldn't stop grinning. The sun felt warm and alive on her skin. She was electric today, tingling all over. Her brain fizzled with a sensation of uncontrollable freedom. She knew she should feel guilty for having slept with Carter, but she just couldn't find room for the guilt inside her.

Life, the world, it was all so beautiful. She had to keep checking herself, stopping herself from imagining a life in some hazy future where Lilah didn't exist anymore and she and Carter were an actual couple. It felt wrong but it also felt unfathomably right.

By the time she'd made it to the Slats and cut in the three blocks from the beach, walking along the sandy side streets of her neighborhood toward the little house where she lived with her mother, she'd almost given up on trying to care about the damage she might have wrought on Carter and Lilah's relationship. He'd seemed so miserable. She hoped that when he thought about what they'd done, he'd see her as a force for good in his life.

Her mother was already up, sitting at the table on the deck of their house. She looked free and easy as ever, her blond-streaked hair hidden under a floppy straw sun hat, her hands around a warm cup of herbal tea. Enjoying the moment. Practicing her Buddhist presentness.

They waved at each other as Jules made her way up the creaky wooden stairs, and Jules felt lucky again that her mother was more a friend than a parent, the kind of person who let her come and go as she wanted.

Flopping into the chair across from her, Jules closed her eyes and drank in more of the sun. The female singer-songwriter music her mother liked so much lilted softly through the open window from the kitchen. The Shawn Colvin Pandora channel, Jules suspected.

"Good night?" her mother asked.

"The best."

Her mother scooped some organic strawberries into a bowl and slathered Greek yogurt on top of them.

"Here," she said. "Breakfast. Tell me all about it."

She could honestly say that her mom was her best friend. Her dad had died six years ago of a heart attack, when she was eleven, and since then it had been just the two of them. They talked about everything. Her mom never judged. And through her, Jules had learned that the world had a way of working things out as long as you didn't try too hard to war against it.

Jules picked at the fruit in front of her. "Well, there's this boy," she said.

A wisp of a smile floated across her mother's face. "Of course there is."

Jules laughed. She'd had this very same conversation with her mother many times before, but from the other side, listening to her describe her excitement about this or that new guy in her life.

"But he's one of the good ones. He's funny. And kind of goofy-cute. But there's, like, a seriousness to him. I've told you about him before, actually."

"Oh?" The hint of a smile, just a ripple across her lips that was so hard for Jules to read, emerged on her mom's face.

"You remember way back in sophomore year . . . that party I went to on the beach?"

"Weren't you already hanging around with Todd by then? It seems like there was always some party or another on the beach."

Jules couldn't help making a sour face at the memory of all that wasted time with Todd and his surfing buddies. "No, before that. With Lauren? It was like a bonfire with a bunch of upperclassmen. Remember? I came home just totally upset? I had to beg you not to report it to the school?"

She was talking about the time she and her friend Lauren had gone to a beach bonfire and been harassed by a bunch of guys who thought it was funny to paw at them and pull at the drawstrings of their bikinis. They'd actually managed to get Lauren's top separated from her body. And then they wouldn't give it back. It was all a game to them. Keep-away.

Her mom's gaze narrowed as she remembered being told about this. It was like she was looking through Jules into some place deep inside her that she didn't know how to protect. "This guy was involved with that?"

"No—no, that's not what I mean. Seth Kruger was the guy who stole Lauren's bikini top. Carter was the one I told you about, who raced down from out of nowhere shouting, 'What the fuck, assholes,' and dive-bombed Seth to get Lauren's top back."

"Thank God," her mom said, relieved.

"And last night, we just talked and talked. It was all so effortless. He was so sweet. And . . ." Jules drifted off into memories of the touch of his lips on hers. She'd thought about what it would be like to kiss him for years and the reality was so much better than she'd imagined.

Her mom reached across the table and patted her tanned hand with her own. "You really like this guy, then," she said.

Jules looked down at her yogurt, suddenly embarrassed; then she glanced back up at her mother and crinkled her eyes. "Yes," she said, blushing.

"I sense a *but* coming," her mom said.

"He's got a girlfriend. And . . ."

As Jules outlined the parameters of the situation— glossing over the details of what exactly she and Carter had done, but not hiding them, not lying about them—her mother listened carefully, looked her in the eyes, took in not just her words but her vibrations as well, all the subtle physical clues that communicated more than her words ever could. She didn't push Jules or try to steer the conversation. She just listened and watched until Jules was done.

"Is that a bad thing?" asked Jules.

"No," her mom said. "Not bad." She put her hands to her lips like she was praying, and thought for a moment. "First, you should know—'cause you're going to be worried about it later—you're not responsible for the things he does. If he chose to fool around with you last night, something must be very wrong between him and his girlfriend. It's not your fault."

She reached across the table and covered Jules's hand with her own.

"Did you hear me?" she said. "It's not your fault. You don't have to own problems he's created for himself. Okay?"

Jules nodded.

"But," her mom said, arching her eyebrows, "be careful. Guys with girlfriends . . . they have no idea what they want. And they'll charm you into thinking that it doesn't matter. You should know that by now, given the example I've set for you."

"I know," Jules said. "You're right. It's just . . ."

She gazed off between the stilt houses to the sliver

of ocean they could see from their porch and thought about her mother's tumultuous love life, the way she fell in love so quickly, and allowed herself to believe again and again that whichever new, cool, brooding, muscular guy she'd met this time would be different from all the other ones she'd dated. She was so wise about how relationships worked, but so terrible at taking her own advice.

Jules's mom patted her hand, and then gave it a playful squeeze. "It's just that they're so hard to resist," she said.

They smiled at each other, almost but not quite ashamed of this truth.

10

By the time she got to Jeff's house, Lilah had calmed down enough to think straight, at least. She shut the door to the Caravan softly and took care with her footsteps as she made her way across the landscaped front lawn and past the grand stone-inlayed entrance to the house and around the side to the backyard, unlatching the gate to the pool area quietly.

She could hear rap music coming from somewhere deep inside the house. It was muffled, a private sound, not the full, surround-speaker blast she knew Jeff's stereo was capable of, and she figured it to be coming from the rec room in the lower level of the place.

Before slipping inside and tiptoeing down there,

she did some recon, peeking in windows, listening for other signs of life. The place seemed abandoned. There weren't even any crushed red cups or beer cans lying around.

She peered through the windows of the pool house, twisting and straining to catch a glimpse of what might be behind the closed venetian blinds.

And there he was, Carter, sleeping like a baby on the pullout bed.

He was alone. That's the first thing Lilah noticed.

Taking great care not to make a sound, she turned the handle on the door and slowly opened it and stepped inside.

Watching him sleep, so peaceful and content, curled up in the fetal position, his hair standing up in all sorts of odd angles, Lilah had a sudden urge to cuddle up with him. He looked so innocent there, so adorable, with the cowlick at the ridge of his forehead sending a pinwheel of sandy hair down over his eyes.

She felt ashamed of herself. If she was going to be crazy and possessive and unrelentingly moody, she thought, if she was going to go out of her way to ruin every fun thing they did together, why *wouldn't* he start questioning their relationship. If she wanted to stop him from outgrowing her, she knew, she should shower him with kindness and unconditional love.

But as quickly as this impulse had bloomed inside

her, her neediness and insecurity returned. Where had he been last night? Well, here, at Jeff's house—she could see that now. But why hadn't he answered her calls? She had to know.

She saw his iPhone on the windowsill, right there in front of her. And seeing it, everything inside her seized up. She had no choice. She had to have the cell phone in her hands, to see what was on it, what clues, what secrets. She had to. She'd never be able to breathe again unless she knew. That's how she felt. That's why she did what she did next.

She grabbed the phone. She pressed the button on top and it came to life. A text bubble on the welcome screen informed her that Carter had sixty-eight missed calls, seventeen missed texts. She flicked the switch to put the phone in silent mode. She slid the bar to unlock the phone. She didn't need a password.

Her heart somersaulted again and again, leaping with another convulsion each time she took another step toward learning what the phone contained.

The calls were all from her. That was a relief.

The texts—well, the first sixteen were from her, but there was one more. Someone named Jules Turnbull. Did Lilah know her? It had come in at eight thirty this morning, just as Lilah had been on the phone with Carter's mother.

Lilah's whole body felt like it was going to erupt in

flames. She was sure that Carter would wake up any second. But she punched through to the message. She couldn't stop herself.

ALL HAIL UPENN DORKS! That's what it said.

And there was a photo attached. Lilah's hands were shaking so much that she could barely control her finger enough to manipulate the screen.

She loaded the photo. She could barely see it through her rage. One of those handheld, off-kilter selfies. Carter, crossing his eyes, sticking his tongue out, his arm draped over the shoulder of some stupid girl. That must be Jules Turnbull. *Good name*, Lilah thought. *She looks like a cow.* Then she realized who this Jules Turnbull was: the girl who acted in all the school musicals.

Where were they? Lilah peered closely, trying to figure it out, but the flash on the photo lit up their faces so much that whatever was behind them had gone totally black.

There was a possibly innocuous explanation for the photo. Lilah realized this. "ALL HAIL UPENN DORKS." The two of them mugging for the camera. It was totally possible that they'd been talking and they'd discovered that they were both going to the same college and they'd simply taken a photo to commemorate this fact. But really? There must be more to it than that.

And why had this Jules bitch already received her acceptance letter when Lilah was still on the waiting list? Keeping this secret was tearing Lilah up inside, and here was this girl, latching on to Carter and flaunting her precious accomplishment in Lilah's face.

Lilah wanted to throw the phone at Carter's head. Then once he was awake and she had his attention, she'd throw more things at him. Curses. Accusations. She'd demand to know exactly what was going on. But just then, she heard the screen door to the main house slide open.

Closing out of the text screen and turning Carter's phone off as fast as she could—not an easy task, given her overwhelming panic at maybe getting caught—she put the phone back on the windowsill and stepped out onto the deck.

Jeff. That's who had come out of the house. She made sure to screw her face up into a smile, to wave at him in the most innocent way she could muster.

He'd unhooked the skimming net from its hiding place along the baseboard of the pool house, and seeing Lilah there with her outsized, frightened smile, he threw her a loose-limbed wave.

"Feeling better?" he asked.

Lilah pushed her smile even wider. "Hi, Jeff," she said. And then, since she couldn't think of what to say next that wouldn't sound aggressive and resentful, she just stood there and focused all her attention on her smile. His eyes were hidden behind his Ray-Bans, and she couldn't tell what he was possibly thinking.

For the next fifteen minutes or so, Jeff went about his business of checking the chlorine levels in the pool, putting new cartridges into the drains, and skimming the leaves and palm fronds from the surface of the water.

Lilah lingered around the deck chairs, watching him. She managed to smirk as he balanced the long-poled skimming net on his finger until it toppled into the water. But always, there was a slight tremor of nervousness to her, twitching, barely visible below the surface.

"You guys have fun last night?" she finally asked.

"Foosball. *Futurama*," Jeff told Lilah. "We didn't end up crashing until, like, five a.m."

"Yeah?" she asked. "Who all was there?"

"You know, the usual. Me, Andy, Reed."

Lilah changed tactics. "When did the party wind down?" she asked.

"I don't know," Jeff said. He was getting annoyed; Lilah could tell by the jerky way he was jabbing the skimmer at the water. "Right around when you left, I guess. It's not like I spent the whole night staring at the clock."

"And then it was just the four of you, huh?"

"Just the four of us. What's with the interrogation, Lilah?"

She climbed out of the deck chair in which she'd been sitting.

"Nothing. Forget it. Listen," she said, "if he ever

wakes up, tell him I stopped by. Let him know that I'm feeling *much* better, okay?"

"Sure," Jeff said. "He'll be happy to hear that. If you only knew how torn up with worry he was last night."

The shit-eating grin on his face as he waved good-bye made her want to kill him.

11

On Monday after school, as she made her way up the grassy hill toward the gleaming, modern theater building, Jules saw Carter sitting on one of the brushed-steel benches out in front of the massive glass entrance, his headphones on, his head bobbing to the music only he could hear. She knew he must be waiting for her. And despite her mother's warning that she should be careful, she couldn't stop her heart from beating just a little bit faster.

He was all alone up there, bent forward, resting his arms on his knees, his eyes hidden behind sunglasses, his messenger bag slumped on the bench beside him.

Continuing up the path, she tried to play it cool and

pretend she hadn't noticed him. When she was halfway there, he threw her a wave, and she waved back, casual, like he was just some guy she knew.

Not the guy she'd been secretly fantasizing about since that day sophomore year.

"Jules?" he said when she was almost on top of him. He pulled his headphones down so they dangled around his neck. "You have a sec?"

She paused in front of him and adjusted the duffel bag full of dance clothes off her shoulder, but she resisted the urge to sit down next to him.

"A sec, sure," she said. "But I've got to meet Lauren for jazz practice in, like, five minutes, so . . ."

"No, that's cool. I just—" Carter said. He took his sunglasses off and hung them from his shirt pocket by one arm. He caught her eye and held it. She was transfixed by the facets of color in his hazel irises, the way they seemed to expose a tender sensitivity hidden inside him. She could have gotten lost in them for hours. "How are you?" he said.

She could hear a slow-groove hip-hop beat pumping faintly from his headphones.

"I'm . . . I'm great." She reminded herself not to forget he had a girlfriend, no matter how sweet he might sound.

"That's good to hear. I—sorry, let me turn this off."

He fumbled with the controls on his iPod and the music went silent.

"I figured we should talk. You want to sit down?" he said.

When she did, he grew bashful. He fumbled with the strap of his bag, and if anything, he seemed embarrassed—ashamed. She could sense what a risk it had been for him to come find her. Sitting next to him on the bench, she waited.

Finally, he looked directly at her again. "I just . . . I want to be . . . honorable, I guess," he said.

"I'm listening," she said.

"So, look. Things with Lilah are—I don't even know what they are. We're going to talk later this afternoon. So, we'll see. I need to figure things out in my head . . . and . . ." He blushed. "I mean, I should get my shit together before I start messing with yours. It's not fair. It's not fair to you and it's not fair to Lilah. You know what I mean? I shouldn't be starting new things with new people when I'm in the middle of a great big confusing thing already."

He pulled his floppy side-parted hair out of his face, and he looked at her again. There was something so earnest, almost tortured about his expression.

"What I'm saying is—"

"I get it. Hey, I don't want to get involved in some

crazy cheating thing, either."

"So," he said. "Friends?"

She wanted to take his hand in hers and tell him to let her know if he changed his mind. But she knew better than to do that.

Instead, she smirked. "Friends," she said.

Jules held out her hand mock-formally and waited for him to shake it.

He did, one stiff pump, and then he let it go.

"Really," he said. "I'm sorry."

"It's okay," she said. "Friends means not having to say you're sorry. Haven't you heard?"

"That sounds sort of familiar. I think I did hear that somewhere." He strained to smile. "But, still. I am."

"I hope you figure everything out," she said.

He stood up and nodded. "Anyway," he said, "duty calls. I gotta go find some starfish for my senior project." Seeing the confused but quizzical expression on Jules's face, he explained. "Their limbs. I'm trying to figure out how they regenerate."

"Ew, gross," she said, shuddering.

When he laughed, she felt amazing, perhaps even better than she did when he first put his hands on her in the ocean.

"See ya, Jules."

Throwing his bag over his shoulder and across his

chest, he paused for a second, taking her in. Then he galloped away down the hill.

"Hey," she called after him, "another thing *friends* means. Doing stuff together. Like hanging out. So give me a call sometime, okay?"

He turned around and ran backward for a stretch.

"You got it," he replied.

12

The first thing Lilah said when she saw Carter padding through the hot sand toward her lifeguard station later that afternoon was, "Where were you?"

"I was working on my project," he said. "Look." He held up a plastic bag containing three small spiny starfish that he'd collected from the shallow water down by the old piers on the south side of town.

"Well, you're late. You said in your text that you'd be here at four. I've been sitting here bored out of my skull."

"Lilah," Carter said, squinting up at her, high in her chair, "come on. Give me a break. I said *around* four. It's four thirty."

She nodded at this, guarded, skeptical.

"I'm here now," he said.

"I see that."

He dug at the sand with his toe, staring at the middle schoolers out in the waves on their boogie boards, wondering how to approach the conversation he knew he had to have with her. He still hadn't decided whether it was better to stay with Lilah and try to work it out, or to break up. She was the only serious girlfriend he'd ever had, and he'd never considered how to deal with what happened when their relationship began to fall apart. What he knew was that he didn't want to hurt her.

"You think maybe we should talk about what happened at Jeff's party?" he asked.

"Sure," she said. "Talk."

She pulled her phone out of the oversized white bag she kept next to her on the lifeguard platform and started fiddling with it.

Carter waited. He told himself to control his annoyance, to have patience. Finally, he said, "Lilah? What are you doing now?"

"Playing Angry Birds," she said without looking up.

"So you don't want to talk."

She looked at him pointedly. "Go ahead, talk if you want," she told him. Then she went back to her game.

"Can you put the game down, then?"

She ignored him.

In the silence that followed, Lilah's punching and

sliding at the screen became more and more emphatic, like all of her anger and sadness and fear were trapped in her finger, trying to get out. It took Carter a moment to realize that she was holding back tears.

"Lilah?" he said, trying to show his concern with the tone of his voice.

"I mean, you could have at least answered the phone," she hissed.

"I was busy!"

"Yeah, Jeff said. Busy watching *Futurama*."

"I guess so, yeah."

"You didn't have one second to say hi? I was trying to say I was sorry!"

"Lilah, I was upset. I mean, think about it. You'd just told the whole school that you thought I was an asshole."

"God," she sighed. "I must be horrible. I must be, just, a horrible human being, if you're afraid to even talk to me on the phone."

Carter winced. "I'm not afraid to talk to you on the phone. It's just . . . the things you do and say sometimes. It's like you don't *want* things to get better."

"I do," she said softly. "I do want things to get better."

She struggled with all her might to stop the tears from falling down her cheeks. She understood that he felt he had been wronged. But didn't he understand that she'd been wronged, too? She ached all over from how badly she'd been wronged.

"Do *you* want things to get better?" she asked, her lower lip quivering.

He wasn't sure how to answer that. Of course he wanted things to get better. But he wasn't sure that was possible anymore. And he couldn't get the memory of the night he'd spent with Jules out of his mind.

Lilah suddenly seemed so fragile up there on her red wooden stand, so exposed. Her freckles had proliferated from the hours she spent in the sun. They covered her arms and shoulders in a heavy patchwork of brown. Her legs, too. If he was honest with her about the doubts he was feeling, this might be the last time he ever looked at her this closely. He tried to memorize this image of her so he'd be able to hold it in his head years later when he thought back on his high-school years and his first love.

Then he noticed that there were small, one-inch-long scratches on her thighs. Six of them. Two tight parallel rows of three.

"Lilah," he said. "What happened? To your legs?"

She quickly covered her cuts with her hand. "I thought you were going to leave me. After what I did," she said.

The thought of what she might do if he broke up with her sent a cold spike plunging through his heart.

"I do want to try to make things better," Carter said, trying to convince himself that he meant it. "I'm not going to leave you."

"Really?" she said. Her voice broke with the word and the tears finally began to stream down her face.

"Yeah," he said. "But, Lilah, if we do this, you have to be honest with me, okay? It can't be like the past few months. You have to talk to me. And . . ." He nodded toward the cuts on her thighs. "You have to find a way not to go to that place in your head anymore. Can you promise me that?"

She nodded.

He reached up and held his hand out to her. He gave her fingers a couple of quick, comforting pulses and then let go.

"I should be paying attention to what's going on out there on the waves. Don't want anybody to drown on my watch," she said, glancing out toward the kids on their boogie boards.

"You're right," said Carter. "Lilah, just remember. It's all going to be okay."

Standing on her lifeguard chair, Lilah watched him go. As he grew smaller and smaller, his blue-and-green striped polo shirt shrinking into just a speck of color at the edge of the promenade, she wondered why she hadn't mentioned Jules's name to him. Why hadn't she asked him about the photo on his phone?

She'd been afraid that if she did so, she'd make everything worse. Now that he was giving her another chance, she swore to herself that from here on out she'd be the best girlfriend ever. She'd find some way other than pressuring him to vigilantly protect what was hers. And, who knows, maybe she really had misinterpreted the photo.

Maybe . . .

13

A week later, Carter waited for Jules on a bench under the massive iron sculpture of the Seminole warrior wrapped in blankets and cocooned in a canoe, about to be sent off to sea by his mourning tribe. It towered over the lush green mall where Shearwater Boulevard circled around and met the beach. He felt he owed it to himself—and to Jules—to make good on his promise to be friends with her. He'd told Lilah he was going to be hanging out with his "buddies"—not quite a lie, but not the whole truth, either.

When he saw Jules heading down the boulevard toward him, dressed casually in a tight aquamarine top and a pair of low-rider jeans that she'd cuffed high and turned into waders, he was struck again by how beautiful she was. The desire he'd tried to forget came flooding back. He could feel it in his knees and his elbows, a tingling weakness. Reminding himself that he needed to control these feelings, he stood up and waved.

"Hey there, friend," he called.

She made like she had a pistol in her hand and aimed it at him. "*Ptewt-ptewt,*" she said, imitating the sound of a silencer.

Identical grins cracked over their faces. Then they glanced away, Carter staring at the toe of his red-and-white old-school Air Jordans, Jules biting her lip and flipping her long black hair over her shoulder.

When she reached the sculpture they struggled to negotiate their greeting. Carter went to shake Jules's hand at the same time as she leaned in for a hug. Then, each of them seeing what the other had done, Carter went for the hug and Jules for the handshake.

"Well, whatever. We tried," said Carter. "How long has it been since you've been to Harpoon Haven?"

"I can't even remember. I used to hang out there in middle school, I guess. You?"

"I've been there once. Freshman year." Carter paused, unsure if he should say more, but in the service of friendship, he felt he should be honest. "With Lilah."

Jules secretly winced, but she didn't push the topic.

As they wandered up the promenade toward the

lights of Harpoon Haven, they made sure to keep a couple feet of distance between themselves. They breathed in the warm salt air, soaked in the cool breeze coming in off the ocean.

Then, once they were inside and making their way through the first arcade of games that ringed Harpoon Haven's small collection of rides, they let the carnival atmosphere carry them along.

Jules pointed at a stand surrounded by children. "The goldfish game!" she yelped, and she raced ahead of Carter toward it. They put all their energy into getting the Ping-Pong ball into the goldfish bowl, taking turns, lobbing the balls at various arcs and angles, laughing and cursing each of the balls as it ricocheted off the lip of another bowl.

And when they gave up on that they moved on to throwing darts at balloons, dropping basketballs into the undersized hoop, shooting the cutout ducks with the air rifle. Jules pretended that she wasn't as touched as she was by Carter's careful, protective way of navigating her through the throngs clogging the alleyways, that she took less joy than she actually did in watching Carter flare with competitive spirit as he tried to get the beanbags into the fifty-point hole.

"You don't understand," he said. "I really, really, really want that AC/DC mirror."

"These games are all rigged," Jules said with a laugh.

"Let's go do the Tilt-A-Whirl and see if we can make ourselves throw up."

And off they went.

An hour and a half later, having exhausted the rides, they ended up standing at a high, round table near an ivy-covered wall of the Harpoon Haven food court, a cardboard box of popcorn between them.

"So, if you could be anywhere in the entire world, doing anything you wanted right this minute, where would you be and what would you be doing?" asked Carter.

Jules tapped her lip with one finger and thought about this. She plucked a few kernels of popcorn from the container and dropped one of them onto her tongue.

"Eventually?" she said. "I'd want to be on Broadway, starring in *Wicked*. Or the next *Wicked*, whatever that might be. You know? Working with the writer and the director to develop and put on a new amazing show."

"You don't want to be a movie star?"

Jules shook her head. "No." She dropped another piece of popcorn onto her tongue. "I mean, I wouldn't turn it down, obviously. But I don't know. There's something so narcissistic about Hollywood. I'm not so interested in being famous." She studied his face for a reaction. "I know, you think it's stupid. Everybody does. They say, 'Why do you want to be an actress if you don't care about being famous?'"

Carter bobbed his head slightly as he contemplated what she was saying. The seriousness with which he listened to her was disarming. She wasn't used to guys taking the time to try to understand the nuances of her hopes and dreams. "I don't think it's stupid," he said. "But what do you like so much about acting?"

"The craft, maybe? Like, the work. Just being in the room. Exploring the play or musical and working through the hundreds of decisions that have to be made to turn it into a great work of art. It's hard to explain."

"I think I get it," said Carter. "It's like what happens when I'm deep in an experiment. I see this goal out there ahead of me, like, this possibility that I can't quite reach. And it's like time disappears. It's like *I* disappear. I can spend hours standing over the microscope, taking notes on every little change going on in the petri dish and putting together all the ways these changes do and don't prove my hypothesis. The only way I know that time's passing at all is that I have to choose a new album on my iPhone."

"Exactly. That's what happens to me when I'm onstage. There's a presentness. Like I'm right there at that moment and nothing else exists."

She looked up at the white lights strung in loops above the food court and realized that right now she was feeling the same presentness she'd just described. She took in this moment, with Carter across from her, amazed at how easy, how natural it felt. She would have been happy if it never ended, and she wondered if Carter was feeling the same thing.

"I'm so glad you get it," she said. "Todd used to just laugh when I talked like this. He'd tell me I should stop thinking so much."

Their eyes found each other and she sensed some sort of fire burning in Carter.

She couldn't stop herself from saying, "Hey, can I ask . . . is this . . . are we on a date?"

Carter blushed. Then he winced and she knew she'd gone too far. A sadness flushed through his face and the skin between his eyebrows furrowed with nervousness.

"Can we call it hanging out? Doing stuff together like friends?"

They locked eyes and a charge of emotion flowed back and forth between them, strong enough for them both to feel it gripping their hearts.

"Sorry," said Jules. "I shouldn't have asked that."

"No, it's . . ." Carter searched for a graceful way to navigate out of this awkward moment.

He picked up a handful of popcorn and shook it like dice. Then, with a glimmer in his eyes, he lobbed one at Jules.

"Popcorn war!" he said, lobbing another one.

Jules grabbed a handful of her own. "Is that how it's gonna be?" she said. She threw two kernels like darts at

Carter. He caught them with his free hand and threw them back. Then he was up, ducking and weaving around the rapid-fire assault of popcorn she was shooting his way.

They were both laughing now. The awkwardness had passed.

14

Earlier that evening, Lilah had gotten a sense—an intuition—that Carter was hiding things from her again. Hanging out with his "buddies" was just too vague.

She'd been following him from a distance ever since she'd seen him lingering around the Native American sculpture on Shearwater Boulevard. She'd seen him stand up and awkwardly say hello to Jules. She'd watched them walk along the promenade, chatting, listening so sickeningly intently to whatever each other was saying. She'd watched them turn into the Harpoon Haven amusement park and play carnival games and eat popcorn and laugh at each other's jokes.

She'd watched and watched and watched and even

though they never did anything overtly—never kissed, never held hands, never even really touched each other—there was something in the way they looked at each other, some shyness, some overcharged nonchalance, like they were consciously *not* touching each other, avoiding the thing that they wanted most, and it made Lilah sick to her stomach. Literally. Her body felt weak and dehydrated. Her stomach acid rose at the back of her throat. She was nauseous.

And yet, she couldn't turn away. She couldn't leave. She felt compelled to punish herself for as long as it took for Carter and Jules to prove all her worst fears true. When they did, she'd explode. She'd spontaneously combust, like those Buddhist monks in Thailand or Cambodia or wherever.

When the moment came it was so subtle that she almost missed it.

Carter and Jules had been leaning against a bright-pink, low cement wall, talking—who knows what about. Something had been decided—that was clear from their body language. They'd reached the end of whatever it was. And Carter had looked down at his hand for a second; then he'd looked back at Jules. She'd begun digging in her purse, in search of something. He'd watched her. He'd just watched her, not saying a word. And then he'd reached up, slowly, and with one finger, he'd tucked a loose strand of her hair behind her ear.

That was it. That was all it took for Lilah to realize that Carter was falling for this girl. That he was no longer hers.

What she felt was fear. And rage. And a despair so huge and heavy she felt like it might smother her, weigh her down, pull her into the ground, where she'd be buried forever. She was dizzy with it. She couldn't breathe.

Tears streaming down her face, she fled to her mom's car. She watched her hands shake as she pulled out of her parking spot and drove slowly, slowly, slowly home. She kept losing herself in thought, catching herself just as her car listed one way or another. But she made it eventually.

The lights were on in the family room. Her parents sat in their usual places—Mom on the couch, Dad in his club chair—watching, probably, one of those tedious BBC comedies they liked so much. No way could she let her mother see her like this. No way could she deal with the hundred thousand questions her mother would ask.

She snuck in, called out—croaked, really, she could barely get her mouth to form the words—"I'm home," and raced up the stairs to her bedroom.

Locked inside, she turned on the overhead light and looked around the room. It was such a sad place. The bright, happy colors and hopeful decorations just seemed to make it sadder.

She flopped onto the bed, lying on her back, and

yanked her pillow toward herself. She covered her face with it and pressed down. How great would it be if she could hold it there long enough to knock herself out, to stop her breathing. How great would it be if she had that kind of courage.

Instead she screamed into the muffling fabric, screamed until her throat hurt.

Then she flung the pillow away and sat up in a daze.

She bounced between searing outrage—how could he cheat on her? How could he have dared? Was she so horrid, so deformed and ugly inside, that she didn't deserve his love anymore?—and annihilating self-hatred—what did Jules have that she didn't? Sure, she was pretty, she knew how to do her makeup real nice, but what was she really? A loser theater chick. She probably thought having pillow fights with her gay BFF Peter Talbot was what love was all about. And, still, Carter was out on a date with her. It mystified Lilah, baffled her.

She peered into the mirror above her vanity and twirled the mascara brush across her eyelid. When had she sat down here and started putting on makeup? She wasn't sure. She'd been so lost in thought that the things she was doing with her body were a blank. Apparently, she'd dusted her eyelids with a subtle, shimmering purple eye shadow. She'd covered her cheeks in dark crème blush.

Leaning in close, she studied the pores of her skin

and wondered if Carter would think she looked pretty. Not as pretty as Jules, probably. She fished a tube of lipstick out of the mess of makeup and beautifying tools and loose necklaces and earrings piled on the vanity.

Jules wasn't the only one who could tart herself up. If that's what Carter wanted, well, she could do it, too. She'd show Carter how sexy she could be.

As she applied the lipstick, Lilah noticed how thin her lips really were. Not at all plump and luscious like Jules's. She rubbed more lipstick on. And more. And more. Incrementally increasing the size of her lips.

The tears were rolling down her face now, taking the mascara she'd just applied down with them. She'd fix that later. Right now, she had to get the lips right. She stared with tunnel vision at her mouth and applied a little more lipstick.

When she adjusted her focus to assess her entire face, she saw a grotesque clown mask staring back at her. The lipstick was streaked all over her cheeks, a big, garish splash of red from ear to ear. The mascara had turned into two huge, polluted deltas beneath her bloodshot eyes. She was hideous. Everything about her. Hideous.

How could she have ever thought Carter would stay with a person like her?

Repulsed by herself, she fell onto the bed and there was Lionel the Lion, the stuffed animal that Carter had won for her—*her*, not that bitch Jules, *her*—which was the way things were supposed to be. But they weren't like that anymore. She punched the toy in the face. She punched it again. She punched it until its nose was smashed backward inside its face. Then she flung it away, too.

She knew what she should do. She should pull herself out of this stupor, at least for long enough to take one of the pills that Dr. Timmler had prescribed for her. She didn't want to. She hated taking the pills. She hated the way they numbed her mind and separated her from the reality of her emotions. But they were meant for moments exactly like this one.

When she reached for the bottle on her bedside table, though, a letter her mom must have placed there distracted her. It was addressed to her, unopened, she saw with relief—for once her mother had resisted snooping in her mail—and the upper left-hand corner displayed the blue-and-red shield of the University of Pennsylvania.

Finally, something good has happened to me today, she thought as she tore the envelope open. But when she read what was written in the letter inside, she just sobbed all that much more.

15

It was almost midnight. A full moon hung above the water, shining its silvery light across the sand-strewn ground of the Slats. The time had just flown, and Carter and Jules now stood in the shadows under Jules's house, in among the bleached wood stilts that held it up above the flood line.

Though neither of them wanted to admit it, it was time to say good-bye.

"I'm glad we did this," said Carter.

Jules cracked that ironic, hard-to-read smile of hers. "We can do it again, anytime," she said.

Carter ran his hand through his hair in that way that

she now realized he did when he was preoccupied with some hidden worry.

"Yeah," he said. "That would be nice."

They lingered there. Jules leaned against one of the stilts. Carter held himself a few feet away from her, keeping his distance as though if he got too close he'd fall into her and never be able to pull himself away.

"I guess . . . see ya," she said.

"Yeah," he said.

Neither of them knew quite how to leave the other. What was appropriate? Where was the line across which friends became something more? They weren't sure. It was hard to see the lines on such an abstract map.

With a wry smile, Carter said, *"Friend."*

And then he held out his hand to shake.

Jules wilted a little, letting the actress in her perform a deflating gesture that seemed to convey, *Really, that's the way we're going to play this?* But she took his hand and shook.

Their hands clung together, their fingers slipping lightly around one another. Gradually, almost despite themselves, they moved toward each other until they were inches apart, their noses grazing, their eyes locked and searching the depths of each other's secret selves. It was like their bodies were acting of their own volition, like they had no control at all over what was happening.

Carter pulled his head away briefly, but then he gave

in. Their lips brushed against each other's. They kissed. A feeling of inevitability and rightness passed between them. Carter could feel the soft give of her mouth against his skin.

Flash memories of that night after Jeff's party sparked in Carter's mind, the feel of their naked skin in the water, how they were entwined in each other's arms. A small ache lit in his heart.

He yanked himself away.

"I can't do this," he said. He had both hands to his head, his elbows out at his sides, like he was trying to keep his brain from exploding.

Jules tried not to let her disappointment show. She leaned back against the stilt and waited for his explanation.

"It's . . ." He lost himself in Jules's face for a moment. "It's not fair to Lilah."

"You're gonna try to work it out with her, then?" said Jules sadly, trying to appear understanding.

He couldn't tell Jules he was afraid of Lilah hurting herself. That would have been too much of a breach of trust. But he owed Jules an explanation. He chose his words carefully. "I have to," he said. "She's going through something. I'm not even sure what it is, but I owe it to her to see her through it."

Disappointment ticked at the edge of Jules's mouth. "Good luck with that," she said, not sure if she meant this or if she was being sarcastic.

"I can't, um . . ." He cleared his throat. "We probably shouldn't hang out for a while."

Jules nodded in sympathy, but then she pushed back just a little bit. "That sucks. I thought you and I had fun," she said.

"It's not . . . don't get me wrong," said Carter. "The problem is that I had too much fun. And—"

"Yeah, I know. Lilah."

Jules quickly stepped around the beat-up old Honda that she'd inherited from her mother, putting some distance between the two of them.

Carter watched her, waited. When she reached the wooden stairs that would take her up to the house, she turned. She was out of the shadows now. The moonlight caught her hair.

Flashing a little wave, just a quick flap of her fingers, a whisper of a smile fluttering on her lips, Jules disappeared up the stairs.

And just like that, their date that was not a date was over.

Carter took the long way through Jules's neighborhood, past the bungalows and stilt houses. As he wandered along the sand-strewn road, passing shuttered boutiques and fried-alligator depots, Carter mulled over the events of the night. He'd managed to resist. There was satisfaction in this, but also, weirdly, sadness. He wondered if he'd just walked away from his one true chance at happiness. He wished that being true to Lilah didn't feel like such a betrayal of himself.

Eventually he reached the edge of downtown, where there were sidewalks and bright streetlights and all the gleam and glitter of a thriving Florida beach town.

Cutting toward the beach, heading loosely toward Shearwater Boulevard, where his car was still parked in one of the rows of public parking lining the turnaround, he allowed himself a small smile. At least he'd had that one glorious night with Jules. He'd be able to keep that memory tucked inside himself forever.

16

April 2, 5:17 a.m.
NEW TEXT FROM LILAH BELL
Remember this? ☺

Under the word balloon, Lilah had attached a photo. The weathered, wooden planks of a bench on the promenade. A familiar message carved there by Carter's hand. CARTER + LILAH is what it said.

April 2, 8:02 a.m.
NEW TEXT FROM CARTER MOORE
How could I forget.

April 2, 8:03 a.m.

NEW TEXT FROM LILAH BELL

Luv U! ☺

April 2, 8:38 a.m.

NEW TEXT FROM CARTER MOORE

Me too.

17

That Thursday afternoon all the seniors were let out of seventh and eighth periods to go to the theater building for the senior awards ceremony.

Jeff got Class Comedian. He did a pratfall up the steps and when he was handed his plaque, he pulled out his Elvis impression and said, "Thankyou, thankyouverymuch."

The legendarily douchey Donny Calhoon got the Ladies' Man award.

Jerome Atkins, who was six foot eight and headed to Duke on a full scholarship, got Class Athlete.

When Jules was awarded Best Actress, Lilah's

stomach roiled with nausea. To make up for this, she clapped extra hard.

Carter clapped, too, but less enthusiastically. He was afraid Lilah might see his feelings for Jules.

She leaned toward him and said, "She's amazingly talented, isn't she?"

"She was good in *Camelot*," he said, shifting in his seat uncomfortably. They'd never spoken about Jules before. This was the first glimmer he'd received that Lilah even knew she existed. He studied her face for some hidden agenda, but he couldn't find any hint of suspicion.

"I'm happy for her," Lilah said. She snaked her arm around Carter's and squeezed.

She tried not to notice how his whole body tensed in response.

The awards went on and on. The school had a policy in place to ensure that every single graduating senior was given something, even if it was something lame like Nicest Smile or Class Mechanic.

Lilah and Carter were named Class Couple. When their names were called, they looked at each other in astonishment. Scattered applause broke out in the auditorium.

"Are they making fun of us?" she asked him.

"No. Of course not," he reassured her. "Why would you think that?"

"You know. Jeff's party. My cannonball off the roof."

"The voting for these awards took place long before that," said Carter. "Anyway, everything worked out, right?" He hoped that the reassuring smile he sent her way looked convincing. "Don't we deserve this?"

"Yeah," she said. "We totally do."

Lilah clutched Carter's hand like she was afraid it would fly away as they made their way toward the stage. She didn't let go as they climbed the steps, even though holding hands made the climb more difficult, like they were tied together in a three-legged race.

The award meant something profound to her. It was more than just a cheap hunk of wood with their names on it. It was proof. It was validation. She wanted the world to see that Carter was all hers. She wanted Jules, especially, to see this.

Ms. Robison, the principal, had handed them their plaques and patted them on the shoulders. Carter could feel the pressure of his classmates' eyes on him. He leaned in and kissed Lilah on the cheek. It seemed like the right thing to do, and he knew it would make her feel extraspecial.

For a few seconds, they stood there, staring out at the audience, all their classmates together in one place. Seeing them together, a big, united group, brought up sentimental thoughts about how soon they'd be going their separate ways.

Carter scanned the room, putting names to the faces. He wasn't looking for anyone in particular—or he didn't think he was—but when his eyes found Jules, he paused there and savored the sight of her. She had such a glow to her. He couldn't help but get lost in her beauty and wondered what it would be like if she were standing on stage with him rather than Lilah.

She nodded at him. A tenderness passed over her face, and he sensed that she could see through him.

He grimaced, ashamed of himself and suddenly feeling like a huge fraud.

She gave him a big thumbs-up, then her sideways smile broke over her face and her eyes danced in that laughing way of hers.

Lilah, possessively attentive to Carter's every move, already prickly from simply having had to see Jules onstage earlier, caught what was going on between her boyfriend and the girl. And though the smile plastered to her face was as unmovable as that of a Miss America candidate, a little part of her heart curdled; a few more of her internal organs were blackened with the hatred that had invaded her body after Jeff's party.

Her grip on Carter's hand clenched. Then she caught herself and regulated her breathing, controlled the muscles of her face. No matter how bitter and panicked she might be feeling, she had to keep it hidden from Carter. She had to present herself to him as sunshine and lightness and joy, hide her true feelings, protect what was hers, take care of the problem behind the scenes, and make sure her man thought things were all fine.

When the ceremony was finally over, Carter said good-bye to Lilah and raced off to find Jeff and the guys.

Lilah didn't protest. This had always been the plan. He and his friends were headed off to the Sunnyside Diner to get burgers and make sugar sculptures on the table. Whatever. With him out of the way she could show Jules exactly how things were going to be.

18

Lilah thought of weasels. How they snuck in and foraged through one another's dens, stealing what they wanted, trashing one another's homes. It was up to you, if you were the one being preyed upon, to sink your sharp claws into your opponent's belly and tear out her internal organs before she succeeded at destroying the little you had to call your own.

She could see Jules walking alone down the hill away from the theater, her head slightly bowed, that long black hair blowing over her shoulders and her worn leather book bag heavy on her shoulder, looking so innocent, so scrubbed clean, an all-American girl, if you didn't know, like Lilah did, how scheming and blackhearted she really was. Didn't she have any friends? But why would she.

She was headed toward the parking lot across the street.

Lilah picked up her pace, making up ground. By the time she got to the parking lot herself, she'd halved the distance between them.

She could see the car that Jules was targeting, a beat-up green Honda Civic with a cracked windshield—it must have been at least ten years old. Didn't it just figure. The girl probably thought Carter was rich and that if she could pry him away from Lilah, he'd give her all the things that her poor daddy couldn't. Well, too bad for her. Except for the charity he hardly ever got from his father, Carter had nothing to give. And even if he did, Lilah reminded herself, his gifts belonged to her.

Lilah walk-ran, moving as quickly as she could. The crushed shells crunched and gave under her sandals. Broken pieces of shell kept finding their way in and stabbing at her bare feet, forcing her to slow down and shake them out.

Jules, in her oh-so-precious low-top pink Chuck Taylors, didn't have this problem. She was almost at the car now. Lilah's window of opportunity was closing on her. Her only advantage was that Jules didn't know she was chasing her.

Slipping off her sandals and running barefoot toward

the Honda, Lilah called out, "Hey! Hey, actress!"

The car was so old that it had to be unlocked manually, and Jules had just inserted her key into the door when she heard Lilah's calls. Jules could tell, more by the directedness of the sound than from the words themselves, that she was being summoned. When she saw that it was Lilah, and that she was limping barefoot toward her across the rough surface of the parking lot, she smiled and waved and continued what she was doing.

"Don't you dare run away. I need to talk to you."

Jules flung the door open and leaned on it, bracing herself for the antagonism to come. She took a long breath, calming herself.

"Do you know who I am?" said Lilah. She'd caught up to Jules now. She was within punching distance.

"Uh-huh. Lilah, right?"

"I don't mean my name. I mean *do you know who I am.*"

Wary of being trapped, Jules said, "Uh—"

"I'll give you a hint. You saw me onstage, like, half an hour ago holding Carter Moore's hand."

"Okay," said Jules. She stretched the word out to convey her skepticism.

"So . . ."

"So, what? You're Carter's girlfriend. That's great. I'm happy for you. He seems like a really great guy."

Lilah's heart rate surged. This coyness from Jules was

intolerable. Didn't she know when she'd been caught? "Don't play dumb, *Jules.*" She spat the name out like it was a piece of rotten fish.

"I mean it," said Jules. "He seems like a nice guy. I wish you all the best."

Lilah threw Jules's words back in her face. *"I wish you all the best.* No you don't. Don't give me that. If you wished me all the best, I wouldn't be having this conversation with you."

"Are you threatening me?"

"No. I'm saying, just so you know, Carter would never be interested in a skank like you. You might as well give up now. Find some other guy to give your gonorrhea to."

Jules couldn't believe that this was really happening. She found it hard to believe that Carter would have told Lilah about their night together. He'd wanted to protect her. So why this, now? Where was it coming from?

"Look," she said, "I don't know what's going on between you and Carter. I don't really care, actually. It's none of my business. He's your boyfriend, not mine. I've only ever talked to him, like, once, for five minutes. But really! Look at yourself. No wonder your relationship is a mess."

"How would you know if my relationship is a mess?" said Lilah.

"Why else would you be chasing after random girls

and accusing them of . . . whatever you're accusing me of. I don't even know."

Lilah's rage surged through her like a tidal wave, drowning out any comeback she might have found for this. She stared at Jules, her hate boring into the girl. "Stay away from him," she finally said. "Just stay the fuck away from him."

Jules flinched. Then trying to shrug it off, she settled herself into the driver's seat of her car and said, "Whatever you say. If I were you, I'd spend less time harassing me, and focus on fixing things with Carter."

She turned on the ignition of her car and it sputtered to life.

"You going to move so I can get out?" she asked Lilah.

Reluctantly, Lilah stepped out of the way of Jules's car and watched as it rolled away and turned out of the parking lot. She wasn't sure now what she'd been hoping to achieve, but she knew she hadn't received satisfaction.

19

Jules was sitting on the hardwood floor of one of the rehearsal rooms in the theater building an hour later, her legs extended in an impossibly wide V as she stretched for dance practice. She was trying hard not to be shaken by her confrontation with Lilah, but her pulse was still racing. While she'd leaned on her acting skills to make Carter's girlfriend think she had nothing to hide, nothing could be further from the truth. As Jules leaned over and grabbed her ankles, her lower back extended. She held the position until her body relaxed and her mind cleared.

When she rolled back up to a sit, she looked to her

friends Lauren and Peter, who were stretching next to her, touching their noses to their knees and locking their hands like stirrups around the soles of their bare feet. She went back and forth in her head about whether or not she should confide in them—could she trust them to keep her secret? She hadn't really needed any help, but now with Lilah getting up in her face, she was beginning to doubt herself.

And feel kind of alone.

"So, what if you had a friend," said Jules, "who'd fallen in love with a guy who had a girlfriend and was pretty sure he'd fallen in love with her, too? What are the rules on that?"

"A friend, huh?" said Peter, leaning back on his elbows so he could look at her. He'd pulled his shaggy blond hair out of his face in a rhinestone-encrusted headband.

"Yeah. A friend." Done stretching, Jules sat up and tucked her legs in yoga style so that one calf rode over the other.

Peter arched his eyebrow in the villainous way he'd perfected junior year for the school's production of *Ten Little Indians.* "Do we know this friend?"

Jules turned beet red. "A friend of my mother's," she said quickly.

"So this is entirely hypothetical?"

"Sure. Let's say it's hypothetical," said Jules.

Rolling onto his stomach, Peter propped his chin on his hand and asked, "Who did this friend fall in love with?"

"Just answer the question."

"Jules! Give us a hint at least. You have a *friend* who's fallen in love with a married man. You can't just tease us like this, right, Lauren?"

He looked to Lauren, who was leaning against the floor-to-ceiling mirror with a smirk on her face. She was a reserved girl who liked to get all the facts before she made a judgment. She was silently taking the conversation in, like she often did. "I don't think she said a married man," she said, correcting Peter.

"Please. Boyfriend, married—either way, it's *scandalous*!"

"I'm trying to be serious," said Jules. Then she added, "Hypothetically."

The teasing grin on Peter's face said everything she needed to know about how useful he'd be in helping her figure out how to deal with her situation. She knew he couldn't help himself. If the gossip was juicy, he just had to know everything. And usually, she'd have been happy to fill him in. But this time it was too personal.

"Lauren," she said, "you have any advice?"

Lauren stretched her spine. She pulled the band off her ponytail, shook out her hair, and put the band back on. "It depends," she said. "How well does your friend know this guy?"

"Pretty well. They've hung out a few times."

Peter flopped up and impulsively slapped the floor between him and Jules. "Hung out, or hooked up?"

"They've maybe kissed a little bit," said Jules, downplaying the reality of her and Carter's steamy night on the beach. "But more importantly, they've had these deep conversations. The kind where you feel like you really connect with each other."

"How long has the guy been with his girlfriend?" asked Lauren, scooting over to sit nearer to Jules.

"Awhile."

"Awhile, like—how long?"

"Forever," said Jules.

"And does he love her?"

"It's complicated."

"She's his girlfriend," said Peter. "So, duh." He stood up and adjusted his black stretch pants. "What music should we use today?" he said. He hunched over his iPod, studying his playlists as he headed to the corner where the sound system was set up.

Jules and Lauren shot him annoyed looks and then ignored him.

"My friend doesn't think he loves the girlfriend anymore, but he won't leave her. She's *going through something*. That's what he said. He's afraid of what would happen if he broke up with her, I think."

"And is she? Going through something, I mean?" said Lauren. "

"She's a little . . . disturbed, maybe," said Jules, unsure if she was downplaying this detail.

Glancing back from across the room where he was fiddling with the cords of the sound system, Peter called out, "Does she know about the hooking up?"

"Hanging out," Jules corrected him. "Hard to tell. There's no way the guy would have told her about it, but . . ." She resisted going into the whole thing with Lilah, but she couldn't deny it was bothering her, so she went on. "She's sort of volatile. She, like, confronted my friend in this really angry, freaked-out way."

Peter gave her a pointed look. "In that case, I wouldn't touch that with a ten-foot pole." He pushed a button, and the horn intro to "On Broadway" began piping through the speakers hung around the room.

Jules and Lauren stood up and got into position behind Peter. The three of them struck identical poses, one knee cocked, elbows sharply out, hands spread like fans in front of their faces.

"He's right," Lauren said, turning briefly to shoot Jules a sympathetic look. "Unless the guy comes to your friend and says he's ready to leave the girlfriend for her . . . it sounds like the sort of thing that might explode on you. You don't want that drama, do you?"

"You're probably right," said Jules with a sigh. They'd told her what she'd already suspected. "I'll tell my friend. She'll appreciate it."

As she started dancing in sequence with them, Jules held on to the little hope she had left—that Carter would change his mind and decide he wanted to be with her. Until that moment, if it ever even came, she'd have to do everything she possibly could to resist seeing or even texting with him. She knew that the only chance she had of getting over him was to go cold turkey. It would be hard.

Dance, she told herself. *Dance. Dance it out.*

20

One warm spring evening, Carter and Lilah took a long drive. With the top down on the BMW, they rode southwest through the palm groves that clustered at the edge of town on the road toward Everglades Park. The wind whipped Lilah's hair into a tornado above her head. She gave him directions on a need-to-know basis, keeping their destination secret.

"Do you remember this?" she teased him. She was wearing a ruffled, short black skirt and she took his shifting hand, placing it on her smooth, bare thigh. The cuts she'd made in her skin had healed some, and Carter hadn't seen any new ones since their talk on the beach.

"Maybe," he said. "I did this drive, like, fifty times

back when I was learning about ecosystems."

"Yeah, but you only came out here once with me," she said.

"I'm not sure that's true, Lilah," he said. "I feel like you came with me a bunch of times."

"Well," she said, her voice edging toward annoyance, "there was one time that was more important than the others."

Over the past few weeks, they'd wandered every inch of Dream Point: the bench at the end of the promenade, of course, but also the corner of Flamingo and Hummingbird Lane, where after driving slowly around town for hours, he'd found her wandering aimlessly, lost in dark hopelessness after she'd been booted off the swim team. And the Native American statue, where they used to meet before either of them could drive, and Enoteca Medici on Flamingo Row, where they'd gone for dinner before prom. And so many more locations. It was like all she wanted to do was revisit their history together. Carter found it sort of sweet, if a little depressing.

"You gonna tell me?" he said eventually.

"You'll figure it out," she said.

Carter focused on the road for a while. He tapped his finger against the steering wheel to the beat of the Mac Miller song streaming through the car's speakers.

"Right there," she said as a McDonald's appeared up ahead of them. "You remember now?" When Carter shrugged, she elaborated. "The summer after sophomore year, just after your dad gave you the BMW? We drove out here? And we stopped at this McDonald's along the way."

"We did?" Carter said. He had no memory of stopping at McDonald's. Why would he? A McDonald's was a McDonald's was a McDonald's.

Lilah could sense Carter's weariness. Hoping to reel him back to her, she filled the gulf between them with words. "That was the first time," she said, "when I understood what it would be like to be a grown-up with you. You knew so much about the plants and animals we were seeing. Just listening to you talk about what we were looking at—I felt like I could do that forever. And remember, we found that little falling-down wooden hut and . . ."

She grinned at him and covered his hand with her own, nudging it slowly up her inner thigh.

"I thought we could drive out there and see if we could find it again."

He remembered the day, how beautiful it had been, how romantic, holding hands as they walked along the faded wooden walkway through the swamps, keeping their eyes out for alligators and whooping cranes, hoping against hope to see a panther, and then the thrill of sneaking into that hut, of taking all their clothes off and having sex out there in that place where anyone might come along and catch them. He wished he could summon those feelings again, but mostly all he felt around Lilah now was weariness over trying to fake being happy, and worry that she might harm herself again.

"Lilah, really," he said to her, "it's, like, six p.m. It's not like we're going to drive for another hour and wander around the swamp tonight."

Carter drove past the McDonald's without stopping, and Lilah turned to see it go by.

"We could watch the sunset together, at least," she said.

"We're on the wrong side for that. You can't see the sunset through the mangroves," he said. "It's just going to be all shadows."

Then, as her face buckled with disappointment, he felt horrible about himself for having said this. *Watch yourself, Carter,* he reminded himself as he patted her hand and tried to comfort her.

"It's just," he said, "maybe it would be better to go out there on a Saturday, when we had time to actually do stuff. What do you think?"

"Sure," Lilah said. "Fine. Turn around if that's what you want."

They pulled off onto a dirt road that had been built over the swampy marshland.

As the car rolled to a stop, Lilah leaned into him and whispered huskily into his ear. "We could pretend to watch the sunset. Or find something else to do. Since we're here."

She pulled back and bit her lower lip, daring him to surprise her.

They got out and Carter sat on the hood of the car, Lilah taking his hand and pulling his arm around her as she leaned against him. The sun had begun to set, and a hundred mirrors glimmered on the water below the reeds, and the swamp grass rustled out in front of them, and a blue heron flapped its wings and rose into the air.

He tucked a wisp of her hair behind her ear and she winced inwardly, remembering the night she saw him do this to Jules. But she didn't show it. What was important right now was that he felt wanted, that he knew she was still capable of pleasing him.

She ran her hands along the muscles of his shoulders. She undid the top few buttons of his pale-blue linen shirt, and gazing lustily into his eyes, she kissed his chest. She undid another button and kissed him again, a little lower on his chest.

He pulled her softly up to a standing position and she was relieved when she saw that his face had softened and flushed with the first wispy stirrings of desire.

They kissed.

Each touch of Lilah's lips to Carter's skin reminded him of the night he'd done this with Jules. The vision of her in her tank top and her low-slung red skirt, swaying her hips, that mischievous dare twinkling in her eyes, pressed itself into Carter's mind and wouldn't leave. He kissed Lilah more deeply. He slid his hand under her blouse and ran his fingers along the smooth skin of her stomach, tracing the lacy contours of her bra. But no matter how hard he tried, he felt like he was just going through the motions, his heart quiet and tortured at the same time.

Lilah sensed how far away Carter was. "What's wrong now," she said, disgust edging into her voice.

"I'm sorry," Carter said, pulling away from her and rebuttoning his shirt. "I've got about ten thousand things on my mind."

The pitying look on his face was excruciating, humiliating to see. He was right there in front of her, claiming to be her boyfriend, acting like her boyfriend. But he didn't *want* her. Why? There could only be one reason.

"Yeah," she said bitterly. "And none of them is me. It's like you don't even like me anymore."

"I do like you, Lilah," he said. "I'm . . . I'm trying my best."

She barely nodded. "Sure," she said. "Whatever. It's ruined now, anyway."

As Carter drove back toward Dream Point, they barely said a word to each other. The golden magic-hour light seemed to mock them. Carter felt hopeless, trapped. He wondered if he'd ever find the love he used

133

to feel for Lilah again. He daydreamed about Pennsylvania, far away from this little beach town, sitting at his desk with a stack of books in front of him, gazing out his window at the fall leaves, smelling the burnt air of a real autumn for once. But no matter how he tried to see Lilah by his side, the person he saw himself wandering through campus with was Jules.

He reached over and squeezed Lilah's hand.

"We've just got to make it to August," he said unconvincingly. "And then we'll escape together to UPenn. Everything will get better then."

Tears welled in Lilah's eyes. "Yeah," she said quietly. "Maybe. That would be nice." But she knew this wouldn't solve the problems between them.

She turned toward the door and watched the palm groves stream by. Her face hardened. Her tactics weren't working. She'd have to try harder. She was sure that these problems had been caused by Jules. She'd have to change strategy. She'd have to find some way to show Carter that Jules wasn't worth his love, to nullify all threats to her relationship.

21

April 22, 10:46 p.m.

NEW TEXT FROM CARTER MOORE

Daisy on Idol?! U cd totally kick her ass!

April 24, 11:12 a.m.

NEW TEXT FROM CARTER MOORE

How R U anyway? Haven't seen U around lately :)

22

A fire was growing inside Lilah. It burned and burned. The only way to get rid of it was to light something else up—Jules. She'd incinerate her. When she was done with Jules, Carter would see that he'd been wrong to have ever been charmed by the girl. He'd remember that *forever* meant forever. He'd understand that Lilah was where his heart belonged.

First step: some recon. She couldn't ask anyone from school. She didn't want to have to explain herself, and anyway, there wasn't anyone she felt close enough to there to confide in. She'd have to use her network of acquaintances at work.

The next Thursday, on the shift change for the

Dream Point Public Beach lifeguards, she lobbed her bag up to the red wooden platform and clapped her hands to let the day guard, Sammi Beck, know that she was ready for a hand lifting herself up.

Sammi got in her stance, bracing her foot against the block along the edge of the platform, and reached out her hand so Lilah could hop and catch her foot on the lower rung of the ladder, pulling herself up quickly with a one-two kick against the tower.

"Anything exciting today?" asked Lilah, surveying the clusters of sunbathers spread out around her. She was cordial with Sammi, though they only ever really spoke during these shift changes.

"Same old, same old," said Sammi. "There's a convention of some sort going on at the Hilton SeaView, but so far they've mostly stuck to their side of the beach. And some guys built a pretty tremendous sand sculpture earlier. A mermaid. It's gone now, though. The tide took it away. See that mound out there? That's all that's left of it."

Lilah wasn't really listening. She was preoccupied with the question she wanted to ask Sammi. But she nodded and followed the line of Sammi's finger out toward a wet hill of sand half-submerged in the waves, pretending to care about what the woman had to say.

"I should have brought a magazine," said Lilah.

Sammi made a disapproving face. "The after-school rush will be here in no time," she said. She was part of the old guard, leathery and tan, one of the lifers who'd been doing the job for ten years or more, and she had a way of acting like being a lifeguard was the most important thing anyone could ever do with their life.

"That was a joke," said Lilah. "I wouldn't really read a magazine on duty."

Sammi shrugged. "Anyway," she said, packing the zinc lotion she always plastered across her nose into her bag and looking again to see if she was forgetting anything. "Don't forget to do your checks."

"I always do." Lilah was running out of time. "Hey, have you ever heard of a girl named Jules Turnbull?" she asked.

"Jules Turnbull. Hmm." Sammi looked toward the sky and thought. "Cara Turnbull's daughter's named Julie, I think. Tall girl? Long dark hair?"

"Yeah. You know anything about her?"

"Not a lot. I sometimes see her working at Waxidasical. Her mom's been part of the beach scene forever. She runs a kind of a new-agey place up the beach. Harmonic Convergence."

"That's it?"

"She dates one of those surfer dudes. Todd Norris, maybe?"

"Wait—Todd Norris? With the bleached hair?" Lilah had seen him out on the waves a hundred times from her perch on the lifeguard chair.

"Why are you so interested in her?" asked Sammi.

Lilah fumbled for an answer. "I don't know. She seems nice. She's a *very* talented actress."

"I wouldn't know," Sammi said. "I'll tell you this—Todd Norris is *hot*." She wagged her fingers like she'd burned them.

Once Sammi was gone, Lilah gazed out at the waves tumbling against the sand and contemplated what she'd learned. It all started to come back to her—Todd and his buddies taking turns hopping onto their boards as the sun faded. Their girls hanging on the beach, watching them. Todd dragging his board out of the surf, leaning over one of the girls—a dark-haired girl, she sat apart from the others—kissing her.

That had been Jules.

And now that she thought about it, Lilah had seen them together a lot over the past year or so. An odd couple, but maybe Jules had another life besides her theater posturing. Maybe there was a beach bum living inside her as well.

Lilah suspected that Todd might know the answer.

23

April 30, 3:22 p.m.
NEW TEXT FROM CARTER MOORE
U OK? Missing UR witty texts.

May 2, 2:03 p.m.
NEW TEXT FROM CARTER MOORE
Saw U just now at cap and gown try-ons?

May 2, 2:06 p.m.
NEW TEXT FROM CARTER MOORE
Im sure it was U. I waved, but then you ducked away. Hmmmm.
Worried. Text me back please?

24

"Dude." Todd Norris was talking. Guardedly. Squinting at Lilah, high up in her chair. "That girl's not my problem anymore."

He was chewing gum and he blew a bubble, popping it with his tongue. He was a spectacular specimen of manhood—toned, tanned, a little scruffy, a brooding intelligence rumbling under his come-what-may exterior.

"You broke up with her?" asked Lilah.

"Naw, she dumped me."

"That sucks," said Lilah.

"It's cool. Whatever, dude. I mean, yeah, it sucks, but . . . that was way back in January. I've traveled on." He illustrated his "traveling on" with his hand, gliding it slowly forward across a flat plain of salt air in front of him.

"Tell me," Lilah said. "What did she do?"

"January second. The day after New Year's. It was like a resolution or some shit." He hadn't been able to tell this stuff to anyone, not without totally losing his cred. But he didn't mind telling Lilah—she was too far off the radar of his surfer buddies to matter.

"Is that what she said? A New Year's resolution?" Lilah asked. "What happened? You don't make a New Year's resolution for nothing. They're not just totally arbitrary."

"She's a diva. Who knows what she was thinking. What she *told* me was that she was 'getting too attached.' Getting too attached! Dude! That's supposed to be a good thing, last I checked. Not to her, I guess. She blabbered about college and early acceptance and whatever. 'Long-distance relationships never work,' she said. Whatever. Like what happens next fall has anything to do with what's going on now."

"Where's she going?" asked Lilah, leading him on.

"Fuck if I know. Some school in Pennsylvania. She got an arts scholarship or something."

Maybe Todd, whose whole world consisted of this beach, didn't understand, but Lila knew exactly what "some school in Pennsylvania" meant.

"University of Pennsylvania," she said.

She was careful not to show the way this information pierced her. She thought of that photo on Carter's phone. Then she flared deep inside and pushed the photo out of her mind.

"You think she was, maybe, cheating on you?" she asked.

"Oh, I don't know, man," said Todd, blowing another bubble. "Her friends are all gay."

Lilah had been trying to control her rage so that it wouldn't all come out in one violent burst, but she couldn't hold back any longer. "'Cause I think she was cheating on you."

Chuckling, Todd said, "Yeah. Sure. Not likely."

"You know Carter Moore? My boyfriend?"

"Maybe, I guess. I don't know."

"I think she was cheating on you with him."

The turn in the conversation had Todd flipping his gum around on his tongue. This wasn't what he'd expected to hear when Lilah had waved him over to the lifeguard stand. He'd been expecting something more like a compliment on the way he'd cut through the waves, maybe a little flirtation. He'd thought she was digging him. That's why he'd played up the sympathy vote.

"Wait, is he that rich, preppy dude?" he said.

Lilah cocked her head and pursed her lips in a tight smile, egging him on to imagine the possibilities.

"You've got to be kidding," Todd said.

Lilah lifted her sunglasses from her eyes and perched them on her forehead. She gave Todd a long, hard stare. "Not kidding," she said. He was chewing his gum quickly with his front teeth, like it was the only thing keeping him from losing his cool. "Sucks to be you, doesn't it?" she said.

He shook his head. "Sucks to be me?" he said. "You're the one who's still dating that asshole."

"Exactly," Lilah said. She took a gamble, a calculated risk. "What I want to know is if you'd maybe want to help me get even."

As Todd thought about her request, Lilah grew conscious of how long she'd been talking to him. The shadow of her chair stretched out in front of her. She'd barely glanced at the ocean all this time. What if someone had drowned? She wouldn't have noticed and she didn't care.

"I'd make it worth your while?" she added.

"Yeah?"

"Sure," she said with a half grin.

"How so?"

She stood up and stretched her arms behind her back, pushing her chest out as she did. Then she sat on the edge of the platform, dangling her naked legs over the edge so he could check them out.

"What would you have in mind?" she said, flicking her foot suggestively in his direction.

She couldn't believe she was really doing this. She felt like a criminal. It was kind of exhilarating, actually. And it's not like she would feel guilty for whatever might come next—after all, she was doing all this in the name of holding on to her guy.

Todd blew another bubble, considering the implications of what she was telling him. A smile rose up from deep inside of him and he shook his head in disbelief.

"You know what," he said. "I think I might have the perfect thing for you."

25

When she returned from the back room where Waxidasical's surplus product was kept, Jules saw Lilah lingering up front, half-hidden behind the twirl racks of sunglasses.

She played it cool, trying not to let Lilah see how her presence rattled her. After a pause to assess just what Lilah might be up to, she pretended to ignore her. Anyway, what was she going to do? Go up and push Lilah out of the shop? Not her style. Better to act like she thought that Lilah had just stumbled in, oblivious to the fact that Jules worked here. For now all Lilah was doing was trying on sunglasses, peering into the tiny mirrors mounted above each rack before rejecting pair after pair.

The six boxes of Mr. Zogs Sex Wax stacked in her arms weren't easy to carry. They required attention. Walk too fast, turn too suddenly, and they'd tip and tumble. One of the boxes would inevitably break. Hockey pucks of wax would go rolling everywhere. They'd skid under the raised shelves and get jammed there. They'd disappear behind the surfboards and boogie boards leaned against the walls. Jules would have to race around after them with her butt in the air like a crazy lady trying to herd cats.

She carefully walked the boxes to the front of the store and slid the stack onto the flat surface of the counter. Then she pulled open the box on top and started arranging the wax disks in the display shelf, not even bothering to glance at Lilah.

Eventually, Lilah sidled up to the counter with a pair of rhinestone-clad sunglasses in her hand.

"Jules, wow, I didn't know you worked here," she said. Her grin was too wide for this to be coincidence, her exclamations of surprise too emphatic for her to be here by accident.

"Well," Jules said, "now you do. Will this be all? Do you want a croaky for that?" She pointed to the rack of Day-Glo glasses strings next to the register. "I like the purple."

"Oh, no thanks," said Lilah. Her smile curdled, just a little. "There is one thing, though. Is your manager here?"

Jules braced herself. "It's just me today, actually." She strained to hold on to the veneer of professionalism she'd adopted. "Why? Did you not find what you were looking for? Was there something wrong with your experience at Waxidasical today?"

"No, it's just . . ." Lilah glanced around to see if anyone was listening. When she saw that the store was empty except for her, she leaned in and said, "I found this crazy thing the other day. I thought you'd get a kick out of it. It's a little not-safe-for-work, though. Wanna see?"

Jules could sense a trap, but she saw no way out. "Uh, sure."

"Here, hold on."

Whipping out her phone, Lilah stabbed at it and then perched her elbow on the counter, angling the screen between them.

It didn't take two minutes for Jules to understand what she was looking at.

There Jules was, alone in her bedroom, wearing an oversized red-and-white plaid shirt and shimmying her shoulders, vamping for the camera. Her hands stretched out in front of her, beckoning. She—the version of her in the video—unbuttoned a button, vamped some more, unbuttoned another. She was wearing a black bra, and she teased the camera, leaning in to give a quick glimpse of her breasts.

The sound was off, thankfully. Jules didn't have to

hear herself say, "Don't you wish you were here with me?"

"Turn it off," she hissed.

"Wait, though," said Lilah. "We're just getting to the best part."

Jules's heart was beating out of her chest. She knew what came next. She didn't want to see her shirt come off. She didn't want to see the lacy red panties she'd worn that day, or the way she'd debased herself for the camera. She'd made the video herself last summer—she didn't know why now—and given it to Todd as a birthday present.

Fucking Todd.

"Turn it off," she said again, more insistently. She grabbed for the phone but Lilah whisked it behind her back before she could catch it.

"So," said Lilah, "what do you think? It's hilarious, isn't it?"

Jules glowered and waited for Lilah to show her hand. She knew this was about Carter—how could it not be?

"It's just so good," said Lilah. This fake bubbly thing she was doing made Jules want to slap her. "I bet if it got out it would go viral in like a second."

"And why would it get out?"

"Oh, I don't know. Why don't you ask Carter? Or maybe you shouldn't. I think maybe, definitely you shouldn't. I bet, actually, that if you asked Carter—or if you ever talked to him again at all—he might, I don't know, tell Jeff, and then, well, you know Jeff. I don't think Jeff could keep that news to himself. I mean, do you?"

So there it was. This was absurd. If this had been a competition, which it wasn't, Lilah would have won weeks ago. Since their nondate, Jules had barely seen Carter—a brief glimpse across campus here and there, a wave as their cars passed each other on Magnolia Boulevard. She'd taken Peter's and Lauren's advice to heart. She hadn't even responded to his texts.

"Has he seen this?" Jules asked.

Lilah tipped her head and let her smile turn coy.

So, no, then.

The possibilities raced through Jules's mind. Her classmates one by one receiving the video, gathering in groups and gawking at her embarrassingly naked body, pausing, rewinding, watching her hands. The snickers of the boys in school as they passed her in the quad. The lewd, mocking gestures they'd flash her way. And then finally the call from Ms. Robison's office. The walk of shame. Then tense, tearful conversation. The cops would come. The news trucks. She'd be all over the TV. Nationwide, probably. Conservative-leaning networks would dedicate whole hours to what a whore she was and how she represented everything immoral about today's youth. She'd lose her scholarship to UPenn. She'd probably go to jail like that girl in Oregon who got caught sexting naked photos of herself. And more than that, whatever slim chance there was now that Carter would change his mind and choose her instead of Lilah would be gone forever. Her life would be ruined.

It took every ounce of effort she had to hold it together. "You know what, Lilah," she said, "I'll give you some advice. Don't show that video to Carter. Or anybody else."

An emphatic hoot of laughter shot out of Lilah's mouth. "Okay, Jules," she said. "Whatever you say."

"It's mine," Jules said. "You understand what I'm saying? It belongs to me. And I didn't . . ." She searched for the most frightening word. ". . . authorize you to have it. If you distribute it, Lilah, you'll be breaking the law. I'm only seventeen. You know what that means?" She was winging it. Hoping that maybe what she was saying was true. "It means that you're in possession of child pornography. And if you *distribute* it . . . Lilah, if you *distribute* it, that's, like, a major, major felony."

Lilah didn't even flinch. "You're the one who made it, Jules."

"You don't know that. Has it occurred to you that maybe I'm the victim here?"

"I don't think it will matter to anyone who the victim is when they're all watching you get yourself off on camera."

Jules felt like she was going to explode. Or implode.

Or melt into a puddle behind the counter. "Maybe I should call the cops right now," she said.

Lilah shrugged. "If that's what you want." She was so smug. It was intolerable.

Jules pulled out her phone and stared at it. Then she set it down.

"You know what? I'll wait. I'll give you a chance to do the right thing. You need to get over this idea you have in your head about me and Carter, though. It makes you sound crazy. You know that, right? If I wanted to be with your boyfriend, you'd know, okay? 'Cause I'd be with him. And you wouldn't."

"Yeah, Jules," Lilah said sarcastically. "You keep telling yourself that."

Jules could sense she'd hit her target, though. Lilah was no longer smiling.

"You know what?" Lilah said. "I don't think I want these sunglasses after all. Thanks, though. They're a little, I don't know, trashy. Maybe you should buy a pair for yourself."

As Jules watched Lilah hustle out onto the promenade, she realized she was shaking. She wondered if she'd been shaking this whole time and if she'd ever stop.

26

May 4, 11:01 a.m.
NEW TEXT FROM UNKNOWN SENDER
Missing you!

May 4, 11:04 a.m.
NEW TEXT FROM UNKNOWN SENDER
Want 2 skip work and go 2 Sunnyside 4 burgers?

May 4, 11:20 a.m.
SENT TEXT FROM JULES TURNBULL
Maybe. Who is this?

May 4, 11:21 a.m.
NEW TEXT FROM UNKNOWN SENDER
Carter. Lost my phone.

May 4, 11:44 a.m.
NEW TEXT FROM UNKNOWN SENDER
Hello Hello?

May 4, 11:52 a.m.
SENT TEXT FROM JULES TURNBULL
Cant today. Helping mom at crystal shop.

May 4, 11:55 a.m.
NEW TEXT FROM UNKNOWN SENDER
2 bad. U get UR UPenn housing packet yet?

May 4, 12:18 p.m.
SENT TEXT FROM JULES TURNBULL
No.

May 4, 12:19 p.m.
NEW TEXT FROM UNKNOWN SENDER
Why do U lie?

May 4, 12:20 p.m.
SENT TEXT FROM JULES TURNBULL
Huh?

May 4, 12:22 p.m.
NEW TEXT FROM UNKNOWN SENDER
Bitch. U Lie.

May 4, 12:23 p.m.

SENT TEXT FROM JULES TURNBULL

Carter? Why so mad?

May 4, 12:25 p.m.

NEW TEXT FROM UNKNOWN SENDER

Lying bitch.

May 4, 12:29 p.m.

NEW TEXT FROM UNKNOWN SENDER

I hope U die.

27

Downstairs in the rec room at Jeff's house, Carter and the guys were flopped on the overstuffed white leather sofas waiting for Reed to show up so they could head to Miami for their big night on the town. They had the music going—Kanye's new album, which they all thought was his best yet—and on the TV, Jonah Hill was gesticulating and making crazy faces with the sound off.

"I still think we should stop off in Little Havana and go to that hole-in-the-wall sandwich shop," said Carlos. He was lying upside down, his head hanging off the edge of the couch, his feet draped over the back cushion.

"Carlos! Carlos! We've been over this," said Jeff, lobbing a piece of ice from his Coke at him. "It's South

Beach or bust. If you want a Cuban sandwich, there'll be food trucks. You can probably even get one of those Korean tacos if you want."

"Won't be as good."

Jeff sighed. "Nobody wants to spend the whole night trolling around Little Havana trying to find some place your dad took you once when you were eight, Carlos. Right? Andy? Carter?"

"Not if it means less time macking on the crazy-hot chicks in South Beach," said Andy. He jumped up from his place sunken deep in the recliner and did his Andy Mack Attack dance, which mostly meant jiggling his large, awkward body to the music until he tripped over a PlayStation controller on the floor.

Everyone cracked up, even Carlos.

"I think you're outvoted, Carlos," said Carter. "Democracy in action."

"If you want we can drop you off, though," said Jeff. "You can get your sandwich. We'll be hanging out at Arkadia sharing LeBron and Drake's bottle service."

More laughs.

Carter had been dreaming of this night in Miami with the guys since February. He'd Tommy Hilfigered himself out, gone as preppy as you could get: a red-and-blue long-sleeve polo shirt with the Hilfiger shield on the breast, brand-new khakis, old-school, flash-white Puma soccer shoes.

Odds were high that they wouldn't get into the clubs, of course, but either way, they'd be out all night long. Jeff's dad's Mustang would be parked in one of the big public lots and the five of them would be free to wander till dawn. They'd drink rum and Cokes from the Big Gulps they'd fashioned just for this purpose, and kick along the strip, and just see what happened. However it shook out, one thing was sure: the hilarity this evening would be nonstop.

"Jesus," said Carter. "What's taking Reed so long?"

"He just texted me," said Carlos. He scrolled through his phone and read it out loud: "Spaced out in the perfect weather. There in fifteen."

"That kid," said Jeff. "He's always in a daze."

Carter's phone rang. When he saw it was Lilah calling, he ducked through the sliding door into the pebbled garden outside.

"Hi, handsome," she said. Her voice was saturated with forced positivity. "You know what today is?"

"I'm not sure," said Carter. "What?"

"It's the opening night of the Dream Bazaar at Harpoon Haven."

"Great, Lilah," Carter said, bracing himself for what he knew was coming next. "Sounds cool."

"It's going to be a special kickoff celebration. Half off on all rides and two-for-one tickets for the games.

We should go, don't you think? Maybe you can win me another lion."

"I can't," he said. "Remember? Tonight's my trip to South Beach with the guys."

Though Lilah didn't say anything, Carter could hear her pouting on the other end of the line.

"We could do it tomorrow night," he said.

"It won't be the same tomorrow. Tonight's the big kickoff."

"I'm sorry. I promised the guys."

The silence between them felt to Carter like it was laced with tiny razor blades. Each second that went by cut a little deeper. She was waiting him out, as though if she withheld her acknowledgment long enough, maybe he'd change his mind.

"I've been looking forward to this for three months, Lilah," he said wearily.

She sighed. "Fine," she said. "Go. Go have your fun with Jeff and Carlos. Whatever. I'll sit and watch stupid PBS shows with my parents."

"Lilah—"

"Don't Lilah me. You're going to do what you want, anyway. I understand. You'd rather drool over South Beach sluts than hang out with me. Okay, fine. Just, I don't see why I should have to applaud you for it, or whatever."

"Lilah, come on. That's not fair."

The silence. The razors cut to the bone.

"I really need you tonight," she said, her voice breaking. "I'm . . . I feel like I'm sinking. I'm worried about myself."

Carter understood what she was implying. Maybe if he'd been less afraid of the possibility of Lilah spiraling into another of her self-destructive depressions, if he hadn't cheated on her with Jules, he would have stood his ground. Instead, he gave in. He said, "Okay. I'll come over for a second and we can talk. All right? But then, really, I'm going to South Beach."

Lilah's mood turned just like that. Suddenly she was happy and affectionate again. "You're the best," she said. "I don't know what I'd do without you."

After he hung up, Carter stepped back inside and told the guys the score. "Hey," he said. "I'm going to have to meet up with you guys later. I've got to deal with something. I'll text you when I'm on my way, cool?"

"Lilah?" Jeff said.

Carter shrugged, hoping his friends couldn't see the frustration building up inside him.

"Dude," Jeff said, shaking his head, "what's happened to you? I fear for your future."

"I'll tell you what's happened," Andy said. "Mofo's pussy whipped. P-U-S-S-Y whipped."

"Well, see ya," said Carlos. "Wouldn't want to be ya."

Carter knew how they felt. He didn't want to be himself, either.

28

When Carter arrived at Lilah's house, she wouldn't let him come upstairs. She was "getting dressed." Trapped by the dating conventions he'd thought the two of them had outgrown years before, he strained to smile for her parents while he waited for her.

They were putting on their perfect-family act. They gave him iced tea. They complimented him on his Hilfiger shirt.

"You're always so well dressed, Carter. Did you buy that shirt especially for tonight? To impress all the people at Harpoon Haven?" her mom said. She had a way of saying things that sounded like compliments but felt like condemnations.

He sipped at his tea. He murmured that no, it was just a shirt. "But I'm glad you like it. Your opinion is so important to me," he said, and he wondered if she heard the irony in his voice.

They definitely weren't acting like there was anything wrong. And the way they talked about his plans with Lilah—plans he hadn't actually made, but that now looked like they were going to happen nonetheless—made him suspect that he had been tricked.

When Lilah finally came downstairs, she was all smiles and joy. She'd dressed herself up in a bright red-and-yellow halter-top sundress that showed off her breasts. She'd put on too much makeup—not so much that she looked ridiculous, but enough that it highlighted her insecurity more than it did her beauty.

She took Carter by the hand and led him toward the front door.

Resentment boiled under his skin. He'd definitely been tricked.

As soon as they were outside, Carter unleashed his hand from hers and said, "What the hell, Lilah?"

"Don't be like that," she said. "Don't ruin tonight."

They were standing directly in front of the door to the house, and knowing that Lilah's mother had a way of lurking and listening in on their conversations, Carter stalked down the walkway to the curb where his BMW was parked. Lilah followed him, almost skipping behind him. Her body language said that her life was beautiful, blissful. She was putting on a show. Carter wasn't sure for whom.

"It doesn't really look like you're 'sinking,'" he said.

She plumped out her lower lip and batted her eyelashes at him. "I thought after you saw me all dressed up that you'd maybe rather spend the night with me."

"Is that what you thought? Really?"

"That's what I *hoped*."

"Hmm. Okay." Carter twisted an imaginary knob above his ear and made a ticking noise, listening to his brain unwind. "Nope," he said. "Doesn't look like I've changed my mind."

Lilah glanced back toward the house. Something broke in her. The tears were pressing under her skin. "Please, Carter," she said. "What am I going to tell my mom?"

"Why is that my problem? Tell her whatever you want."

"She's been putting a lot of pressure on me lately. Haven't you noticed how nervous I've been? She thinks I'm going to . . . I don't know, hurt myself again."

"Are you?"

"No. Not now that you're here," she said.

"God, Lilah. Why are you doing this to me?" he said.

"Doing what? Trying to keep us together?"

This was blackmail. And emotional terrorism. Carter

could barely contain his anger. "Jesus, Lilah," he said. "I can't even have one single night to myself? You know? Unlike you, I actually like having friends. I want to see them sometimes."

Lilah slumped to the curb and held her head in her hands. Her back quivered like she was crying, and Carter knew he had gone too far. He sat down next to her.

"Look," he said. "We can go another night. Tomorrow if you want. The rides and games will be the same either way."

No answer. Lilah just kept shaking, burying her head deeper and deeper between her legs. Carter rubbed her back with one hand, trying to soothe her, or get her to stop crying, at least.

"I'll make it up to you," he said.

Suddenly sitting up straight, Lilah turned on him. Her eyes were dry—she hadn't been crying after all. She was tight with fury. "You don't get anything, do you, Carter? I *need* you. When you're not around, I feel like . . . like I don't have any reason to exist."

"Do you think that's fair to me?" he asked quietly.

She just stared at him. She was so volatile that she was quivering. He knew he wasn't going to get to South Beach tonight. He knew he should be concerned about Lilah, but he was seeing red.

"Fuck it," he said. "Fine. Lilah, you win."

She waited until they were downtown looking for

parking to speak to him again. "Tell me you're not going to be mad all night," she said. "I was hoping this would be special."

He looked at her. Did she not understand what she was doing to him? "I'm here," he said. "What more do you want?"

"Oh, I don't know. A little love. Some sense that you're excited to be here with me."

"Well," he said, "you can't always get what you want."

As they wandered through the arcades of Harpoon Haven, Carter felt like he was standing outside his own body, watching himself step over crushed soda cups and half-eaten cones of cotton candy with Lilah. Eating fried dough with Lilah. Listening to Lilah gush over things they'd done years ago, how romantic it had been, how sweet and beautiful those memories were; and with every word out of her mouth, Carter was forced to compare then to now, to the strain and the agony of this prison he was in.

He could see his own future life with Lilah spooled out in front of him like a trip wire. The future she yearned for, anyway. Maybe he'd condemned himself to a life of fear, sitting around in some little house in Dream Point, watching gobs of TV because it was the only thing he could do that didn't throw Lilah into a suicidal panic, begging her for permission just to even talk on the phone with Jeff.

And he couldn't help thinking about the last time he'd been here, with Jules. He couldn't help thinking about how relaxed, how alive, how simply happy he'd been that night. How magical Harpoon Haven had seemed when she was there by his side, how hard it had been to resist kissing her, how much he wished she was here with him right now. It was as though Lilah had engineered this night explicitly to make him as uncomfortable as she could.

Lilah noticed. Of course she noticed. Finally, while they waited in line to ride the Tilt-A-Whirl, she said, "You could at least pretend to be having a good time."

He stifled the sarcastic responses that flooded his mind and waited awkwardly for the line to inch forward.

"Carter. Why'd you even come out with me tonight if all you're going to do is brood and make me feel like shit?"

This was too much. "Are you seriously asking me that, Lilah?" he said, almost spitting the words in her face. "You gave me no choice."

"You've always got a choice."

"Not when you threaten to hurt yourself if I say no, I don't."

"I never threatened to hurt myself."

The other people in line were noticing. They turned their faces away and cocked their ears. Smirks and frowns played over their faces.

"Sure, whatever, Lilah," Carter said. He took a step forward, keeping up with the line.

Lilah kept up with him, pressed like a yappy dog at his heels. "Don't whatever me." When he didn't acknowledge her, she repeated herself. "Carter. Don't whatever me. It's like you don't even love me anymore."

"Jesus Christ," Carter muttered.

This acting like he was above it all just egged Lilah on. She stomped on his foot to force his attention.

"Hey!" He turned on her.

Maybe he was pissed, but at least he was paying attention to her now. "What's the point of your being here if all you're going to do is punish me the whole time?" she said.

He wasn't sure who he pitied more, her or himself. And in that moment, while he struggled to control his rage, he realized that there was nothing he could do— nothing he'd ever be able to do—to save Lilah from herself.

"You know what," he said, "you're right. I'm done punishing you." He ducked under the metal barricade and stepped off the line.

As he walked away, he heard her shouting after him, "Hey! Carter! Where are you going?!"

He turned and called back to her, "Where do you think? I'm going to South Beach."

29

As he sat in front of his meticulously organized desk, Carter watched the minutes click by on his computer screen. Finals were set to begin the next week, and though he'd already been accepted to UPenn, he still worried about bombing them. He wasn't the kind of guy to coast through the finish line. He'd lined up his textbooks and notebooks in an order based on his testing schedule, and created a careful plan of action for himself, blocking out the time needed to study for each subject. But each time he attempted to review his notes, they seemed like they were written in a foreign language.

His chest wouldn't stop throbbing. It felt like it was going to burst, a feeling like people describe when they talk about heartbreak, but Carter's heart wasn't breaking. It just hurt. He'd started feeling this way that night with Lilah at Harpoon Haven, and in the four days since, the feeling had intensified. It was constant, a mixture of anger and resentment and worry and fear that congealed into a dark image of Lilah in his head. A pressure so extreme that he could hardly concentrate on anything else.

Carter forced himself to stay in his chair, becoming more and more frustrated with himself. He'd already played thirty-six games of Spider Solitaire—the only thing he could bring himself to concentrate on—and he knew if he kept this up, he'd still be staring cross-eyed at the screen at three a.m., winning nothing but a few digitized fireworks and the promise of a bleary day at school tomorrow.

What he needed was Jules. Just to talk to her. Just to be in her presence for a while.

He sent her a text to remind her he existed, but she didn't respond.

Ten more games of Solitaire and still no response.

He yearned to tell her she haunted him each and every day. To tell her he'd been wrong. He'd made the wrong choice. But he knew he couldn't do that. Not while he was still caught up in this mess with Lilah.

He sent her another text.

Nothing.

He couldn't stand it anymore. If he'd broken up with Lilah way back in March, after that perfect "nondate" with Jules, maybe Jules wouldn't have forgotten him already. There was no way he was going to be able to save Lilah, anyway. He was just making himself miserable trying.

He had to move. He had to fix his life.

He sped through the backstreets toward Lilah's neighborhood. It was just ten. Her parents would be nodding off to the evening news. She'd be upstairs in her bedroom, avoiding them.

When Lilah's mom answered the door in her pink flowered pajamas and her fuzzy white slippers, she gave a pinched little sigh. "Oh, Carter, we weren't expecting you," she whispered. "We're all in bed right now."

"I know. I'm sorry. I'll be just a second. I've, uh, got something I forgot to give her earlier. A book, uh . . ." He was winging it. Making it up as he went along. "*The Grapes of Wrath.*"

He wondered what she saw as she gazed at him with her sleep-weary eyes—the quiet, gentlemanly guy who answered her daughter's every beck and call, or the rabid dog that he felt like tonight, burning with pent-up rage. Did she see the sweat beading on his forehead? The spite flashing behind his smile?

She nodded and stepped away to let him into the house.

Avoiding eye contact, he squeezed past her and tip-toed upstairs. He knocked softly and then pushed open the door to Lilah's room.

Lilah, who had been sitting at her computer but not really working, saw him in the mirror above her makeup table—so awkward there in the doorway, his hands patting at his waist like they didn't know where to go, his whole body tense. She could tell just by looking at him that he wasn't here to say sorry for his behavior at Harpoon Haven.

"Hey," he said.

It took her a long time to respond. She had to wait until all her shields were in place. She didn't want to surrender to her tears all at once. She didn't want to give him the satisfaction of seeing that.

Once she was composed enough to enter the battle, she turned slowly, slowly away from her computer.

"Hey," she said.

And so there they were. A warm relief swept through Carter's body. He was finally doing what he should have done months ago.

"Think you might have a minute to talk?"

She tipped her head ambivalently. She was going to make this as hard as she could for him.

"Should we go outside?" he said. "Maybe sit out front?"

"Sure."

They took the long walk down the hallway, down the steps through the darkened foyer to the crystal-inlaid front door. There was no touching, no eye contact, no discussion as they marched. They wandered past the rosebushes and the azaleas and all the other nonnative flowers displayed on Lilah's family's artificially lush, landscaped lawn, and found two spots, not quite next to each other, on the white concrete curb.

The time had come. Lilah braced herself. She felt dead inside, cold as stone.

Carter adjusted his position so he was facing her and took her hand in his. "I've been thinking and thinking about this," he said, "and you're right. There's . . . everything's screwed up."

Each fumbled word out of Carter's mouth hit Lilah like a separate punch in the gut.

"And after what happened on Friday . . . it's just . . . it's not going to work. It's never going to work."

She knew he'd been thinking this for a long time, but hearing him say it out loud still stunned her. Her heart had no room in it for these words from him. Yes, things had been hard; things had been pretty horrible. But that other thing that had sustained them throughout the previous three years still existed. It had to exist. She could still remember it, so it must exist.

"I really tried. I can't tell you how hard . . ."

But it didn't exist. The new reality was sinking in.

She excised her hands from his with a snap.

He said it again. "I'm sorry." That's all he could say. Like saying *I'm sorry* did anyone any good.

She'd tried so hard. She'd put up with so much. And she'd managed the Jules situation so carefully. How dare he? This wasn't allowed to happen to her.

"Did you?" she said. "Did you really try? Is that what you call fucking that bitch Jules Turnbull behind my back while I'm *vomiting my guts out at home*?" She was losing control. She didn't care. "'Cause that's what you did, isn't it? Isn't it?"

Carter didn't respond. He refused to make eye contact with her.

"You thought I didn't know about it, didn't you? You thought, *Lilah, she's just a naïve little girl. I can get away with any shit I want to with her.* But guess what? I'm not as stupid as you think."

The way his eyes bulged at this revelation told her that she'd scored a point on him.

"I don't think you're stupid," he mumbled.

"What, then? You obviously thought you could get away with it."

Carter ran his hand through his floppy, sandy hair. "Does it really matter?" he said. "I was trying . . . What was I supposed to do, Lilah? I was afraid of what you might do if I broke up with you."

The way he was spinning his guilt, denying nothing,

but implying that this was all somehow her fault, disgusted her. And still, she was desperate to get a confession from him. "So it's true. Just admit it. We both know it's true. You've been screwing that skank behind my back all this time."

Warring with him was better than nothing. Better this than the howling winds of loneliness that would sweep through her once he left.

Carter looked Lilah dead in the eye. Whatever compassion he'd been feeling before, whatever instinct he'd had to protect her emotions, was gone.

"She's not a skank," he said.

There was a beat, a delayed reaction, then Lilah felt everything inside her turn to liquid. She was seeing spots, surging with adrenaline, no longer aware of anything in the world except his taunting presence there in front of her. Her ability to think had been flushed away.

She shoved him, and when he didn't tip over she shoved him again harder, slapped at his shoulder, his chest.

"Fuck you!" she hissed. Then she shouted it. "Fuck you!"

She leaned back and kicked at him with her heels.

He just sat there, watching her, so dispassionate, his face so empty of emotion. She felt a hatred beyond anything she'd ever felt before.

"You lied to me," she said. "YOU LIED TO ME!

And I loved you." She wasn't sure if she was pleading with him to change his mind, or accusing him, or what. "Say something, you asshole," she said. "Don't just—say something!"

But he didn't say anything. He just kept on watching.

She hated his face and his stupid preppy clothes and his high-tops and the way he seemed to have so much pity for her.

She leaped up and stormed away—three, four steps— then the rage broke in her again and she turned and ran back to him. She slapped and shoved at him again. She kicked him. She was howling. "Why?" she said. "Why? What does she have that I don't?"

"Lilah," he said. He was so above it all.

"I'm not your Lilah anymore. You said it, not me. You . . ." Coherent speech was beyond her. She was uncontrolled emotion.

"Lilah, stop it. Calm down."

"No. You don't get to decide when I calm down." Another surge of rage and she went at him with all the strength she contained. When he held her off with a stiff arm, she clamped her fingers into his arm and dug into his skin with her nails. He'd hurt her; why shouldn't she hurt him back?

The answer was: because she couldn't. Now that he'd told her and it was all over, she'd lost her power over him. This final lashing out just made clear to him how right his decision to leave her had been.

Finally, exhausted, totally emptied out, Lilah dropped to the curb and imploded into sobs.

She'd hate him forever, and maybe he deserved this.

He stood up. He took her in one last time: sprawled, half-coiled on the curb, her face flushed and streaked with mascara and tears. He felt bad for her and he wished he could comfort her, but he knew he couldn't.

"I'm sorry," he said. "I'm really, truly sorry about everything."

And he was gone, leaving her there in front of her parents' house with nothing but her jealous rage to console her.

30

Carter took the steps up to the porch at Jules's house three at a time and he had to check himself in order not to pound on the front door like a crazy person. His heart beat like thunder in his chest. He felt like everything—his whole life—depended on this moment.

Why was nobody answering? The lights were on. There was someone home.

It was a little after eleven. He hoped he wasn't being rude or something.

Finally, the faded curtain drawn across the window in the door shifted a little and he saw an eye peering out at him. Then the door opened a crack and Jules's mother slipped out onto the porch. She pulled the door shut tight behind her.

"Can I help you?" she said.

Carter knew from Jules that her mother was a bit of a blissed-out hippie, and she definitely looked the type, with the colorful frayed sarong tied around her waist and the bright-yellow bikini top and long, flowing, sandy-blond hair, but something in the set of her jaw intimidated him.

"Yeah, hi, I'm—hi!" Carter knew he was speaking breathlessly fast, but he couldn't slow himself down. His thoughts were exploding at an unrelenting pace. "You're Jules's mother, right? It's nice to finally meet you. I'm Carter. One of Jules's friends. I was hoping I could maybe talk to her for a second."

"I know who you are, Carter," she said. "Jules can't come to the door right now." For a second, she gazed at the aloe plant mounted on the porch railing. Then she went on. "She's not here."

"She's—oh. Can you tell me where she is? It's sort of important that I talk to her."

She was sizing him up. She had a quiet grounded-ness about her, a sense of something tough and strong underneath her spiritual exterior, and he could feel her hardening as she considered what to say next. "Don't you think you've said enough to Jules already?"

There was something not right about this

conversation. Carter scratched his head. He was confused. "I . . . er . . . ," he said.

"Aren't you at least a little ashamed to be showing up here like this?" Her tone of voice remained gentle and calm despite the harshness of her words.

"I don't—" he said, but the woman cut him off.

"Of course. You don't know what I'm talking about. Okay." She patted Carter on the shoulder. "I've seen guys like you before. You never know what us girls are talking about."

"But I don't—"

"Believe it or not, Jules has a certain amount of self-respect."

"I—I'm confused."

"I could show you the texts you sent her. Refresh your memory."

"Texts?" He searched his thoughts for what she might be talking about. Had he crossed some line he didn't know existed? Maybe he should have stopped bothering her when she hadn't responded to the messages, but they hadn't been mean or anything like that. They'd been goofy stuff, just normal hellos and things. Sweet. He'd meant them to be sweet. "I'm really sorry if something I wrote to Jules upset her somehow. I mean—"

"Uh—no. Try that on some other girl. You knew exactly what you were doing."

"Look, can I just talk to her, like, for a second? I'm

having sort of a crisis here and she . . ." He paused and tried to pull himself together. "Jules is the only one who knows what I'm going through."

Jules's mother ran her hand through her long wheat-like hair. She crossed her arms pointedly across her chest and began tapping her finger against her elbow. She wanted him to leave. That was obvious.

"There's some misunderstanding, I think," he said. "Can I see what you're talking about? You said you'd show me the texts. I can explain, I think, if I see them."

Jules's mom shook her head. It was beyond a no. It was a cosmic disappointment. She was disgusted by him. "You know," she said, "Jules had high hopes for you. She told me you were one of the good ones. I guess not. It's a shame."

He stood there, baffled, fighting the urge to defend himself. But there was no use. He could tell. There was nothing he could say. She was going to stand there and stare him down like a lioness no matter what he said. And protesting any further would just make it worse. He had the sense that she could eat him alive if she wanted to.

"You should go now, don't you think?" said Jules's mom.

As he made his way down the wooden staircase to the street, Jules's mother stood guard, watching him, waiting for him to be gone.

Back in his car, he couldn't bring himself to put the key into the ignition. To turn the car on and roll away would be to say good-bye to Jules forever.

He sat there for a long time, staring up at the lights coming through her window, wishing there was some way to let her know how completely he'd fallen in love with her.

31

Hidden behind a beaded curtain, Jules watched Carter walk sadly back to his car. She wondered if he could see her perched on the window seat, wondered if he could feel her longing reaching across the distance between them.

He moved very slowly. His head hung low between his shoulders. She could sense the reluctance to go in his gait and in the way he dug his hands deep into his pockets.

Opening the door of his BMW, he looked up at her window, searching for her. He ran his hand through his sandy hair in the way she'd seen him do so often. Then he settled in the driver's seat, still gazing up at the window.

She was holding the strands of light-tan beads apart with a finger in order to see what was happening out there, curious about whether or not Carter saw her through the crack.

"Jules," her mother said, touching her shoulder. "You should come away from the window now."

She knew her mom was right, but she couldn't stop looking, not as long as he was still out there. "In a second," she said.

Her mom squeezed once and then let go of her.

She gave Jules a bit of space, seating herself across the room at the dining table, which was strewn with crystals of different sizes and colors, a new shipment she'd received that she'd been in the process or sorting when Carter had arrived at the door. Though she pretended to be working on this project now, Jules knew her mom was mostly focused on her.

Nonetheless, she kept her vigil at the window. The urge to lean out, to call to him and tell him that she still thought about him more often than she should, was almost too much to bear. Did he know she was reaching her heart down to him the way he was reaching his up to her? She wanted to ask him why he'd sent those ugly texts. What had she done to turn him so against her? Did he know about the video Lilah had on her phone? Did he hate her for it? So many questions she'd never be able to ask.

Eventually Carter started the ignition of his car and

the headlights went on. He rolled out of the sand-strewn side of the road and slowly drove away.

Jules let the beads drop. When she looked at her mother, she saw her quickly pick up a lump of azurite and shift it into a new pile, pretending to be engrossed in her task.

"Did you have to be so hard on him?" Jules said.

"Somebody had to," her mom said.

"I don't even know for sure that it was him who sent the texts."

"You don't know it wasn't."

"It might have been the girlfriend."

"In that case, you definitely shouldn't be talking to him," her mother said. "Has he broken up with her?"

"I don't think so."

"So . . ." Her mother rolled her open palms out toward her as though to say, *You know what you should do.* The compassion on her face as she silently gazed at Jules was unending, and Jules knew that this quiet fire was her way of showing concern. She wanted what was best for her. And Jules hadn't even told her about the confrontations and threats with Lilah. She couldn't tell her that. She couldn't tell anyone.

"It gets better," her mother said. "Love fades."

Jules shrugged. "Does it?" she said. Before her mother could say anything more, she added, "I don't think I want it to."

32

The facts were simple. They told a story, but no one knew what this story was: A car had been found in the parking lot, vandalized. A Honda Civic—nine years old, already dented and scuffed, one of those hand-me-downs that the less wealthy kids puttered around town in. Someone had taken a key to it. It appeared that at first some sort of words had been scratched onto the hood, but this had been crossed over, gouged out with hundreds of scribbles, and so whatever it said couldn't be read. The rear driver's-side light had been smashed in. The driver's-side mirror was shattered. There was a hairline crack in one of the windows.

The car belonged to Jules Turnbull.

This is all that was known.

Theories about who could have done it and how grew into rumors, which were elaborated upon until they became conspiracies. Then another rumor would spread through the student body, replacing the first and the second and the third, and the excitement would rise again. There was danger here. And scandal. It was better than TV because it was happening right here, right now.

Not everyone felt this way, of course.

Especially Carter.

As he and Jeff ate their soggy tempura in the cafeteria, they traded rumors.

"Todd Norris, her ex-boyfriend," Jeff said. "Gotta be him." He popped a piece of battered broccoli into his mouth. "Can't you just see it? Todd stumbles on a hit of acid. He's totally out of his gourd. Hearing voices. Seeing, like, flying cats or whatever. And he's thinking he's the Silver Surfer or something—riding his board through the backstreets of the Slats, following some song that's floating in Technicolor in front of him, one of the corny love songs that Jules serenaded Peter Talbot with in *Camelot* last fall, and suddenly he's right there at Jules's house, and there's Peter Talbot standing under Jules's window in full knight's armor, singing"—Jeff broke into an off-key melody—"*If ever I would leave you, it wouldn't be in summer*"—and then returned to his fantasy. "And he thinks Peter Talbot is a dragon come to steal Jules away from him, so he takes up his sword and tries to slay the dragon—but Peter's not there. And the dragon's just Jules's car and he's scratched the hell out of it all of a sudden."

Jeff had gotten a smile out of Carter. But the darker, more likely possibilities still hung like thunderclouds in his mind. Carter had yet to tell Jeff that he'd broken up with Lilah. He worried that this might be her doing. He knew her—he'd loved her. He didn't want to believe that she could be so vindictive.

"I don't know, man," he said. "Jules and Todd broke up, like, four months ago."

Jeff made a face. "Love never dies," he said. "Speaking of which . . ." He nodded toward something behind Carter's back.

Lilah. She seemed to have recovered from her fury of the night before. She was joyous, ebullient, her smile so wide it took over her whole face. The first thing she did after plopping her tray of tempura down on the table next to Carter's was to lean in and kiss him on the cheek.

"There he is," she said. "My hero."

She rubbed his back. When she climbed into the bench attached to the table, she let her hand linger for a beat on his shoulder.

Her affection disturbed Carter. It made him tense up. It was like she'd completely forgotten that he'd broken up with her, like in her mind, their relationship was better than it had ever been.

He flicked her off of him with a twitch of his shoulder.

And Jeff, who knew him better than anyone, saw the conflict between them without having to be told. He raised an eyebrow, asking with a nod if maybe he should tease her into submission, but Carter shook his head as though to say, *Let it ride.*

Knowing she'd interrupted something, Lilah pressed herself into the conversation. "What are my two favorite guys up to today?"

"Nothing," said Carter. "We're eating tempura. Obviously. And having a conversation."

"Wow, touchy. Whatcha talking about?" she asked.

"Just . . . stuff. What do you want?"

"Do I have to want something? Am I not allowed to sit and talk with my friends in the lunchroom now?"

It was all too much. She was playing an ominous game here, and Carter wanted nothing to do with it. He squeezed the bridge of his nose and held his eyes shut in an attempt to control his frustration.

"Okay. You want to talk, Lilah? Let's talk. Did you hear about Jules's car?" he said.

"What?"

"Jules's car." Carter stared her in the eye, trying to suss out what secrets she might be holding.

"Somebody took a baseball bat to it," Jeff said.

"You're kidding."

"I'm not kidding," said Carter.

"Wow."

"You really don't know anything about this? It's the only thing anybody's been talking about today."

"I live under a rock," she said. "You know that. Do they know who did it?"

"Do you know who did it?" Carter asked pointedly.

"God, no. I mean, I'm just hearing about this now."

The expression on Carter's face was enough. He didn't have to tell her how skeptical he was.

"It's shocking, huh?" said Lilah. "I mean, she's like the sweetest thing. And she's so talented. You know, I bet it's some girl who's jealous of her acting. Like a psycho *Black Swan* sort of thing."

"My money's on that ex of hers, Todd," said Jeff. "'Like, whoa, dude. Nobody breaks up with Todd Norris, dude. Whoa, what's that? Is that car trying to eat me alive? Thwack, thwack, thwack. I'll show you, car!'" Jeff couldn't help himself. He was in love with his tale about the dragon-slaying surfer.

Carter kicked him under the table. He wasn't really upset at Jeff. It was just that this shtick was too much for his senses to take right now. He was too distressed by the smiley, happy act Lilah was putting on, the sudden compassion for Jules she was displaying.

"Carter," she said now, "you're sort of friendly with

her, aren't you? Have you talked to her today? I mean, I can't imagine. I'd be totally destroyed if someone did that to my car."

"You don't have a car, Lilah," Carter said without thinking.

Then seeing the disbelief on Jeff's face, the words that had just come out of Lilah's mouth sank in. The depths of her deceit. The saccharine strain of her positive attitude. He felt the adrenaline surging to his chest.

"You sure you don't know anything about this?" he asked her.

It was like he'd slapped her. "Is that an accusation?" she said.

"It's a question."

"I can't believe you're asking me this."

"But I am."

Though they were both speaking in reasonable tones of voice, the tension between them caught Jeff off guard. He tracked their conversation with a bemused interest, his glance bouncing back and forth and back and forth like a Ping-Pong ball from Carter to Lilah to Carter to Lilah.

"You know what, I'll see you guys later," Lilah said finally, seeing that Carter wasn't going to soften. She stood up in a huff. "But for your information, Carter, no. I don't *know anything about this*. I hadn't even heard about it until you just told me. Good to know the kind of person you think I am, though."

"If I find out you're lying, Lilah," said Carter sharply, "I swear to God, I'll—"

"Well, you won't, 'cause I'm not."

She stormed off, leaving her barely touched tray of tempura on the table.

When she was gone, Jeff asked Carter, "What was that all about?"

"I broke up with her last night."

For a second Jeff wasn't sure he'd heard Carter correctly. Then he dropped his head to the cold enameled table and slapped his open palm against it twice, laughing.

"Seriously, though, Jeff," said Carter, "do you think Lilah could do something like this?"

Pulling himself together, Jeff said, "Do you?"

"Maybe."

Carter stared at Jeff for a second with pleading eyes. "I mean, should I try to do something about it?"

"Have you asked Jules about what's going on?"

"She won't talk to me."

"Then what can you do?"

"I wish I knew," said Carter. "I'd hate for anything to happen to her."

33

May 9, 1:57 a.m.

NEW TEXT FROM UNKNOWN SENDER

Nice car. Ur face would look good smashed like that.

May 9, 10:44 p.m.

NEW TEXT FROM UNKNOWN SENDER

Is it true abt U + the football team, whore? Yum yum!

May 11, 6:15 a.m.

NEW TEXT FROM UNKNOWN SENDER

Ur life is 1 long botched abortion.

34

Jules stormed through the house throwing things everywhere. She was looking for the duffel bag full of her dance clothes. She couldn't find it anywhere. She'd already ransacked her bedroom, and now she was on to the living room, digging in the couch, checking under its cushions, opening drawers that hadn't been opened in years, picking up and then putting down boxes of her mother's crystals and Polynesian sarongs. She even pulled up the rattan mat on the floor and checked under it, though of course, the lumpy bag couldn't have been hiding there.

The longer she searched, the angrier and more anxious she became. She'd had the bag yesterday; she knew she had. She remembered throwing it over her shoulder and walking up the stairs to the porch with it. The fact that it had disappeared like this seemed impossible to her. It should be right here—but right here where?

Her mother, trying to be helpful, trailed behind her. She held her mug of ginseng tea in two hands, and in between sips, she reminded Jules that getting upset like this was doing more harm than good.

Rubbing Jules's shoulders, she said, "Let it find you. If you really need it, it's sure to make itself known."

"Mom, don't."

"Or you could let me help." She put her nose to her mug and let the scent of her tea saturate her nostrils. "You could at least tell me what it is you're looking for."

Jules shot her a look. She didn't want her mother's help. She was embarrassed to be this upset about something so insignificant as a bag of smelly clothes. It was stupid, really. But she was fixated, frantic. There weren't enough Buddhist aphorisms in the world to calm her down.

"My stuff, all right?" she said. "My dance stuff."

Her mother nodded sagely. She placed her tea on a circular glass-topped end table and took Jules's face gently between her two hands. Peering into her daughter's eyes, she tried to will some degree of calm into her body. "Let's go outside, okay?" she said.

Jules let herself be led out onto the porch.

"Is this what you're looking for?" her mother asked, picking the duffel bag up from the place where it lay, right there in plain sight next to the sunflower on the porch table.

Jules nodded.

No way would she cry. If she cried, she'd have to acknowledge—both to herself and to her mother—that the reason she was upset had nothing to do with the dance bag. Now that the bag was found, she felt weirdly worse than she had when she was sure she'd lost it. She never lost track of things like this. It was Lilah's fault. All of this. Lilah and her stalking. To top it all off, now she was going to be late for school.

She snatched the bag out of her mother's hand and threw it over her shoulder before racing back inside to grab her book bag.

"A little thanks, maybe?" her mother said, calling through the screen door.

"Yeah, okay, Mom. Thanks."

When Jules returned to the porch, her mother was seated at the table. "Can I have your hand, just for a second?"

"No, I'm late."

Her mom smiled at her—the soothing smile, the one that meant, *Take deep breaths and keep calm.* "Well, if you're late already, you might as well skip first period and sit with me for a little bit." She reached out and took Jules's hand in hers. "Is this about that boy? Carter?"

Jules sighed. It was and it wasn't. Just thinking about Carter made her heart ache. She tried to pull her hand away, but her mother held tight. "No. Mom, it's nothing. It's just finals, okay? It's . . . whatever."

"You sure?"

"Yes, I'm sure." Jules looked her mother dead in the eye and lied. "Nothing's wrong. I'm just anxious about my tests. Can I go now?"

And so her mother released her, but not before letting her know with a crinkle of the eyes that she was disappointed at being kept out of the loop.

She didn't understand—she couldn't understand— that Jules was protecting her, and protecting herself. However diligently her mom struggled to live in the now and practiced letting go, Jules knew what a ferocious warrior she could be when she got mad.

And what would that solve? It would just make things worse. This was something Jules had to deal with on her own. School would be over in a week. Then there was graduation. And then she'd never have to see these people again in her life. *Ride it out*, she told herself as she ducked under the house's stilts to her car, which still ran, thank God, despite the damage that had been done to it.

Two blocks later, while she was waiting for the light

to turn at the corner of Beach Street and Bittern Avenue, she took her mascara brush out of her bag like she did every day on the way to school and flipped down the driver's-side sun visor to apply it.

WHORE

The word shouted at her like there was a person sitting on the visor's mirror. It was written in red lipstick, streaked capital letters. And seeing it, Jules felt like she'd been punched in the gut. She felt that way every day, it seemed. It wasn't even the word itself that got to her. It was that Lilah had gone after her car not once but twice, and this time she'd figured out where she lived and where she'd parked. She'd managed to get the door unlocked. Sometime last night while Jules had been asleep, she'd crept around, sitting in Jules's space, invading Jules's world like she'd invaded Jules's mind.

It was all too much. Futilely, Jules punched her steering wheel, her dashboard, the visor itself. All she accomplished with this was to hurt her hand. The tears that she'd swallowed earlier couldn't be kept down. They rose to the surface. They flowed and flowed.

And those texts. Those awful, horrifying texts. It was now more than obvious that it was Lilah, not Carter, trying to humiliate her over and over again. Trying to make her feel like she was nothing.

One more week, she reminded herself. One more week and it would be all over. And then who knew, maybe once she got to UPenn, she'd bump into Carter. Maybe they could start over without all the torture Lilah was putting her through. But this fantasy didn't solve the problems. If anything, it made her feel so incredibly alone.

35

May 11, 9:33 p.m.
NEW TEXT FROM LILAH BELL
U miss me yet?

May 11, 9:37 pm.
NEW TEXT FROM LILAH BELL
I miss you.

May 11, 9:47 p.m.
SENT TEXT FROM CARTER MOORE
I'm busy, Lilah.

May 11, 9:47 p.m.
NEW TEXT FROM LILAH BELL
Busy with your new girlfriend?

May 11, 10:19 p.m.
SENT TEXT FROM CARTER MOORE
No. Starfish regeneration.

May 11, 10:23 p.m.
NEW TEXT FROM LILAH BELL
[photo attachment: CARTER + LILAH]
Forever! ☺

May 11, 10:25 p.m.
SENT TEXT FROM CARTER MOORE
You have to stop this. I mean it.

36

After school on Thursday, Jules and Peter Talbot made their way to the theater building for one last look around. It was a trip she'd been both looking forward to and dreading, a sort of pilgrimage, one last good-bye to the place around which her high-school career had revolved. Tomorrow would be the last day of school. She'd be busy with the graduation rehearsal, and the celebrations and yearbook signings. And the rehearsal was going to happen right here in the theater—there'd be too many people around for her to savor the place the way it deserved to be savored.

She and Peter went through the practice rooms, gathering scarves and leg warmers and forgotten pages of rehearsal scripts. No one, not even Lilah, could ruin her enchanted memories of this place.

As she stood in front of the floor-to-ceiling mirror in which she'd watched herself dance for four years, she ran her hand along the smooth, worn surface of the bar where she'd propped her foot how many hundreds of times.

"I'm going to miss this," she said to Peter. "You think, maybe one day in the future, other girls learning how to do high kicks will hold on to this bar and think, *Wow, Jules Turnbull once did this very thing in this very same room?*"

"There'll be a plaque," he said. "To make sure they don't forget. It'll say: *This bar was used by the glorious Jules Turnbull when she was a student at Christopher Columbus. Feel free to use it to practice your routines. Maybe one day you'll be as good as she was. But probably not. She was just that good.*"

They vamped together in front of the mirror, did the "I'm the Diva, Watch Me Roar" strut they'd created together after watching Beyoncé in the Super Bowl half-time show.

The beat-up old saddle from *Oklahoma* was still propped in the corner of the room. Peter cocked a half grin at her when he saw it. "Hey, baby girl," he said to Jules, "want to take one more spin around the rodeo?"

When she hesitated, he struck a bowlegged cowboy

pose, holding his hand out to her, waiting. She curtsied, and the two of them began to do-si-do, exaggerating the moves, mocking them as they performed them. They barely got a minute into the routine before they fell into each other, laughing.

"All right, enough of that," said Jules. "It was stupid enough when we did it onstage. But look at this: they haven't ripped the *Camelot* tape up yet."

"It's weird, isn't it?" Peter said to her. "This place isn't going to belong to us anymore."

"Yeah. We'll be off to new practice rooms in new theater buildings."

"You will," he said. "I don't know about me."

"You're going to quit?"

"No, I just . . . I'm not sure. You've got real talent. I think maybe I'm just—I was good enough for this. Good enough for high school, but . . . " Peter smiled nostalgically.

"You'll never know unless you try," she said.

He winked at her. "Anyway, UPenn, here you come."

"Yeah," she said. Ever since the night they had their "nondate," the thought of UPenn evoked thoughts of Carter, who she knew would be there, too. She wondered if things would be different then. Less fraught. Maybe they'd bump into each other at some dorm-room party and get to talking, and then, who knows. The thought brought a wistful smile to her lips.

Peter raised an eyebrow.

"What?" she said.

"You look like you've got a secret," he said.

She blushed. "I guess you'll never know," she said. "Come on." She tugged him by the hand. "We should get our stuff."

They went through the rooms collecting their belongings: T-shirts, an old bra, a couple books—*The Poetry of Robert Frost: The Collected Poems, Twilight: New Moon*—she'd wondered where she'd lost that one.

Backstage in the theater itself, they found that the tables in the wings were still piled with the props from *Camelot*. There were the goblets and the torches and the shields and the swords they'd had so much fun fighting with during breaks in rehearsal.

"Should I steal one?" asked Peter.

"You think?"

He made a face, like to say, *Why not.*

"How about this," she said. She took one of the fake roses from the bouquet she'd carried onstage in the final scene, and tucked it into the lapel of the stylish suit jacket Peter wore every day like a uniform.

"I guess that's it, then," said Peter. "'Bye, theater." He waved at the rafters. He blew kisses toward the balcony. "I hope you save a little dream for me."

As they headed up the aisle toward the exit door, Jules stopped.

"You know what," she said. "I forgot my makeup kit."

Peter glanced at his watch, biting the corner of his lip.

"Sorry, I know you have to go," Jules said. "Don't wait for me. I'll catch up with you later."

She headed back to the dressing room alone.

A couple minutes later, makeup in tow, she made her way slowly back to the stage, lingering, gazing out at the auditorium, wondering if it would be too corny of her to sing one last song to the empty seats in the audience. She was getting a little teary. There was no one here but her, just her and the ghosts of the characters she'd played, and it was sort of spooky to think that she was all alone in this place that was usually so full of song and laughter. She kept thinking that one of her previous selves, Miss Adelaide from *Guys and Dolls*, or Cecily from *The Importance of Being Earnest*, was going to step out of the shadows and into the flat, bare-bulb glare from the stage lights and start talking to her about the adventures they'd had.

And then, just as she was about to take the leap and sing her heart out, just let the emotion flow, the room went pitch-black and the silence around her seemed to grow even more silent.

A cold chill went down her back. She couldn't see anything. She willed herself not to jump to conclusions. It was probably just Peter playing a joke on her.

She called out to the darkness. "Peter?"

There was no answer.

"Hello?" she said. "Peter? Not funny. At all."

When there was still no response, not even the tell-tale giggles that she would have expected from Peter, she called out again, a little more shrilly. "Peter. Come on. Turn the lights back on."

A piercing squeal of feedback shrieked through the auditorium.

Jules's eyes weren't adjusting to the dark. The panic and adrenaline building in her heart overwhelmed her other senses. Her voice cracked as she called out again, "Hello? Can you please turn on the lights?"

"Where's your boyfriend, Jules?" A snarling, menacing, whispering voice. "Or don't you have one anymore? Did you drive him away by sleeping with all his friends?" It wasn't coming from any one place. It floated around, moving from speaker to speaker. It was female. It was Lilah. Who else could it be? But it didn't sound like Lilah. It sounded like someone bolder and smarter than Lilah.

"I bet that's what you did. I bet you thought it would be fun to take them out to the beach when you thought no one was looking, and spread your legs for them, but guess what? People are always looking."

Jules could almost make out the shadow shape of the edge of the stage, the three steps leading down to the aisle. She felt her way across the stage, not trusting her eyes, afraid to fall.

"Everybody knows what kind of a skanky whore you are. Those guys you fucked behind your boyfriend's back? They're too disgusted to even admit what they did with you."

She tripped. At least she was down the stairs now.

"It's gonna be fun to see what happens when you get pregnant. How will you figure out who the father is? They're all going to deny that they've ever met you."

From here, she could see a little bit better. She ran up the aisle toward the light booth, where Lilah or who-ever it was had to be.

"Or maybe some of them will admit that they let you suck them off, but nobody's gonna be willing to say they're the father. Why would they? Who would want to help you raise your AIDS baby? That would mean they'd have to hang around with you."

Jules threw open the door to the light booth and lunged toward the green and white and red blinking lights in the darkness of the room. Her arms stretched out in front of her, she groped at the air, but there was nobody there.

She flicked on the light. No Lilah, no nothing—just the soundboard and the MacBook that controlled it. A sound file. Not a single person in sight.

"Nobody's ever going to love you. Guys don't fall in love with whores like you. They just use you and then throw—"

Jules finally got the sound file streaming from the computer to turn off.

She slumped to the carpeted floor of the light booth and clenched her head in her hands.

Maybe it was a good thing she hadn't found Lilah there. If she had, there's no way she would have been able to stop herself from wrapping her hands around the girl's throat and strangling her. And then what would have happened? She'd have been free of this torture, but her life would be ruined in a whole new way.

This had to stop. It had to.

She'd never felt murderous before in her life. She was a nice girl. A kind girl. She was charming and witty and she tried not to take life too seriously. If this went on much longer, she was going to lose the best parts of herself. She'd become bitter and angry, a paranoid mess. She could feel the change happening already.

She ached for someone—anyone—she could talk to. Not for the first time, the thought of calling Carter went through her mind. She was sure that he'd understand how she was feeling and know what to do about all this. But that just reminded her of the sexy video she'd made for Todd. It had seemed so playful and fun when she'd filmed it. Now as she remembered the images it contained, she couldn't help thinking that Carter would hate her forever if he saw it. The whole thing seemed filthy and ugly, a powerful and cruel blade hanging over her, ready to chop her head off if she made one wrong move.

And what if the sound file was right? What if she was all alone and no one cared? What if she really was the disgusting girl that Lilah was trying to make her feel like she was? She admonished herself: *Shake it off, Jules. Be tough. Don't let the hater get to you.* But no matter how often Jules told herself to be strong, Lilah *was* getting to her. Big-time.

37

As Jules jogged across the quad and neared the bank of lockers outside Mr. Wittier's biology room, the air thickened and became sticky with a rancid smell. She covered the bottom half of her face with her shirt, but the smell seeped right through, gagging her. A smell so powerful that it was a physical force, heavy and damp and revolting.

She wondered what Mr. Wittier could possibly have going on inside his classroom to create such a smell. It hadn't been here three hours ago, when she'd stashed her backpack in her locker before graduation practice. Mr. Wittier was a weird guy—there was something musty and vaguely autistic about him, and he wore the same stained brown cords every single day—so she wouldn't have been surprised if he'd brewed up some sort of evil-smelling mushroom concoction in his lab, but this quickly? And hadn't she seen him running crowd control in the auditorium during the rehearsal?

She held her breath and soldiered on. She just wanted her yearbook. A quick in and out and then she'd race back to the theater building to collect her signatures. She could find someone there to tell. God, it was gross.

Gulping air through her mouth, she ran the combination on her lock. She threw the door open, and it was like she'd opened the gates of hell. The intensity of the smell quadrupled—it was coming from her locker.

The stench was overwhelming, acidic and sweet and putrid like rotting meat. It made her light-headed. Her stomach rioted and she willed herself not to throw up.

She could barely see straight, it was so intense, but she could see enough to know that someone had been inside her locker. On the shelf where she stacked her schoolbooks this someone—and she knew who it was—had lodged a leaky plastic bag full of heavy, orangey-brown liquid. It was dripping all over her yearbook, down the stack of books under her yearbook. It pooled on the shelf and drizzled down the wall of the locker.

There was a sheet of lined notebook paper taped to the bag. Someone—Lilah, it had to be Lilah; goddamned Lilah, again—had written on the sheet, block letters in ballpoint pen. Jules could see the force of her rage in the way she'd traced over the words, heavy scribbles and stabs.

It said:

EAT MY PUKE, BITCH!

The rage and despair surging through Jules's body were so overpowering that the things she did next were more animal instinct than considered choices.

She whipped the bag of vomit out of her locker and threw it with all her might across the lawn, out into the middle of the quad. As it flew, its nasty liquid contents were let loose in a spray, like from a runaway hose. Flecks flew everywhere. They got on her shoes, her legs, her skirt.

It was revolting. Her stomach turned over like something angry and alive was kicking inside her, trying to get out. She could feel the acidic taste working its way up the back of her throat.

And she realized then that waiting and hoping was never going to make Lilah stop.

She pulled her phone out of her purse and made the one call she'd been resisting all these weeks, the one she both most and least wanted to make, the one that terrified her because it required a trust she wasn't sure she could believe in—it could easily solve her problem, and just as easily make it worse.

She called Carter.

38

"You smell that?" Jules shouted, while Carter was still half a quad away.

"Yeah, what the hell?"

"You see that plastic bag there? Go pick it up."

Carter did what she said. He fought through the stench and wandered out to the bag and picked it up by the tied handles. Then, realizing what it was he held in his hand, he dropped it with a shudder and looked back at Jules.

"Nice, right?" she said. "Welcome to my life."

When Jules had called, she hadn't told him why she wanted to see him. She'd just said, "Come to my locker. I have something to show you." He hadn't imagined that this was what she'd meant. Since the incident with her car in the parking lot, he'd resisted contacting her out of respect for what he thought were her wishes. He knew nothing about the torture she'd been through since then, and throughout the walk across campus his head had been full of visions of her maybe having some kind of a peace offering for him. He'd hoped that this would be his chance to explain his feelings to her and maybe find out why his texts had made her so mad.

"Where'd it come from?" he asked her.

"It was in my locker."

"Jesus." He ran his hand through his hair as he tried to come up with the right thing to do in this situation. "This is horrible, Jules."

"'Jesus? This is horrible?' That's all you've got? Weak, Carter. Very weak."

"Jules, I swear, I would never do something like this," he said.

"I know it wasn't you!" She was shouting now. Carter couldn't quite tell if she was mad at him specifically, or blind with rage at the whole situation. "It's your fucking girlfriend. You want to know what else she did? She took a baseball bat to my car, and then she broke into my car a second time to write nasty notes in lipstick for me to find. And she sends these awful texts. My God, you should see the texts."

As Jules rolled through the rest of the list of Lilah's

crimes—the various confrontations they'd had, the stalking in the theater, all of it—feelings of horror and shame surged through Carter's stomach. He berated himself. How could he not have known? How could he not have guessed that Lilah would do something like this?

"I'm so sorry. I didn't know," Carter said, his pulse racing. "I wish I had. I would have stopped her."

He tried to take Jules's hand, to comfort her, but she was worked up and didn't trust him to console her. She yanked her arm away.

"Why didn't you tell me about all this before?" Carter asked.

He caught her eye and held it.

"Why would I do that?" she said. Tears were brimming below the surface, but she swallowed them down. "You chose her."

An ache plunged through Carter's heart. There'd been so many misunderstandings. So much misplaced ill will. How could he ever begin to peel it all back and allow the deep caring buried beneath to show through again?

"But I didn't," Carter said finally. "I broke up with her. I mean, it took me longer than it should have, but . . . that's what I'd been hoping to tell you that night when I went to your house and—" He caught himself. Now was not the time for declarations.

For a moment, the two of them stared at each other.

The miscommunications of the past few months hung between them in balloons of regret. Jules's rage had melted a little, but Carter sensed that she still didn't want to be touched.

"This is all my fault," he said.

She shook her head. "No. It's not, but . . ." She didn't see any way to ensure that he understood how cruel Lilah had been without telling him about the video. "Look, there's this stupid video I made last summer. It's—it's X-rated, okay. It's a video of me touching myself and whatever. It was stupid. The second-stupidest thing I've ever done. And Lilah somehow got her hands on it. She's been threatening me with it."

She yearned for him to tell her that he didn't judge her. Her every muscle was tense with the effort to hold herself together.

Carter placed his hands on her tanned shoulders, holding them firmly but tenderly.

At his touch, Jules flinched. She felt like she might turn into a puddle of water.

"That's terrible," he said. "I wish you would have told me."

"You don't think I'm a slut?"

"No. Why would I?"

"I thought, because of the video . . ." She wanted to give in to his warmth, to let him comfort her, but she knew she couldn't—she shouldn't—not right now, not like this. She could feel her body pushing itself toward him.

Jules looked away, out toward the plastic bag leaking into the lawn. Then she lifted his hands off her and said, "I'm not sure I can trust you right now, Carter."

"I'll get the video back," he said. "I promise I will. But you just have to understand. Lilah's—she's very unstable. She must have stopped her treatment or something. And her parents are pretty clueless. I doubt they even notice anything's wrong."

Carter didn't want to sound like he was defending Lilah at all—he just wanted Jules to know that she hadn't done anything to deserve this.

"Why didn't you tell me?" Jules asked, her voice cracking.

Carter knew he had to backpedal here or risk losing even more of Jules's trust. "I'm so sorry. I should have. From now on, let's tell each other everything, okay?"

Jules recognized that disarming earnestness on his face, that sense she'd had before of his inherent goodness, his desire for all good things to be given to her. All the things about him that tugged at her heart. She wanted to believe in him. She didn't have any reason *not* to—no reason except her fear of Lilah.

"I'll get her to stop," Carter said, with a sudden vehemence. "I swear to you, Jules, I won't let anything bad happen to you. Ever again."

39

Lilah could tell that the shadowy figure trudging across the beach toward her was Carter long before she could make out his features. She recognized his adorably slouchy posture, the cute way he kept his hands buried in his pants pockets, the way he periodically pulled his mop of hair across his forehead.

When he was finally close enough for her to make out his features, she stood up on the platform of her lifeguard chair, waving at him, willing the pitter-pat of her heart to stay calm. He'd returned to her like she knew he would.

There was worry on his face, a wary nervousness. But of course. After everything he'd put her through in the past few months, he must wonder if she would ever forgive him.

Didn't he know she would?

Didn't he know there was nothing he could do in the whole wide world that she wouldn't eventually forgive him for?

She'd dreamed of this moment. She'd always known it would come. If she just waited him out, if she held sturdy and tight to the rock of their love—it was a mountain; it was immovable—he'd come slinking back, carrying his regret and shame heavily on his back.

He was her prince, and he'd made her a princess. Finally, he was remembering that.

She did a quick survey of the people on the beach: a couple of middle schoolers whipping a tennis ball back and forth in the surf, a prematurely balding dad building a sand castle with his daughter, a large group of twenty-somethings camped out under a tangled mass of umbrellas, blasting their reggaeton and drinking something out of red cups. The Frisbee throwers. The boogie boarders. There were a lot of people here this afternoon, actually. But she didn't care. They'd have to fend for themselves. She had bigger concerns today than their physical safety.

Hopping down from the lifeguard stand, she ran to Carter. In her mind, she'd already forgiven him, they'd already made up, the tears had already been shed, and the apologies had already been accepted. There was nothing left to do but embrace each other now, wrap each other up tight and kiss and kiss and kiss, press their foreheads together and gaze into each other's eyes and promise and swear that nothing—not Jules, not college, not anything in the world—would ever again come between them and their love.

When she was close enough to touch him, she leaped and clasped her arms around his neck, wrapped her legs around his waist. He instinctively held her up and she went in for the romantic, end-of-the-movie kiss she'd been rehearsing in her mind over these past few weeks.

"It's okay, Carter," she said. "I've been waiting for you to come back to me."

And nothing. Carter's lips didn't part for hers. They tightened, actually. They clamped shut. He didn't whisper *I've missed you* or *I'm sorry* or *I've finally realized I can't live without you.* He leveled a cold, hard stare at her. He went stiff under her grasp and released her thighs from his hands, and she fell under her own weight to the sand.

Then he didn't help her up. He dug his hands back into the pockets of his pants and gazed down at her with an expression on his face that scared her. There was no love there—just a cruel, hard, and spiteful bottled-up rage.

For a brief instant Lilah was in shock.

"What the fuck, Lilah?" he said.

"You're not happy to see me?"

"No, I'm not fucking happy to see you."

She didn't need to be told what he was angry about. Part of her had known that he wouldn't understand the fierce beauty in what she was doing for him. Before he could build his case against her, she launched into her defense. "She's going to cheat on you. You know that, right? Jules is a sex addict. She sucked off the whole football team last year—I know because her ex-boyfriend told me. Todd Norris. He told me how disgusted he was when he found out." Why wasn't he responding? When had he started hating her so much? "I'm protecting you, Carter. Don't you understand?"

"I don't want or need you to protect me."

She pled with him. "Carter, please. You have to believe me."

"I believe that you *think* you're protecting me, Lilah. I believe that you've got yourself so twisted around in your head that you seriously believe that this is what you're doing, but you've got to stop. And I want you to leave Jules the fuck alone."

A fresh surge of outrage went tumbling through her.

"She's a total whore," she said. "Here. I'll prove it."

She climbed to her feet and whipped her phone out of the waistband of the shorts she wore over her swimsuit and cued up the video that Todd had given her. As the video began streaming, she shoved the phone in Carter's face. He tried to grab it, but she yanked it away, held it above her head, taunting him with the writhing, jiggling image of Jules on its screen.

"You see? Carter? You see? Internet porn. She'll be doing videos for the Bangbros by the time summer's over."

The emotions were swirling around on his face, changing shape and texture. He seemed about to cry, and she interpreted this as proof that he finally understood she was—even in his betrayal—looking out for him, shielding him from the dangers in the world, loving him.

But this wasn't at all what was going through Carter's mind. He wasn't going to cry. The emotion Lilah saw on his face came from a place of horror—at himself, at her, at the fact that after all the time he spent trying to be good to her, Lilah was way beyond his or anyone's help.

The video itself wasn't so disgusting. It was just a sweet, slightly awkward girl exploring her own sexual boundaries. That Jules had dared to try this made him love her more. But Lilah had taken something private and innocently misguided and turned it rancid and ugly. In Lilah's hands this video became something frightening, a bunker buster aimed at Jules's future.

"Give it to me."

"Ha."

He leaped forward, grabbing at her hand, and waving the phone above her head, she took a step back.

"Lilah, give me the fucking phone."

He jumped and slapped at her hand until finally he connected and sent the phone sailing across the beach. Scrambling, they both dove for it. Carter got there first. Holding it out like a live grenade, he ran into the surf, high-stepping through the water in his shoes and socks, and he threw the phone with all his might into the ocean.

He kept his distance from Lilah as he turned back to the shore. She was clearly stunned. Her mouth hung open and she had that tilt to her head like she got when the events she was witnessing overwhelmed her sense of what was possible.

He jabbed his finger at her as though this would somehow make his words stick more successfully. "I'm serious, Lilah. If I find out you've got another copy, I'll report you."

As she watched him trudge away in his wet, sand-caked Adidas, this refrain circled through Lilah's brain: *Don't you understand, Carter? I love you. I love you. Carter, don't you understand? I love you.*

She'd make him understand—and everyone else, too.

40

Graduation day finally arrived.

The auditorium had been decked out in the red-and-gold school colors. After dark, rolling clouds threatened early, the sun had come out and the humidity and heat sank to levels that seemed almost miraculous for South Florida. It was a perfect day for the pageantry and pomp that marked the life change everyone was about to make.

People's spirits were high. Parents sat in back, brandishing their cameras and video cameras. The hipper among them held their smartphones in the air. They found their friends, waved, mouthed their *wows* and their *Can you believe they're so grown-up alreadys*. Carter's mom had brought her best friend from work, Sue, so she'd have someone to sit with, someone to lend a hand that she could clench when her son walked across the stage and she was inevitably overcome with emotion. (His father, true to form, had skipped out on the proceedings.)

Jeff's parents came dressed like they were at an art opening—his father wore Tom Ford, and perfectly round, plastic tortoiseshell glasses; his mother wore a Stella McCartney pantsuit that women half her age might not be able to pull off. Lilah's parents had arrived two hours early to stake out seats in the front row of the balcony, and once the ceremony began and the seniors marched in, they clutched the railing, tracking Lilah's every move below them like if they lost track of her, even for an instant, she'd somehow get lost and not end up graduating. Jules's mother, looking laid-back in a diaphanous pastel-blue dress, kept herself apart from the other parents. Watching her daughter graduate—and go to college, no less—was a special gift and she wanted it all to herself.

The 462 graduating seniors, penned in like chickens in alphabetized rows in the orchestra seats, squirmed under their robes and fidgeted with their caps and joked and rolled their eyes through Ms. Robison's corny, quasi-uplifting speech. It touched on all the usual points about how special this particular group of students was, and how much they'd be missed, and how, though they maybe couldn't picture it now, their lives would continue after they graduated, they'd go on to have all sorts of interesting experiences, and, eventually, maybe they'd come back to Chris Columbus having accomplished things they couldn't even dream of now. It was a fine speech, if a little rote, and though they pretended they didn't care about the words they were hearing, the students were glad to be told these things today.

Finally, it was time for the diplomas to be handed out. The school had done something special this year. Instead of having Mr. Cruz, the gaunt and awkward assistant principal, read people's names off as they marched across the stage and shook Ms. Robison's hand, the A/V department had put together a kind of video slide show through which each student could introduce him- or herself from the big screen hung above the stage.

Joseph Accevedo

Bethany Adams

Rebecca Amato

They said their own names, and sometimes they waved for the camera, or smirked, or in the case of Ranjit Aranjun, otherwise known as Reed, bugged their eyes in inspired goofery.

Lilah Bell

There she was, smiling demurely, just the smallest nervous glance off camera to signify her discomfort.

Paco Bermudez hadn't bothered to take his sunglasses

off for the camera. The Paco on-screen threw some sort of hand sign, and the real Paco walking across the stage below him threw the same sign simultaneously.

On and on it went.

Andrew Drucker

Macalia Finnegan

Teresa Hernandez

Carter Moore

Friends and enemies and people Carter and Lilah and Jules had somehow never noticed the existence of traipsed across the stage and got their diplomas.

Peter Talbot

According to the program in Jules's mother's hand, there were nine more names before Jules took the stage. Her seat wasn't the best. She was wedged into one of the back two rows and the man in front of her must have been six-foot-five. As she angled for a better view, and finally slid and climbed over people's knees out to the aisle, where she could stand and watch, the roll call continued.

Then it was finally time. Jules strode toward Ms. Robison. Tears of pride welled in her mother's eyes.

And on the screen, Jules's face smiled out at the camera.

Something was different, though. She didn't say her name. Instead, she blew a kiss and ran her tongue lewdly across her upper lip. And she wasn't in front of the same bland, marbled background as everyone else had been. She was in her room—her mom recognized the *Book of Mormon* poster on her wall.

This was wrong. Something was wrong. From her place on the stage, Jules didn't realize it, but her mother could see that this wasn't right at all, and she grew suddenly very, very afraid.

The video continued. It didn't have any sound. Jules stepped back from the camera and it was revealed that she was naked from the waist up except for a black lace bra. She swayed her body seductively, licking her lips. She pointed at the camera and curled her finger as though she was enticing it to move close and kiss her. She shimmied her breasts and ran her finger seductively along her smooth, flat abdomen.

Carter searched out Lilah. She was eight rows in front of him, and he could barely see the back of her head. For Jules's sake, he feared what was coming next: the big reveal, the public shaming. He would have stopped it if he could have, but there was nothing he could do but sit there and feel responsible.

When her name wasn't announced and the applause didn't come, Jules looked out at the audience, and it was then that she registered that she was in trouble. All of them—every single person in the room—were staring at the screen above her head. The expressions on their faces told her all she needed to know. Such ugly expressions.

Some enthralled, some disgusted, all of them captivated by her humiliation. She glanced at the screen above her head to see herself unlatching the strap of her bra.

Lilah's heart tumbled with delirious glee as she watched the scene transpire. She smiled. She couldn't help it. She grinned like she'd just won a trip around the world.

It was obvious to everyone, even the people onstage, that this was a cruel hoax of some sort, but no one knew what to do. Ms. Robison was blinking up at the light booth, waving her hands futilely, shouting for Arnold Chan, the hapless sophomore who was still stationed there, to cut the video. "Turn it off! Turn the damn thing off!"

But it didn't turn off. The Jules on the screen peeled her bra from her body, and there were her breasts for the whole world to see.

Jules went from shocked mortification to piercing tears. She felt invaded, assaulted. She felt like her life and everything it had ever contained were crashing down and burying her alive. She was beginning to hyperventilate. She ran. She didn't even get her diploma; she just ran. Peter Talbot tried to take her arm and console her, but she shoved him away. She ran and ran. If she didn't get outside soon, she'd suffocate.

41

By the time they got the video turned off, chaos had broken out in the auditorium. The parents in the balcony were crushed toward the ledge overhanging the orchestra, shouting in outrage at Ms. Robison, who could think of nothing more effective to do than stare up into the stage lights and call up—in a voice drowned out by the rabble—at Arnold Chan in the booth. Some of the seniors were hooting at the screen, reveling in Jules's embarrassing exposure. Others seemed to be in shock, disgusted. All of them were out of their assigned seats, searching for friends with whom they could squeal and vocalize their disbelief.

In the midst of all this, Carter climbed over the

aisles, squeezing past his early-alphabet classmates; past Reed and Andy, who wanted him to join them in their witticism competition; and finally, lunging for Lilah, sitting prim in her seat, not speaking to anyone, not even pretending to be surprised by the craziness happening around her.

He slid down in the empty seat next to her. "What the hell?" he said. "Lilah, what the fuck?"

She turned in her seat and gazed at him, the delirious smile still frozen on her face. After a beat, her grin widened even farther, and then she giggled—not in a demonic way, no—what was spookiest about her behavior was that she seemed almost innocent, naïve, and gleeful.

"We're not gonna do this here," he said. He grabbed her wrist, maybe a little too roughly, and pulled her to her feet. "You're coming outside with me. *Now.*" Then he dragged her through the throng and down the aisle toward the exit, ignoring Ms. Robison's pleas to the crowd to take their seats again so the ceremony could continue.

Lilah went willingly. She was getting what she wanted: attention from Carter, if not exactly in the form she'd hoped for. *I've got him now. At least there's that. I've got him now.* Every time the thought went floating through her mind, she'd break into a new bout of giggles, and Carter's grip on her arm would tighten.

Outside the theater building, he surveyed the campus—first for Jules, who he couldn't find, and then for a secluded spot where he could lay into Lilah without being disturbed by the entire senior class and their parents.

There, at the bottom of the hill, behind the flowering hibiscus bushes that divided the soccer field from the classroom quads. That would do.

"Where are we going?" asked Lilah.

Carter told her to shut up. He marched her down the hill, trying to think of what he could possibly say or do that would convince her to accept reality, or at least stop trying to alter it.

And so, there they were, behind the hibiscus.

Carter let go of her arm and scowled at her. He was pulsing with rage, too angry for words.

"She totally deserved it," said Lilah. "And now everyone knows."

"Everyone knows what?" His words were taut and clipped.

"That she's not the cool, glamorous actor girl she pretends to be. That she's a whore and a home wrecker."

"No, Lilah. No. She's not a home wrecker. Look at yourself. You think I wouldn't have broken up with you regardless?"

"I don't know why you're so angry with me, Carter. I'd think that now that you know what kind of girl Jules really is, you'd understand that it's not worth throwing what we have away for her."

Carter was dumbfounded by the logic Lilah could have possibly followed to come to this conclusion about her actions. *"You have to stop this."*

"I don't understand why you're being like this, Carter."

He let out a howl of frustration and rage. "Because you're trying to destroy someone who didn't do anything to you!"

"Are you kidding me? She knew you had a girlfriend. *Everyone* knew. We're class couple! People shouldn't go around stealing other people's boyfriends."

"She didn't cheat on you, Lilah. That was me. You understand? That was *me*. So why are you taking this shit out on her?"

"Forever. Remember? You promised me that when you carved our names into the bench on the promenade."

It was like she wasn't even hearing him. Nothing was getting through to her.

"Things were different back then. And when things got rough, I wanted to help you, Lilah, but I can't do it anymore. You need professional help."

Lilah's lips quivered with emotion. All the pain in the world seemed to have coalesced in her eyes. Her desperation—her delusion—was alarming.

"I don't believe you. We're going to be together forever. You've just forgotten how much you love me."

"No, Lilah. I haven't forgotten anything. It's over. Nothing you do is going to change that. So stop messing with Jules to get back at me! You know, I could have you thrown in jail."

Tentatively, conscious of how volatile his rage was right then, Lilah moved in closer to Carter. She placed a hand on his heart and held it there.

"You do still love me. It's in there somewhere. It's hidden right now, but it's there. I know it."

He swatted her hand away. "You're delusional, Lilah."

"You just need to be reminded," she said. "Here . . ." She returned her hand to his heart and ran it down his chest. Then she unzipped his graduation gown.

"Stop it," Carter said.

But she didn't stop it. She was fumbling with his belt now.

He tried to push her off him, but she had his belt unbuckled and she was on her knees, working on his zipper.

She gazed up at him. Tears were welling in her eyes. "I bet Jules wouldn't do this for you, would she?" she said.

People were beginning to exit the theater building now. A trickle at first, the VIPs who'd processed down the aisle. They congregated outside the door waiting to shake the hands of the seniors and their parents. Soon the hill would be clogged with people, stiff cardboard hats would be flying into the sky, discussions about the video of Jules would commence, and Carter and Lilah would still be here hiding behind the hibiscus, exacerbating an already bad situation.

Before Lilah could go any further, Carter pushed her off him and yanked himself away, rezipping his zipper, rebuckling his belt. "I said stop it. I. Do. Not. Love. You."

She was stunned for a moment. It was like he'd hit her.

Then she lashed back. She went at him, slapping and scratching and hitting and bawling.

Carter wrapped her up in his arms, restraining her.

People were looking now, glancing in their direction.

"Get your shit together now, Lilah, and admit that you were behind all this," said Carter. "Come on. I'll take you myself."

Keeping her caged in his arms, he jostled her, trying to turn her around and begin marching her toward the theater building.

Lilah flung her elbows, tried to punch him in the gut. That he'd sell her out like this boggled her mind. She'd kill him if she could—at least then he couldn't go and love someone else. But his hold was strong. She couldn't budge inside it. She tried kicking at his shins, but he held his ground. She had only one weapon available to her, and so she used it. She bit him. She grabbed him between her teeth, took hold of him in the spot where his shoulder met his neck, his trapezius muscle, right above his jugular. She clamped his skin, his muscle inside her jaw. She dug deep. She broke skin. She was willing to take a part of him with her if that's what was needed.

"Jesus, fuck, Lilah!"

He shoved her away from him with all his might. She stumbled. She fell. And she stayed down, curled in a ball, silently sobbing.

At this point, there wasn't an ounce of sympathy he had left for her, and part of him felt guilty for it. But another part of him wanted to leave her there like that. However, with everyone looking, that seemed like a bad idea, so he went through the motions of seeing if she was okay, leaning in, reaching out to help her up.

And when he was close enough to touch, she pounced. She shoved him back. She was strong. She was a swimmer, a lifeguard. There was power in her arms.

Carter reeled back, his feet churning as he tried to keep his balance.

The particular path on which he traveled took him toward the hibiscus at a diagonal angle. The bushes were bedded in a landscaped row and the soil beneath them had been replaced with wood chips. There was a small divot, a moat where the grass gave way to these chips, and in this moat, there lived a family of voles. They'd dug their tunnels. They'd shoveled the dirt away in places so that they'd have entrances and exits to their homes. They'd created holes in the earth, and one of these holes happened to be in the path along which Carter stumbled.

His foot caught and twisted.

He felt a sharp pain.

And as Lilah fled the scene, sobbing hysterically, he went down with the feeling that something was broken.

42

An hour later, Carter was in the emergency room at St. Francis Hospital, getting his foot X-rayed and having a bright blue cast put on the broken ankle the doctors discovered under the skin.

An hour after that, he was at home, lolling around the living room with his leg elevated, watching old episodes of *Futurama* on Comedy Central.

One thing was for sure. He knew—he just knew—that he would never talk to Lilah ever again. He'd stay away from her part of the beach, stick close to Jeff and the guys. His presence in her life would just cause her more problems. He hoped she would get the professional help she needed.

But what about Jules? He wished there was some way to protect Jules, too.

And then it occurred to him: *Fuck. UPenn. Four more years of this shit from Lilah.*

He'd requested that he and Lilah be put in the same section for the August orientation weekend. That would have to change. Immediately.

He hobbled as quickly as he could down the hall to his bedroom, and rifled through the folder he'd filled with all the correspondence and brochures and admittance materials he'd received until he found the orientation contact number.

He punched in the numbers and was routed to an electronic greeting system. Once he'd followed the prompts through enough corridors, he was put on hold for a live person. As he waited for the admissions officer to get to him, he could feel the rage that had raced through him earlier that day surge back into his blood.

"University of Pennsylvania admissions office, Kelly speaking. How may I help you?"

"Hi, my name is Carter Moore. I'm wondering if I can maybe change orientation sections."

"Well, you realize they're all pretty much the same, right? Is there something specific you're concerned about?"

Carter explained his predicament. He knew he sounded crazy, that this wasn't really the school's problem. But Kelly in admissions was respectful and courteous. "Well, let's see," she said. He could hear her fingers clacking at the keyboard. "Lilah Bell. Hmm."

He felt like he needed to apologize for bothering her. "You can't do it, right. I'm just going to have to deal."

"Carter, do you and Lilah still talk at all?"

"Sort of. I mean, she broke my ankle today, if that's what you mean by talk."

Kelly in admissions didn't laugh at this, thankfully. "You won't have to worry about that sort of thing here," she said. "Lilah Bell isn't going to UPenn."

"She is, though. Can you check again?"

"I'm looking at it right here. Lilah Bell. Dream Point, Florida. I'm not supposed to tell you this, but here's what it says. Wait-listed, February nineteenth, and then denied, April eighth."

Confused, Carter at first refused to believe what he was hearing. "That can't be right," he said. "She told me she got in. We celebrated together."

"I think maybe you've been misinformed," said Kelly.

Then the reality caught up with him. He'd never actually seen Lilah's acceptance letter. In a flash, he saw the anxious panic she must have felt when she found out she had been wait-listed. Here was an explanation for the nervousness, the defensiveness, the unending arguments they'd been having back in February and March. She'd been terrified. She'd been staring at the end of their relationship long before the possibility had crossed his mind, and that must have pushed her over the edge.

Still, did that excuse anything that she'd done over the past few months? Did that give her the right to terrorize Jules and attack him when he told her enough was enough?

"I see," he said. "Well, I guess that's all."

"Wait, since I have you on the phone," said Kelly. "Your friend Lilah Bell is . . ." The professional tones in her voice cracked and a new emotional velocity entered her speech. "We all know Lilah and we're not very happy with her. I personally have had about twenty conversations with her. And they're not fun conversations. She calls us up virtually every single day and curses us out for having rejected her. She's writing letters to President Hassinger, trying to get us all fired. I mean, it's not going to work, but . . ."

"Jesus. That's horrible," he said.

"Your friend Lilah could get herself in real trouble if she keeps acting like this."

"I—like I said, I don't really talk to her anymore."

After he hung up the phone, Carter lay back on his bed and thought about the things Kelly had just told him. He thought about his broken ankle. He thought about the cruel things Lilah had done to Jules.

For the next hour Carter lay there motionless, running through scenarios, working through all the possibilities, regretting more and more that he'd ever gotten involved with Lilah. If the way he'd treated her today didn't stop her, he was pretty sure nothing would. She'd be chasing him forever, destroying everything and everyone he ever touched.

43

On Monday afternoon, Jules's mom closed the crystal shop early and drove over to Lilah's house for a discussion. She shifted her weight back and forth as she waited for someone to answer the door, struggling to hold on to her Buddhist presentness.

The door opened a crack and Lilah's mother, her hair blown out into a perfectly coiffed helmet, peeked through. The expression on her face was guarded and pinched. When she opened her mouth, her voice was nervous and sharp. "You're—"

"Jules's mom."

Lilah's mother pushed the door open wider to let Jules's mom in. She was an anxiously polite woman with strangers, and her emotions twitched at the corners of her mouth as she led Jules's mom into the kitchen and pulled out a chair at the sun-drenched table for her.

"Please sit down," she said. "Would you like something? Coffee? Tea?"

"No. I'm fine."

Hovering over the counter and compulsively wiping nonexistent crumbs from its marbled surface, Lilah's mom asked, "Have you decided what you're going to do yet?"

Jules's mom shot her a dumbfounded look. "What would you do if you were me?" she asked. "I can't let this continue. I have to press charges."

Lilah's mom suppressed a frown. This woman might be messy in ways that made her cringe—those jeans shorts, that loose-fitting spaghetti-strapped top, a sense of style fit more for a coed than a mother—she may have instinctively disliked the woman, but the details she'd presented on the phone were too specific; they explained Lilah's nervous, secretive behavior over the past couple months too perfectly. Much as she didn't want to believe it, she knew the things Jules's mom had told her must be true.

"There's no other option?" she asked.

"Do you see any other option?"

"I was hoping—Lilah's always been a troubled girl. Since we talked this morning, I've learned that she hasn't been following her treatment. I'm going to make sure that changes, of course, and . . . I thought maybe, if I promise to monitor her . . . I'm hoping we can maybe work this out between ourselves."

Jules's mom contemplated this for a moment, her pulse slowly beginning to pick up speed. Her beliefs preached mercy and compassion, and though she could be vigilant when she needed to, she strove to be a force of positivity in the world. But no matter how troubled this Lilah girl was, she had hurt and degraded her daughter in front of hundreds of people. Keeping her composure right now was taking up all the energy she had.

"Does she understand how wrong what she's done is?" she asked, her hands trembling a little. "Whatever mistakes Jules may have made, there's no way she deserved that kind of public humiliation. And the stalking? I can't even begin to wrap my head around it."

"I know. It's hard to know what goes on in Lilah's head. Her father and I, we've tried so hard with her. But it's . . . she's too much for us. Too much for anyone, actually."

Jules's mom raised an eyebrow. She would never say anything like that about her daughter, no matter what her problems were. It almost made her feel a little bad for Lilah. Her parents had obviously given up on her.

"We're sending her back to the doctor. In a few days," said Lilah's mom.

"I'd say that's long overdue. Wouldn't you?"

Lilah's mother narrowed her eyes and opened her mouth as though to defend herself against this sharp criticism, but then closed it again and nodded. "Let me go get Lilah," she said. "She's upstairs. We'll be down in a moment."

Lilah's mom disappeared around the corner and up the stairs, leaving Jules's mom alone to study the watercolor fruit on the wallpaper. The house was beautifully decorated, everything so appropriate, the correct tables in the correct places with just the right bland pictures mounted above them. She felt like she'd walked into a Pottery Barn catalogue, and again her heart went out to Lilah. It must be hard to live in such a sterile house. She herself had grown up in a home like this one. She understood the expectations a place like this held, the pressure to keep up appearances whether you agreed with them or not. But none of this justified the horrible things the girl had done to her daughter.

Lilah's mom returned as promised, trailing Lilah behind her.

So there she was, the girl who'd been making Jules's life such hell for these past two months. She didn't look the type, unless maybe she did. Her straight shoulder-length hair was too perfectly combed, too carefully situated under her headband for a day of lounging around the house. Her skirt was too well pressed. Her blouse too buttoned up. She looked like a doll that had been dressed up by someone else. But underneath this costume, Jules's mother noticed, was an insolence that couldn't be disguised. She kept picking at her clothes. The looks she gave her mother behind her back were icy, like something a prison inmate would give the jailer who'd just taken his privileges away.

"Lilah, this is Mrs. Turnbull," her mother said, with a hint of an edge in her voice.

"Cara is fine," said Jules's mother. "Do you know who I am, Lilah?"

Lilah immediately put the pieces together. Mrs. Turnbull, who wanted to be called Cara. With a loosey-goosey beach-bum attitude about her. She slouched in her chair. Her long arms and legs flopped out every which way. There was someone else Lilah knew who was comfortable with herself like this. Someone who'd stolen her boyfriend. She wondered what this Cara thought of her daughter now that she knew the girl made porn videos of herself.

"Don't you have something to say to Mrs.—to Cara?" said her mom, tapping her finger nervously on the table.

The words, as they came out of Lilah's mouth, had a rehearsed quality. "I'm sorry for all the things I did to Jules. I won't do it again."

Jules's mom glanced skeptically at Lilah's mom. The woman's expression had a pleading, fretful quality to it.

She felt bad for her for a second. She could imagine how terrified she'd be herself if she thought Jules was about to go to jail. But from the few minutes she'd spent in this house, Jules's mother couldn't help but assume that this woman had neglected her child, or at least turned a blind eye when Lilah began spiraling out of control.

"Are you sorry, Lilah?" Jules's mom asked. "Do you have any idea what you've put my daughter through?"

Lilah braced herself for the lecture she knew was about to come, squeezed her lips tight, waiting for it to be over.

Jules's mom listed all the things Lilah had done and explained all the ways she'd broken the law. Vandalism. Threats. Stalking. Harassment. Not to mention theft and illegal distribution of child pornography.

Lilah let the words wash past her. She had to sit here. She didn't have to pay attention.

As the woman went on and on about this stuff, Lilah refused to even glance in her direction. She focused on the grandfather clock against the wall, on the carnival glass her mother had mounted above the table, on the stupid dolphins she collected, lined up on the window ledge, and pretended to listen. Her leg bounced uncontrollably.

"Do you understand what I'm saying to you?" asked Jules's mom.

Lilah rolled her eyes. This was such bullshit.

"He was *my* boyfriend. You know that, right? Mine. Not hers. *Mine*," she barked, suddenly looking directly at the woman, letting her hatred flash out toward her before turning back to the wallpaper.

Lilah's mother called her name, once, in warning. Then, turning to Jules's mom, she pleaded, "Like I said. Too. Much."

"I'm sure Jules has some regrets, Lilah," said Jules's mom, ignoring the girl's mother entirely. "But if you don't show some remorse for the terrible things you've done to punish her—show *me* that you realize you went way over the line—then I promise you, from now on this situation will be handled by a group of lawyers."

Jules's mother didn't like to use threats. It wasn't something she believed in. But she had to drive the point home that she wasn't someone to be messed with, or afraid of what Lilah might do. She held all the cards this time.

"Tell her you're sorry now," Lilah's mother said tersely. "Tell her you'll leave her daughter alone."

"I already did that," said Lilah.

"Well, do it again."

Lilah did as she was told. "I'm *really* sorry. What I did was wrong. I won't bother Jules anymore," she said ironically, sarcastically, not even trying to give the impression that she was doing anything but going through the motions.

Jules's mother looked at Lilah's mother again, and then back to Lilah. She wasn't sure she could trust either of them, but she took a cleansing breath and tried to open her heart to the possibility that the universe would undoubtedly make sure justice was served.

She would help it along a little, though.

"I think the best course of action is to get a restraining order against you. Do you understand what that means?" Jules's mom said to Lilah.

Lilah refused to let the relief she felt leak out. "I'm not stupid," she said. "I watch TV."

"Good, so you know that if you come within one hundred yards of Jules, they'll arrest you. And then there won't be anything anyone can do to help you."

"That won't happen, right, Lilah?" said Lilah's mother.

As Lilah screwed a fake smile onto her face and nodded at Jules's mother, she felt reinvigorated. She might be beaten for now, but that didn't mean that the war was over. It just meant she had to bide her time and prepare herself for the battle to come. And make sure she didn't get caught next time.

44

All Carter could think about was Jules. In the days after the catastrophic graduation ceremony, while he sat around the house with his broken ankle propped up, he'd gone over and over the details in his head, chastising himself for not having seen what was happening sooner, lambasting himself for not having protected her from the danger he'd unleashed in her life. And yet he couldn't stop searching the usual spots—Google Chat, Facebook, Twitter, the rest of them—for some sign that she was okay now.

What he found was nothing. Not a trace of Jules. She'd disabled her chat. She'd gone off Twitter. She'd deleted her Facebook account, and he knew it wasn't an issue of her unfriending him, because when he had Jeff, who'd never been her Facebook friend, search for her, he came up with the same nothing result.

He ached to text her, but no text could contain the depths of his remorse.

Finally, he conscripted Jeff to drag him and his broken ankle around town in search of her. They'd gone to her house, but there'd been no one home. They'd gone to Waxidasical, where they'd discovered that she'd quit unexpectedly after one too many snarky comments from the customers. They'd trolled the sun-bleached streets of Dream Point, hoping she'd materialize on Flamingo or Pelican Drive like she'd been waiting there for them to roll by.

There was one place they hadn't tried where Jules might be. Harmonic Convergence, her mother's crystal shop. Carter wasn't even sure if she ever helped out there, and he could just imagine the hard time her mother would give him if he showed up to bother her daughter again.

They had to stop every hundred yards or so for Carter to rest and adjust his crutches, but eventually they made their way past the carnival crowds around Harpoon Haven, past the sleek hotels and the tiki bars and takeout joints, all the way to the far end of the promenade, where the freakier, less brightly scrubbed shops were located.

They walked right past the bench where he had

carved his and Lilah's names. Seeing it, seeing the names still etched in the wood, Carter shook his head in regret.

Then, finally, they were standing in front of Harmonic Convergence, staring up at its flaking, hand-painted sign, listening to the tinkle of the wind chimes mounted above the door. The airy curtains in the window and the wall of beads hanging across the open door made it difficult to see who was inside the space, but it somehow felt like destiny that Jules would be there. It would only be fitting for Carter to have to face her mother and show he wasn't afraid before being allowed to hold her in his arms.

"Wait here," he told Jeff, and then he pushed the beads aside with a crutch and stepped inside.

And there she was.

She sat on a high stool, nestled in among the cases of glimmering rocks in a back corner of the small room. She was wearing one of the flowing, low-slung Mexican skirts she liked, aqua blue, and she was reading a book of monologues for women.

She was so absorbed in this book that she didn't notice when he entered the store. She looked so peaceful there. He almost didn't want to disturb her. Just to look at her—that would almost have been enough. Just to take her in and savor the fact that she was alive.

When Jules guardedly looked up, they gazed at each other silently for a moment. With his crutches, he looked vulnerable and sad. She wanted to forget the past few months. Forget that Carter had told her that he wouldn't let anything bad happen to her, ever again. When he'd said it, she knew it was something he could never promise. He just wanted so much to make things right. And him showing up here, all battered and broken from the altercation she'd heard he had with Lilah after graduation, proved he was still trying to look out for her.

But so much had happened, perhaps too much to get past, although deep down she hoped that wasn't true.

"Hi, friend," Carter said, hoping the inside joke would make her smile.

He ran his hand through his hair, flopping it in that cute way of his.

"You're hard to find nowadays," he said.

"That's by design."

"I sort of had to stalk you to track you down."

Okay. She acknowledged that was a pretty good joke, but only with a smile. She wasn't ready to let her guard down yet.

"Think I could persuade you to take a little walk?"

"I'm the only one here."

"I'll make Jeff watch the shop."

"Oh, Jeff's here, too?" she said, her voice laced with sarcasm or disappointment—Carter couldn't tell which.

Carter gestured toward his ankle. "He's my driver."

Jules considered her options. "Okay," she said. "Briefly."

Outside, Carter instructed Jeff to go man the cash register. He and Jules leaned against the railing on the promenade. They watched the waves lapping against the beach. Neither of them knew quite where to start.

"Are you gonna get in trouble? For the video, I mean," Carter asked.

She shook her head. "I'm eighteen now, and luckily, the time stamp on the video is dated to the day Lilah uploaded it to the school computer system. There's no way to prove I was underage."

They gazed out at the beach some more. A seagull bounced around below them, pecking at something half buried in the sand.

"That's good," Carter finally said.

They watched the seagull again. There weren't many sun worshippers this far out—most people clung to the northern end of town, the ritzy areas near the hotels. There were so few people around that they could almost imagine they were totally alone.

When Carter spoke again, he risked slightly more. "I'm so, *so* sorry, Jules. I tried to stop her," he said.

Jules cautiously turned to face him. "I know. I can't . . . I can't believe you broke your ankle. Are you okay?"

255

"I don't care about me, I care about you," Carter said. "I don't expect you to forgive me or anything. I fucked up. I get that. But I want you to know I tried, at least. I threw her phone into the ocean. I didn't realize she'd made other copies of the video and . . ." He went dreamy for a second, trying to find the words that would honestly, nakedly explain himself. "I keep wondering why I didn't see what Lilah was up to sooner. It's like I was afraid to see it. I think the mistake I made was in not admitting from the start that I loved you, not her. And I won't—"

His confession came out so casually, more an explanation than an admission, that Jules almost missed it.

"What—wait—what?" she said.

He came out of his dream and was as confused as she was. "What, what?" he said.

"Did I just hear what I think I heard?"

"I don't know. What did you hear?"

"That you, um, love me."

Carter blushed. "Oh," he said. "Yeah. I guess I did say that."

Jules's heart did a backflip. She remembered, in flashes, the hero who'd raced in to help her and Lauren sophomore year, that sensitive charmer she'd seen at Jeff's house and gone on that spectacular "nondate" with—he must still be in there somewhere, right? Seeing him now, leaning on his crutches, that blue boot thrust out in front of him, she couldn't help but feel like she was seeing the Carter that she'd fallen in love with reemerge.

He was looking at her, nervously waiting to see how she'd respond.

"This is—wow," she said. Then, after a beat, she looked at him slyly out of the side of her eye and added, "It's good to see you . . . friend."

"It's good to see you, too." Carter took a risk. He picked her hand up and held it between both of his, studying her elegant long fingers, running his thumbs along her skin.

She let him do it. She didn't resist.

"So, here's the thing I don't understand," he said. "Why didn't you just get your CIA friends to come in and take her out?"

The laugh came easily to Jules's lips, and her heart told her she was going to have to kiss him. It just had to happen. It wasn't a choice.

She narrowed her eyes at him and cocked her head. "I'm going to do something now. And before I do it, I want you to understand that it in no way—"

He looked at her then, saw the soft beauty of her face, the smooth skin of her cheeks, and the high arch of her eyebrows. She captivated him. And some force outside himself pulled him toward her and suddenly he knew what was about to happen. He was kissing her. And she was kissing him back. They poured all the pent-up energy of their months of resisting and avoiding each other into this kiss. Each time it seemed like it was about to come to an end, a new surge of emotion pulled them back toward each other, and the kiss began again and again and again.

When finally they came up for breath, they just gazed at each other for a long, long time.

"You know," Carter said, "I'm going to make sure she stays out of our lives."

"Too late," she said. "My mom's taken out a restraining order on her."

"Even so," he said.

"And if that doesn't work, you're right. I've got my friends in the CIA."

There she was with that mischievous twinkle in her eyes. She was back. The girl he so adored.

They kissed again, and then they stopped to glare at Jeff, who was clapping for them from the doorway of Harmonic Convergence.

PART

RT

two

45

Carter and Jules barreled along the coast road in Carter's BMW, following the blindingly white beaches north toward I-95, away from Dream Point. They were free. It had been two months since either of them had heard a word from Lilah. It was like she'd abandoned her destructive mission on the day she'd learned about the restraining order.

They had the top down on the car and the wind whipped Jules's hair out behind her. The short sleeve of Carter's gray-and-red-striped linen shirt flapped like a flag.

Good-bye, Dream Point.
Good-bye, Miami.

Orientation weekend would begin in five days, and since Carter's dad and his wife were vacationing in Brazil, the plan was to stop off in Savannah, Georgia, and hang out in the house where Carter had grown up before he and his mother had moved down to Dream Point. Carter still had keys, after all, and Savannah was a magical, romantic city.

Good-bye, Fort Lauderdale.

Good-bye, Boca, Palm Beach, Port St. Lucie.

They sang along to the songs streaming from their iPods, or Jules did—Carter refrained from ruining the beauty of her sound with his own squawks and rasps.

They counted license plates. *There's one from Mississippi. There's one from Alabama. There's one from Ohio, New York, Kentucky. A little green Mazda2 with Idaho plates. Hey, there's Pennsylvania—hello, neighbor, here we come!*

Good-bye, South Florida.

Good-bye, Daytona.

Even though they knew it was corny and a kind of old-person thing to do, they played I Spy to fill up the time. Carter spied something black—a vulture circling above them. Jules spied something yellow—the blocky sign for a Waffle House up the road. They were ironic about it, rolling their eyes and mockingly, emphatically congratulating each other on getting things right.

Carter spied something green—a little Mazda2 with

Idaho plates. "Didn't we see that car, like, an hour ago?" he asked Jules. "It seems like it's been following us forever."

"You see it, too, huh?" said Jules. "So it's not just my imagination."

She turned in her seat to study the car. The sunlight beating off the windshield made it almost impossible to see the driver, but from what she could tell, whoever it was had longish brown hair. "I swear, it's been behind us since at least Palm Bay. That's weird, isn't it?"

"It is weird," Carter said. Each time he'd checked the rearview mirror, he'd seen it again, hovering fifty, a hundred yards behind them. "Do you think—" Jules couldn't bring herself to say Lilah's name out loud. It was like if she said the word, the girl would materialize.

"No," said Carter. "Absolutely not." Seeing the worry invade Jules's face, Carter tried to explain the car away. "It's got Idaho plates, for one thing."

"Yeah, but it could be a rental. Rentals seem to *always* have Idaho plates."

"Well, and it's I-95. It's, like, the only road you can take north from Miami. Every single person leaving town is following the same trail. We've seen that same Walmart semi the whole way as well, so . . ."

"You think?"

"Yeah, I mean, really. How would she even know we're taking this trip?"

"How does she know anything? How did she know I'd be in the theater that afternoon? Or where I'd parked my car when she broke into it?"

"It's not her. I promise. It can't be her."

Carter took Jules's hand in his and held it tight.

To take her mind off the car behind them, he asked her, "Have you ever been to Savannah before?"

"First time," she said. "I'm imagining thick, sultry southern heat and Spanish moss everywhere. And everyone a little love crazy, filled with a longing that nothing can diminish, just like Scarlett O'Hara in *Gone with the Wind*."

"Ha," said Carter. "It's sort of like that. I can definitely promise you some Spanish moss. And there are some unbelievable restaurants. You haven't had soul food until you've had Georgia soul food."

"Collard greens!" she said.

"Chicken-fried steak! And we can check out the bar scene if you want. It's like a classier, never-ending spring break. People dancing on the bar. More Southern Comfort body shots than you'll ever want in your life."

Jules laughed.

"What I'm really interested in is seeing your dad's house. The place where little Carter watched cartoons and learned how to walk."

"Yeah, well," he said, "it's totally changed since then. He did this huge renovation a couple years ago."

He was careful not to mention the many times he'd visited his dad's house before with Lilah, that she knew where it was located and how to get there, that she knew all the secret hiding places in the drafty old building.

A Kanye West song shuffled on and Carter turned it up. He thrust his head back and forth to the beat. So did Jules. They bobbed their heads in tandem and rolled on.

By the time they crossed the Georgia state line, they'd forgotten all about the green Mazda, but if they'd looked, they would have seen that it was still behind them.

46

Finally, seven hours later, the mileage signs counting down to Savannah entered the double digits. They were thirty-six miles out. The beaches and flat expanses of reclaimed Florida marshland had been replaced by rolling fields of grass, grand plantation houses, Spanish moss on the trees.

"So, we've got a choice to make," said Carter. "We can drop our bags and get settled in the house, which might be nice because then we won't have to worry about it later, or we can head straight for the Riverwalk, where all the restaurants are. What do you think? We could go to Paula Deen's and have one of those donut burgers.

It's, like, diabetes on a stick, but hey, we're young, we can handle—"

Out of nowhere, an engine to their left roared out of control, and before they could process what they were seeing, a blur of metallic green—the Mazda, the same one that had been following them earlier—swerved into their lane, cutting so close that Carter had to slam the brakes and twist the wheel with all his strength in order to avoid clipping its fender.

He yanked hard to the right, then the left, trying to stop the car from spinning out.

The tires squealed. The wheels locked up and they were suddenly moving sideways, halfway onto the gravel of the breakdown lane.

A chain reaction: suddenly, every car on the road was swerving. There was honking, screeching brakes. Cars were winding around them like snakes. And then they weren't. Carter had gotten the car under control somehow, straightened out, slowing down to thirty, his fingers turning white as they clenched the steering wheel. Traffic returned to normal, like nothing had happened.

"Fuck," he said. "That was close. I can't believe *nobody* got in an accident! Jules?"

When she didn't respond, he dared to glance in her direction.

He saw the blood on the windshield first, barely a

fleck, just a thin smear of red, but it was enough for his heart to stop beating for a second. Then he heard her groan and he saw that she was slumped forward against her seat belt, holding her head in her hands.

"Jules—oh, shit. Jules, are you—what happened?"

She tried to put a good face on it. Slowly, so slowly, she sat up straight. She turned her head tentatively back and forth, checking to see what had been broken and where. "I think I'm okay."

Blood trickled down her face from a spot over her right eye.

"You don't look okay."

"I hit my head."

Carter drove on. He had no other choice, really.

A few miles up the road, he turned off and pulled into the parking lot of an Exxon Tiger Mart. As he walked Jules around the parking lot, he gauged her behavior. She was wobbly on her feet, a little. She kept touching her temple where she'd hit her head.

"Talk to me. Tell me how you're feeling."

"I'm a little dizzy." She pressed her eyes shut and tried to blink away the pain.

Carter sat her down on the yellow ridge of cement at the end of the empty parking space next to their own. He studied her wound. It was swollen and bruised. He didn't know enough about what to look for to really learn anything from what he saw.

"You know what? I'm going to take you to the hospital. We'll be in Savannah in, like, twenty minutes. Okay?"

"I'll be fine. I just need to shake it off." She buried her head in her hands again. Though she was trying to play it down, she definitely seemed disoriented.

As he drove off toward Memorial University Medical Center with Jules still rubbing her head in the seat next to him, Carter's mind raced even faster than his heart. He struggled to ward off the worst-case scenarios. Internal hemorrhaging. A sudden stroke.

The possibility that Lilah had been driving that Mazda.

47

Carter hung around the waiting room, reading the closed-captioning on the television set mounted near the ceiling. He wished he could be back there in the examination room, but he couldn't. He wasn't a family member and the admitting nurse had refused to allow him to join Jules in the deeper recesses of Memorial University's emergency room.

Alone with just the TV and a bunch of pamphlets about pregnancy and HIV to distract him, he fretted about Jules, wishing the doctors would tell him something, anything.

It was taking them forever to let Jules go. Was that a good or a bad thing? Carter didn't know.

To ease his anxiety, he bummed a cigarette from a weedy guy in a bright red hoodie who was fidgeting a few seats down from him in the waiting room. He stepped out into the swampy heat of Savannah and smoked, something he almost never did—just one here or there, usually at parties.

He couldn't stop thinking about that green Mazda, about the way it had flashed periodically into view behind them all the way up I-95. That wouldn't have been so unusual in and of itself, but if the car that almost clipped them had been the same one, and even though he couldn't prove it, his gut told him it was . . . then *that* was too weird to be a coincidence.

It occurred to him that he could call Lilah's home phone and get some verification of where she was and what she was up to. Yes. That's what he'd do. He'd made a promise to Jules. He intended to keep it.

He found Lilah's home number in his phone. If she picked up, he'd have his answer and he could just hang up. If one of her parents answered, well, he'd see how it went.

When he heard her mother's voice on the other end of the line, a surge of annoyance tumbled through his chest, but he pushed through it and said a respectful hello.

"I don't think you should be calling like this, Carter," she said.

"I'm going to be leaving for UPenn soon," he lied, hoping this tactic would help him get the information he needed. "And I figured I should at least say good-bye. Can I talk to her?"

"Well, that's nice," said Lilah's mother in that way she had of saying things were nice when she actually meant they weren't. "You're too late, though. She's in Mississippi. For freshman orientation."

"Are you sure?"

"Why wouldn't I be sure? We drove her out to Oxford on Saturday."

Mississippi. That had been her safety school.

"You drove her out yourself?"

"She can't really get there on her own, now, can she? It's not like she's got a rich daddy to buy her a car like you, Carter." After that low blow, she didn't even ask if he wanted to leave a message. Instead, she simply said, "Is there anything else I can help you with?"

"No, I guess not. Thank you, Mrs. Bell."

Without another word, she hung up. Relieved, he went back inside and waited for Jules.

Eventually, she was buzzed out through the locked doors separating the waiting room from the examination rooms. She had a small bandage on her temple, but other than that, she looked like she was maybe okay.

When she saw him, she flashed him a weak smile. "So, I guess I know what it's like to be a football player now," she said. "It's a concussion. I'm going to be a little dizzy, so . . . no cartwheels and no . . . see? Because of my concussion, I can't think of the witty thing that goes there."

Carter kneaded her shoulders. "It's okay," he said. "I'll pick up the wit until you're feeling better."

She smiled at this. "I should be back to my old charming self in, like, three or four days."

"I've got good news, too," said Carter. "Lilah's in Mississippi."

Jules looked confused for a second; then her expression hardened into skepticism. "You called her?"

"No. I did some recon. I talked to her mother."

Jules nodded. He could tell that she was having trouble processing what he was saying, and he chose not to burden her with any more details.

"Anyway," he said, "there's no way it could have been her. So we're free."

He sat her down in one of the blue molded chairs.

"Jules, we're free," he said again. "Really. Whoever it was in that car back there, it wasn't her. It couldn't have been. We can relax. We don't have to worry about Lilah anymore."

He could see the strain on Jules's face as she struggled with what he was saying. Finally, she grinned. "I guess, maybe we should go look for that Spanish moss," she said, winking at him.

48

Carter's dad's house was like something out of a movie, a huge antebellum row house right on Oglethorpe Square—one of the many shady parks scattered in a grid across downtown Savannah. It was four stories high, made of dark wood and stone, and on each floor there was an ornate iron balcony from which Jules could imagine southern belles in petticoats waving their handkerchiefs at passing gentlemen. Inside, the place was sleek and modern and sparsely furnished, but it was decked out with all the latest electronics—surround-sound speakers built into the walls, a 3D TV the size of a truck, Bluetooth everything. An awesome and slightly intimidating place to camp out for three days. The muchness of it all was enough to overwhelm any lingering fears she had about the green Mazda and the accident and the possibility that maybe Lilah had followed them north.

She'd always known that Carter hung out with the rich kids, but she'd had no idea that he was this rich himself. He sauntered around the place like it was just normal, like it was a place for living, not staring at in awe.

They made their way up the weathered wooden stairs—they had actual banisters with actual scrollwork—to the second floor, then farther, up and up and up.

"It's creakier than it looks," Carter said as they walked through what seemed like a parlor on the third floor. "These old mansions. There's no way to get rid of the draftiness, no matter how much money you throw into them."

"Yeah, I guess. But it's marvelous."

Carter smirked. "Only the best for good old Paul Moore the third." He turned a glass knob and pushed open a heavy oak door. "Your room, madame."

Wow. A canopy bed. It must have been two hundred years old, at least.

Carter dropped their bags on a bench and then threw himself backward onto the bed. He bounced a few times, then laid back and crossed his arms behind his head.

It was all too much for Jules, such casual luxury. To think that this was really a part of her life now. She dove in after Carter and wrapped her arms and legs around him and kissed him deeply, joyfully. This was already pretty close to the best vacation she'd ever been on in her entire life.

They lay there, all wrapped up in each other, for a while, gazing up at the white, lacy fabric strung like a roof over the bed, just happy to be in this place together. Getting used to it, Jules studied the room. A bleached wooden wardrobe. A cool-looking Eames chair. There was a painting mounted across from the bed, vibrant dashes of color, a dancer. She reached down, extending her arm in a graceful line toward her outstretched toe, so delicate and yet so poised. It looked like—but it couldn't be, could it?—an actual Degas. Jules had imagined dancing for Carter like that and him seeing the same beauty in her that Degas had seen in the woman he'd captured in his paintings.

"Is that—"

"Yeah. It's real."

"Wow. I need to get used to the idea that this is really happening to me."

"Just wait till you see the hot tub on the roof."

She studied the painting, the five thousand shades of yellow and pink it contained. It soothed her, and calmed her excitement. Suddenly, Jules felt the exhaustion release in her body. They'd driven for seven and a half hours. Then there'd been the craziness with the Mazda and the hospital. She had a stiff neck and her head still throbbed. She closed her eyes and felt herself breathing.

There were noises, she realized now: creaks and pitter-patters coming from she didn't know where.

Listening more closely, she wondered if maybe she could discern a pattern. A door turning on a rusty hinge. A step-step-step-pause on a loose floorboard. Then more steps, deliberate. Someone walking on tiptoes through the house.

"Do you hear that?" she asked Carter.

"What?"

"Listen."

There it was again. A scurrying in the room directly below them.

"That," she said. She knew that Carter had told her that he'd spoken to Lilah's mother. She knew that the girl was, theoretically, way off in Mississippi, hanging posters in her freshman dorm room or whatever, but—there it was again, like someone had opened a closet door downstairs or something. "There's someone downstairs," she whispered.

Carter was sitting up, his head cocked, listening.

"I don't know, Jules."

"There!" said Jules. "That *di-di-di-di-dum*. Like someone's moving from room to room."

Carter must have seen how wide her eyes were, because he placed his hands on her shoulders and held them firm like he was trying to physically still her fears.

"Jules, she's not here," he said. "It's going to be okay."

He nudged her close to him and wrapped her up in his arms.

"It's just the house. I promise. It's like a hundred and fifty years old. There's all kinds of weirdness to it. The floors creak. All that wood everywhere is settling all the time and it makes crazy groaning sounds. Squirrels hide their acorns on the roof and then rustle around up there all night looking for them. You'll see. By tomorrow you won't even notice these sounds anymore."

Jules wanted to believe him. What he was saying made total sense. But there was a possibility he was wrong, and no matter how far-fetched that possibility was, as long as she knew it existed, she had a hard time not fixating on Lilah. She thought briefly about a phone call she'd received last week from a blocked number—she hadn't told Carter about this one. She'd heard what sounded like heavy breathing on the other end of the line—or maybe it was just the wind; she hadn't been sure—and then an abrupt cutting off of the line. At the time she'd decided that it must have been her mother, butt-dialing from her work-issued cell phone, which always came up blocked. But now she wondered, *Could that have been Lilah?* No. Well, maybe. She hoped not.

She reminded herself that she had a concussion and that her thinking was a little foggy. For Carter's sake—and for the sake of her own sanity—Jules willed herself to stop being paranoid.

"You're right," she said. "So, how 'bout that hot tub?" She forced a smile. She didn't want him to worry.

"Just what I was thinking," Carter said.

As they neared the wrought-iron ladder that led up to the trapdoor through the roof of the mansion, he came up behind her and slid his hands around her waist. "You like the place?"

"Yeah. I love it," she said.

She turned to kiss him and just as her lips grazed his, a loud clap, like someone had slammed a door with extreme force, shuttered through the house.

Everything in Jules tensed up. She let out a small gasp.

"That wasn't—"

"The wind," Carter said reassuringly.

Jules wanted to believe him; she really did. The problem was—what if he was wrong?

49

No matter how she tried, Jules couldn't shake the feeling that the noises she'd been hearing weren't as normal as Carter claimed. She kept these worries hidden, for his sake, as they changed their clothes and got ready to go out and explore the city. She knew he had a whole list of things he wanted to show her, that it was an important place to him and he wanted Jules to see it through his eyes. It would be horrible if she let her paranoia ruin all this.

Just before they left, he stopped off in the downstairs bathroom, a small space at the far end of the dark, wooded hallway.

Standing outside the closed door, waiting for him,

she couldn't help but peek through the open passageway that led into the darkened kitchen. Was there someone hiding in the shadows there? Lurking behind the refrigerator? Crouching behind the chopping block? She knew she should just believe Carter's assurances, but the kitchen was tantalizingly close, and really, what was wrong with verification? She had the moment now—when would she have another one?

She couldn't stop herself. She darted into the room and threw on the lights. A fridge, an oven, an island counter. No sign of anyone but Carter and her. The white enamel table. No one underneath it.

She checked the leaded windows above the sink. They were locked tight with castor bolts, sticky, like they hadn't been opened in months.

There was a door in the far corner of the room. It led to the house's large backyard. She pulled lightly at the handle, and it didn't budge. She pulled harder. It was sealed shut like the windows. She examined the door—one, two, three separate locks.

Whatever it was that had blown through this room, it hadn't been the wind. No way had it been the wind. The room was closed up tight—stuffy, almost.

There was one more door, built into a short wall, too far out of the way to catch any wind from the front rooms. What was in there? A pantry? A staircase to the basement?

Lilah? Was Lilah hiding right there, right then?

Only one way to find out.

But before Jules had a chance to turn the handle and throw the door open, she heard the toilet flush in the bathroom and Carter was out and calling to her.

"Hey, you ready, Jules? Where'd you go?"

"I'm right here," she said. "In the kitchen."

When he appeared in the doorway, a wave of relief rolled through her.

"What are you doing in here?" he asked.

"Just—nothing," she said.

She could see the worry on his face. She'd have to try harder, be better. They were fine. They were safe. She had to remember this. She knew it was true.

As she followed Carter out of the kitchen, she heard a creak. She was positive it had come from that door. She couldn't stop herself from casting one more nervous glance at the kitchen as they left. There was a chef's knife on the chopping block, she noticed. Had it been there before? It must have been. But she didn't remember seeing it. Either way, she didn't bother Carter with this new worry.

She refused to be that kind of girl.

50

The cobblestone streets and the live oaks and the ancient streetlamps cast their romantic shadows across the city, and as Carter and Jules sat in the candlelit corner table at the Carriage House, the restaurant he'd picked for them, and ate their dinner of beet salad, rack of lamb, and raspberry-chocolate mousse, she managed to escape the fear that the day had filled her with. She stared into Carter's soft, hazel eyes and lost herself in the romance flickering there.

By the time they made their way hand in hand down Congress Street, heading toward the City Walk, she'd put Lilah completely out of her head.

Knowing the state she'd been in all evening, and

worried about the effects of her concussion, Carter worked hard to be tender and careful with Jules. He didn't push to speed-walk like he usually did and instead strolled next to her, gauging the pace by the pressure of her hand in his. When he felt her growing tense, he'd pause and put his arm around her hip and kiss her lightly on the lobe of the ear.

The closer they got to the heart of town, the thicker the crowds became. It started with corner open-air bars—Braves games on the TVs, college kids in cargos and backward baseball caps hovering around pitchers of beer. Then the bars became more crowded, people spilling onto the street, the music getting louder, the distance between each bar shrinking. There were restaurants everywhere. The crowd waiting to get into Paula Deen's place stretched in an unruly line halfway down the block.

Carter steered Jules to the other side of the street, where tourist families with children wandered in a daze, unsure of where to go, where to look, what to do.

"It's like Harpoon Haven, but classier and more real," said Jules. "Like, part museum, part tourist trap, and part real living city just going about its business."

"Yeah. It can get pretty crazy here. You have to teach yourself to look through the mob and see the place itself." Carter thought for a second. He studied Jules for signs of weariness.

"Is it too much for you tonight? How's your head feeling? We can find somewhere more out of the way to go, if you want."

"No, I'm good. I'm fascinated."

"You'll let me know, though, yeah? If it gets to be too much, you'll tell me so I can take you home?"

"Relax," she said. "I'll tell you. I promise."

She let go of his hand and forged on down the street.

When they reached the City Walk, they found themselves in a dense throng of people packed so tight that it was almost impossible to walk. The smell of grilled meat and popcorn filled the air. The din of a thousand conversations, all being carried on at two or three decibel levels higher than they needed to be, crashed over their ears. Packs of drunken college kids collided with moony middle-aged couples and families struggling to herd their children in and out of shops.

Jules paused in the middle of the street to study the ornate facade of a bright-yellow building. It seemed slightly more special than the others near it, like whoever built it had taken just a bit more care. There were curved shingles along the top three feet, and mounted lamps next to each window. If she pretended that the mob of tourists wasn't there, she could almost imagine that she was standing here on this street in 1845.

"What's that place," she said. "Do you—"

She turned toward Carter and found he wasn't there.

He'd been swallowed up by the crowd. She told herself that he couldn't be far, but there were so many people, so, so many people everywhere, moving like rivers in every direction.

Turning in a circle, standing on her tiptoes, Jules searched for Carter's flop of hair, the pale-green, short-sleeve oxford he had been wearing. Her view was blocked everywhere. There was one guy in particular—he was like seven feet tall—who seemed to be in her way at every juncture. Carter had to be somewhere, if she could only see. She hopped in place, and strained to see over people's heads. It was almost like the guy knew where she was going to look, and he was bobbing and weaving to make sure she couldn't see.

She sent Carter a text—WHERE'D YOU GO?—and when he didn't write back immediately, she called him. No answer.

She pushed past the tall guy, deeper into the thick of the crowd, and retraced her steps up the block. Maybe Carter was back there somewhere waiting for her. She wove and dodged through the masses of people but she felt like she was getting nowhere.

Her head began throbbing—the racing of her heart sent blood to her head, reigniting the effects of her concussion.

There were stalls set up in the pedestrian mall, people selling sunglasses and cell-phone covers and bottles of water. She circled around them, calling out Carter's name.

She turned a corner.

Then another.

No sign of him.

She wasn't sure what street she was on and she didn't know Carter's dad's address and she was positive that, if she didn't find Carter, she'd have no idea how to get back to the house.

She stopped for a second. She found a street sign. Bay Lane and Jefferson, whatever that implied. She sent him another text telling her where she was. Maybe if she just waited here, he'd find her.

Standing under the streetlamp, she tried to have patience. She could feel something behind her. The heat of someone's eyes focused on her. When she turned, she saw nothing, just the throngs going their way. Or wait— was that a woman ducking her head, deflecting her gaze so she wouldn't be seen?

Jules moved twenty feet down the street. She leaned against a potted plant. She glanced back. There was definitely a girl back there staring at her, but the mass of people pressing toward her closed in and the girl disappeared before Jules could see who exactly it was.

Like she needed to.

Like she didn't already know.

She tried to squeeze out of the way of the crowd, but

someone bumped her and sent her stumbling, almost losing her balance altogether. When she looked up, she saw that same girl marching on ahead of her. Maybe it was Lilah, and maybe it wasn't. She was wearing a baseball cap and it was hard for Jules to tell from behind.

The walls of the buildings seemed to be bending in toward Jules. She was surrounded by people and she could hardly breathe. But she pushed through, moving against the flow. She squeezed between parents and their children, broke through couples holding each other's hands. She willed herself not to look over her shoulder, not to check and see if Lilah was following her.

She turned another corner and pressed through another crowd.

How far did she have to go before she lost the girl?

But the dizziness. The throbbing in her temple. Jules could only go so fast.

She stopped to steady herself. She leaned her arm against a wall and took as much oxygen as she could into her lungs.

And that's when someone placed her hand on Jules's shoulder and she knew, she just knew, that if she acted fast, she might catch Lilah and put an end to this, finally.

51

Jules shook the hand off her shoulder. She spun around to face the girl. She swung, fighting Lilah off, clawing and batting at her.

But it wasn't Lilah. It was someone else. A girl with the same bland hair, with the same dowdy fashion sense, but not Lilah.

"Jesus, calm down," the girl said, slightly irritated. Then she held her hand out and there in her palm was Jules's cell phone. "You dropped this."

As the reality of the moment sunk in and Jules realized how wrong she was—how crazy she was being—Jules felt trapped. The shock and shame of this were too much for her to take. She felt like she was having a heart attack. Or a stroke. Or . . . anyway, she couldn't breathe. She was hyperventilating. She could gulp the air down, but she couldn't get it to come back out. She got weak at the knees. She slid down the wall she'd wedged herself against, and squatted there, staring with tunnel vision, straight ahead, seeing nothing, just her own humiliation.

"I just wanted to make sure you got it back. Here." The girl pressed the phone into Jules's hand. "It's not like I was trying to scare you or whatever," she said. "I just figured you'd want it."

Jules had managed to get her breathing back under control, but she was too ashamed to look at the girl. "You didn't scare me," she mumbled. "I . . . It's been a rough day."

The girl knelt next to Jules, concerned. "Do you need—"

"Jules!" It was Carter. He'd found her. Thank God. "I went to the address you texted me but—whoa. Are you okay?"

She just shook her head. Seeing him here now, his face filled with worry, made her even angrier at herself. This was not the kind of person she wanted to be.

Turning to the girl, Carter said, "Thanks. You're a lifesaver. She's a little out of sorts today."

"It was nothing," the girl said, pursing her face in sympathy.

She ducked back into the crowd and Carter crouched next to Jules.

"What happened?" he asked.

She didn't answer at first. She was still seized with shame.

"Nothing," she said finally. "It's stupid."

He took her hand in his. He wrapped his arm around her shoulder and guided her head toward his shoulder, holding her tight. They sat like that for a while, huddled under the potted plant against the brick wall as the mob of tourists streamed past, an unending march of legs stepping around them.

"I stopped to look at the awning of this building back there," said Jules. "And then . . ." She told him her story. How she lost him in the crowd. The panic she felt. The walking in circles as she searched for him. "Where did you go?" she said. "It was like all of a sudden you were gone."

"I was searching for you," he said. "I must have not noticed you'd stopped at first, and then I couldn't find you. We must have been walking in circles around each other."

"And . . ." She shuddered. "I keep seeing Lilah everywhere. I can't stop. It's stupid. I'm sure it's just the concussion, but—"

"It's not stupid," Carter said. "She put you through

hell. But listen to me, Jules. She can't hurt you. I won't let her."

She nuzzled her head against his shoulder. It was nice to know he cared, to see his conviction and hear his valiant pledges.

"Come on, let's go home," he said.

"What about the Riverwalk?"

"Not tonight. Let's take it easy. Don't you think? Until you shake off that concussion, anyway?"

Jules knew he was right, but it stung to admit her limitations. "I'm sorry," she said. "I ruined everything."

"No," Carter said, standing and pulling her up. "You didn't ruin anything. I'm just thinking—hot tub?" A mischievous half smile floated across his face. "Whatta ya think?"

52

Carter spotted Jules as she climbed the ladder up to the roof, and he adjusted the temperature and bubbles in the hot tub so that the water was just warm enough, just massaging enough, for her to feel like she was at a spa designed to fulfill her every wish. He set his iPod on the surround-sound speaker system and, conscious of the headache a bass-heavy rap beat might cause her in her current state, cued up the calming new-agey music that her mother played in the crystal shop. He slid in behind her and gave her a back rub, and they gazed out at the rooftops and the wide lanes and treetops of Oglethorpe Square below them.

It didn't take long for Carter's hands to slide from

Jules's shoulders, down her long back, and around to her stomach, her breasts, a full-body massage that made her tremble with pleasure. Giving to her. Asking nothing in return.

That night he held her while he slept. He didn't let go once. He nuzzled his face into the base of her neck, spooned her, and wrapped his body over hers like a shield. She really was safe here with him. She could feel it. And to her surprise, she slept like a baby.

By morning, her headache had receded a bit. She unlaced herself from his arms and turned in the bed, propped herself on an elbow, and gazed at his sleeping face. She could see the small child he used to be, and also the old man he would one day become in the twist of his mouth and the crease of his eyes. She told herself to remember this quiet, peaceful comfort. Despite the complications, this being alone with him here in Savannah was a precious experience. She had to hold on to it.

When Carter was awake, he told her that the plan had changed. They'd take it easy today. Create an optimum condition for her to recover. Then they could go out on the boat tomorrow, if they wanted. The important thing was that she felt better.

So they lounged around the house in their pajamas, playing Scrabble and doing puzzles and gorging on streamed episodes of *Glee* (a show she knew Carter didn't find all that exciting, but that she loved and that she knew he was pretending to enjoy just to please her, just to make sure she understood that he was here to provide whatever her heart desired).

Throughout the day, Carter did everything he could to keep Jules from having to exert herself. He experimented with cooking—something he knew nothing about—serving up burnt grilled cheese for lunch, gummy pasta with sauce from the can for dinner. He hovered over her so lovingly that she felt both pampered and embarrassed. It was like she was one of the priceless sculptures his father collected, mounted under glass, there to be seen and cooed over but never touched, never played with, for fear that she might break.

By evening, when she was feeling fine—totally recovered, by her own ad hoc diagnosis—she finally had to say to him, "Carter, it's okay. It's just a concussion. I'm going to survive."

"I know," he said, but the look on his face said that maybe he didn't. He was sitting on an ottoman, giving her the whole kidney-shaped couch, and they had a *Twilight* movie going on the big-screen TV.

"You'll see. By tomorrow, I'll be fine."

This got a smile from Carter, but he still seemed concerned.

"Really, Carter," she said. "*Hakuna matata.*" She wobbled her hand in front of her like a surfer, her thumb and pinky outstretched. "It means *no worries.*"

"Yeah. I'm just not used to that," he said. "With Lilah there was always something to worry about."

Jules sat up. Now she feared she'd created a problem where one hadn't existed.

"Hey, come here." She tugged softly at his shirt, and he leaned toward her and she cradled his head in her hands and kissed him slowly, sensually. "I know you love me. I'm not going to forget it. Just treat me normal, you know what I mean?"

"M-mm. Okay. I can try to do that." He kissed her more deeply. "How's this?" He pressed his body forward until they both fell back on the couch, and he pressed himself against her and slid his hand under her shirt.

"Better," she said. She kissed him again. "Much, much better."

"Oh good," he whispered. He slid her shirt up and ran his hands up and down her body, kissing her stomach, her rib cage, her breasts.

"I've been so worried, Lilah. You don't even know."

Jules froze. Had she heard that right? She was sure she had. Her lips tightened and her mouth clamped shut and her body went rigid.

"Get off me," she said.

"What happened? What's wrong?"

"I said get off me."

Carter straightened up and retreated to the ottoman.

"Okay, okay. What's wrong, Jules?" he said.

She made him work for her forgiveness. She stared at the screen, watched as the werewolves there pranced through the woods toward their showdown with the vampires.

Finally, she said, "You really don't know?"

He was mystified, clearly, but that just made it worse.

"You really want Lilah? Give her another shout. She's probably here in the house somewhere."

She watched as he put the pieces together, his face slowly dropping with each new tick of mortification.

"Did I—"

"Oh, so, now you're going to pretend that you didn't realize it."

"Fuck. Really?"

Now he was up, nervously running his hand through his hair, staring at her, repelled by what he saw in her expression and how it reflected on him.

"I can't believe I did that. I'm sorry. I'm . . . my God, Jules, I'm sorry."

He came for her and tried to take her hand but she refused to give it to him.

"I can explain," he said.

"Yeah, that's the thing about guys. They can always explain."

"No, really, I can. We were just talking about her," he

said. "She was in my mind because I was thinking about all the ways that you're not like her." Jules waited for the complicating *but* she knew was coming. "And then, okay. She used to come up here sometimes with me."

"How many times?"

"God, I don't know. You have to believe me, Jules. I wish I'd met you freshman year instead of her. You don't know how badly I wish that."

She did believe him. Of course he was telling the truth. But still. "I wish that, too. My life would be a whole lot easier if you'd never met her. I swear to God, Carter."

As soon as these words came out of her mouth, Jules regretted them.

She retreated into the movie again, gazing at the screen, not really seeing or hearing what was happening there, just using it as a way to avoid Carter.

"It won't happen again, I swear to God, Jules."

She stared at him. The whole thing made her feel insecure and rejected, and she absolutely hated that. The dreamy perfection of the day had been bitterly destroyed with just one word.

"I'm sure you didn't mean it," she said. "I understand. It's just . . . after everything that's happened in the past couple days . . . I need some space."

His face flushed red.

Jules let him take her hand and kiss it.

"I'm going to sleep in the other room tonight. I just . . . I need to get my head together."

She gazed sadly at him one more time and walked slowly out of the room.

53

Carterless, shut up by herself in the bedroom with the Degas hanging on the wall, Jules turned in the bed and turned again.

The *ticktock, ticktock* of the grandfather clock hammered at her brain.

She kicked at the sheet. She pulled it up to her chin and then threw it off again. She punched at the pillow and buried her head in it.

It was pointless. She gave up even trying to sleep.

The seconds seemed to last forever. The room seemed huge, full of nooks and crannies where Lilah could be hiding. The open French window let out creaks and moans when the wind hit it—the glass rattled in the panes. A cat mewled somewhere outside.

Every time Jules closed her eyes, the creeping, trickling sensation, like something running its sharpened fingernails down her spine, returned. Her senses were alert, speeding, delirious, letting too much in. The short huff of someone breathing in the corner. That smell—that horrendous smell—that Lilah had placed in her locker. The person in the room would take a step toward the bed, stop, listen, step again.

Then she'd pop her eyes back open and check the time and see that half an hour or so had passed. The feeling that Lilah was in the room watching her would be gone. Just a dream, a dream that wouldn't leave her alone.

She stared at the billowing canopy over the bed, watched it ripple like the ocean as the wind blew across it. She could track the ripples from one end to the other. It should have relaxed her, but it just made her more anxious.

The sensation of being watched returned.

She was sure of it this time. She could see the contours of a human shape by the window. She could see the shadow, long and ghostly, moving slowly across the canopy above her.

Closer.

Closer.

The shadow stretched across the entire canopy, a

hulking specter peering down on her.

The sounds that had been keeping her awake before had vanished. The smell was gone. The wind had stopped blowing. She was in a void—there was nothing there but her and Lilah, creeping closer.

She held her breath and waited.

She was afraid to move—if she moved, she'd lose her advantage. Lilah would know she was awake. There'd be no way for Jules to surprise her when she attacked.

She could feel the body heat emanating from Lilah, four, three, two feet from the bed now.

She could feel Lilah leaning forward, stretching out her arms, her fingers spread like talons ready to tear her apart.

This was happening. This was really happening.

She could feel Lilah's hot breath on her face.

The crazed rage of her expression.

The cold death in her eyes.

Jules, you whore. Did you really think you could live happily ever after?

The arms rose above her.

They descended. Here they came. Propelling toward her. Claws sharp as spears.

She screamed from somewhere deep in her bowels. She kicked at the air and she lunged at Lilah.

And she was awake again and there was nobody there.

The ticking of the grandfather clock.

The creak of the windows in the wind.

A slamming door downstairs, maybe in the kitchen, maybe the same door that had slammed yesterday. It led to the cellar. She knew that now; she'd checked, finally, in secret. A dank, dirt-floored cavern. An easy place to hide, if you didn't want to be seen. She still wasn't convinced doors could slam on their own.

She couldn't take it anymore. She ran from the room, ran to Carter, who was sitting up in bed in the room next door, awoken by her scream.

She crawled into bed with him, and he held her tight. "It's going to be okay," he told her. "It was just a dream."

He willed himself to believe it, too.

She nuzzled her face in his shoulder and clung to him. She couldn't get close enough.

For the next hour the two of them lay awake, listening to each other's breathing, waiting, ready to defend themselves if need be. Even after Jules had fallen back to sleep, Carter could feel the anxious tension moving through every inch of her body.

54

That morning, Carter woke up at ten thirty to find that Jules was clinging to him in her sleep. He understood how bad her night had been, and he could see by the way the dreams twitched behind her eyes that she wouldn't be waking up anytime soon.

Carter felt horrible. It wasn't just the fact that he'd called Jules *Lilah*. That was bad, and he hated himself for having done it, but what was worse was that he couldn't figure out why or how the word had come out of his mouth. It was a dick move. He had to admit it. The kind of thing his father would do and then laugh about later.

And it couldn't have happened at a worse time. Jules

put up a good front—she was really trying—but he knew the concussion was having its effect on her. And the pressure she was putting on herself to shake it off, to forge ahead, be better, be stronger, was just going to make it all that much worse.

She saw Lilah everywhere.

But Lilah wasn't here. He refused to believe in that possibility. And it was on him to show Jules a path toward forgetting her.

He slid out from under her and tiptoed downstairs, throwing on some shorts and a T-shirt. Then he slipped out of the house and race-walked to Amelia's, the Frenchy brunch place around the corner from the house. If he wanted to impress her, if he wanted to bring her joy, it was better not to inflict his own burnt attempts at pancakes on her.

He bought her a Belgian waffle with the works—Nutella, bananas, strawberries, whipped cream—and back at the house, he slid it out of its tin to-go container and onto a plate from his father's china set.

He broke into his father's fancy wine-chilling cabinet and found a bottle of Dom Pérignon champagne. It must have cost at least five hundred dollars, but he didn't care. His father probably wouldn't even notice it was gone, and if he did, so what—Jules deserved the best.

As he was arranging everything on the TV tray, he heard Jules call out to him from the bedroom. "Carter?"

He could hear her moan as she stretched. "What time is it?"

"I'll be up in a second," he shouted. He sped his pace. Coffee. Orange juice. Two champagne flutes.

Balancing all the food and drink on the tray, he wobbled up the stairs and edged the door to the bedroom open with his foot.

There she was, beautiful, her hair a rumpled mess, sitting up in the bed with the sheet draped over her chest.

"Hey there," he said, holding the tray up in front of him. "I got you a little sum-sum."

A smile. Her face just glowed this morning. "For me?" she drawled playfully, pulling her best southern belle. "You shouldn't have."

"Oh, but I did."

He almost dropped the tray right then to leap into the bed. Who needed breakfast when Jules was waiting there so lusciously? There'd be time for that later, though. He set the tray down on the bed and popped the cork on the champagne and poured two glasses.

"To morning," said Carter. "And feeling better."

They toasted.

"You *are* feeling better, right? You look better."

She nodded. "Yeah," she said. "I think so. We'll see."

But the house creaked again, like it always did, and the glow of morning comfort on her face faded. The wary tension of the night before returned.

She picked at her waffle, pushed it around on her plate, politely not eating, and Carter worried that she'd begun to fixate on Lilah again. How to ask her about this, though, without exacerbating things? Better to say nothing. Change the subject. Let her find her own peace.

"I'm thinking today we should take a vacation from our vacation. What do you think? The boat. The water. The two of us, out in the bay by ourselves. Yeah?"

She shot him a look like he'd just read her mind. "Hell yeah," she said.

They toasted again. To sailing. To rich fathers with boats they could borrow.

55

They threw their bags into the trunk of the BMW, stocked up on groceries—LUNA bars and bags of pretzels and chips, peanut butter, jelly, a loaf of sliced bread, a Toblerone to go with the second bottle of champagne they'd snatched from Carter's dad's stock—and then they raced off across the Savannah River and onward to the Wilmington Island Yacht Club, where Carter's dad's sailboat was docked.

Carter checked in at the office and signed the boat out. Then they loaded up and trudged across the sun-bleached parking lot, through the maze of promenades to dock number 15-L.

In their excitement, they didn't notice the little green Mazda with Idaho plates parked in a far corner by the utility vehicles and chain-link fence.

The boat was twenty-five feet long, a beast of a vessel. Carter checked the jib. He checked the mainsail and made sure the boom was secure. Then he untied the ropes and started the engine.

One, two, three, go.

They navigated their way through the no-wake zone and out into the river.

Carter raised the sails and adjusted the ropes in the riggings. He knew just what he was doing. He positioned himself on the deck, and manned all the sails at once as they tacked up the river toward Wassaw Bay.

Jules was surprised by how fast Carter had gotten the boat to go. She hadn't realized that a boat this big could really book. Kneeling toward the front so she could gaze over the edge, she watched the wedge of the stern cut smoothly through the small, nearly imperceptible waves. The sunlight glistened in diamonds on the surface.

Once they were out in the open water, Carter shouted, "Hey, you ready for the fun part?"

Jules rolled over and stretched her legs out in front of her, leaning back to catch the sun on her face. "This isn't the fun part?" she said.

"It gets even better. I need you to come over here and

sit next to me." He patted the hull, showing her where to sit, then tugged the rope sharply to hold the mast tight against the wind.

Once Jules had situated herself next to him, he said, "Hold on tight to the bar."

She did.

As he tied one of the lesser ropes to the boat, he said, "You have to make sure you keep your head low."

She hunched. He grinned at her.

"Here we go," he said.

Carter let the rope slide through his fingers and the sail swung in with a *whoosh*. It pivoted over them, coming so close that Jules could feel the air move across the top of her head. The sail continued on, flying out wide to the point at which the rope Carter had secured went taut and stopped it. Fluttering once, it caught the wind again, and without losing any of its speed, the boat tilted impossibly to the starboard side.

They leaned all their weight against the hull, stretched back until it was almost like they were standing up. The boat took a sharp ninety-degree turn and as it did, a wall of water went up behind them, a spray that arched over the edge of the hull and soaked them.

A thrilling experience. Jules yelped like she was on a roller coaster, and then she laughed and laughed. "Wow," she said.

Carter nodded. She could see how much he loved this all over his face. He adjusted the ropes one more time and snapped them into their safety latches.

They glided forth toward the ocean, far away from everything.

"You feel better?" he asked Jules.

"Yeah," she said.

"There's nothing like a sailboat to take your worries away."

The water glistened with sunlight. The fish jumped and spun. The cormorants skimmed the surface. The seagulls soared overhead.

A school of dolphins came leaping and dancing across the open sea. They seemed to be waving. They seemed to be smiling. For almost an hour they swam along with the boat.

They were happy. Carter and Jules, happier than they'd ever been in their lives. Simply and completely. Jules sitting between Carter's legs, wrapped up in his arms, the two of them gazing out at the calm, endless sea.

And as the sun began to descend to the west and the sky began to glow, they pulled in the sails. They let loose the anchor. There it went—*rumble, rumble*—down to the ocean floor.

They sat on the stern all alone, arm in arm, and

watched the sunset as if seeing it for the first time.

Any nervousness and fear lingering in their hearts had been left behind them, far off on the shore. They were a long way from the past now, a long way from Dream Point.

56

While they were belowdecks, changing into their swimsuits, the skylight on the prow of the boat rolled open. A stowaway climbed the ladder out of the storage compartment at the front of the boat.

First the hands became visible. Then the muscular swimmer's arms. The wavy, dishwater-brown hair. The deep-red lifeguard's swimsuit with the ghostly white cross on it. The whole of her.

Lilah.

She stood there like a fury, the wind whipping her hair. She'd been waiting. She'd been planning. She knew this was her time. She wore a diver's belt around her waist, an eight-inch knife clipped to her hip. She looked to the sky and she could see the future there, written in the bloodred streaks of the vanished sun.

She stretched and flapped out her muscles. Then she dove off the boat into the water. The sea was her home.

Her moment was coming soon.

57

Back on deck, Carter and Jules were giddy. They sat
on the edge of the boat, braced behind the safety railing
with their legs hanging over, bouncing against the hull.
They watched the fish jump in the fading dusk light
and chattered away. The game was What's the Weirdest
Thing You've Ever Eaten?

"Alligator," said Jules.

"Doesn't count! If they sell it on the promenade in
Dream Point, it can't be that weird."

"Okay . . . blood sausage. That counts. It's too revolting not to count."

"Rattlesnake," said Carter. "Tastes like chicken."

"Cow stomach."

"You've eaten cow stomach?" said Carter.

"My mom dated this Cuban guy for a few months, and one time when I was sick he brought me this soup that he claimed would make me better. Mondongo soup. It was made with—he called it tripe, but it was cow stomach."

"Did it work?"

"I don't know. The intestines were cut into these strips, like spaghetti, but they were hairy. It made me gag. Your turn."

"Moose."

"Wow. Moose."

"Yeah. My father went on some crazy hunting trip in Canada. Like a rich-guy trip where the guide takes you around and catches the animals for you, and then you shoot them and feel proud of yourself. He brought me back some moose jerky. He claimed it came from a moose he actually shot, but . . ."

"What does moose taste like?"

"Teriyaki sauce."

Jules shot him a look that was so adoring—teasing and flirty and admiring all at once—that the both of them started laughing and couldn't stop. They felt silly, sloppy drunk, and they hadn't even opened the champagne yet. Just being together—that was enough.

"Look at that moon," said Jules, lacing her arm around Carter's waist.

"Yeah." It wasn't quite full, but it was close. There were no clouds in the sky that night, and the outline of the moon was crisp, its craters in high relief, like it had been shot in HD. It reminded Carter of the moon on the night they'd first met. He pulled her close and kissed her, and for a moment the two of them swooned close, attracted by each other's body heat.

"Should we swim?" Carter said.

Jules unlaced her legs from the railing and stood up. She did a slow dance, spinning on her tiptoes, her arms stretched gracefully above her head. Then the boat rocked slightly and she lost her balance. She toppled over and giggled again.

As they stood by the opening in the guard railing, psyching themselves up to dive, she asked Carter, "You think there are sharks in there?"

"I've never seen one in all my time coming out here. I think we're too far north."

"Jellyfish?"

"No, but I ate jellyfish once."

"Okay, here goes nothing."

Jules dove off the boat as gracefully as she danced. Carter watched as she slid under the water in one smooth arc. Now that his thoughts had floated back to that first night with her, he was lost there, overwhelmed with the memory of the electric shock of that first touch of her skin, the fizz he'd felt in his heart just standing in her presence.

She surfaced fifteen feet out or so and turned toward where she thought he'd be, right behind her, only to discover that he still hadn't jumped. She called out to him, "You chicken?"

"No." What he was, was dazzled by how hot she was. He didn't want to say that, though, so instead, he said, "I'm figuring out which dive I should do."

"It's cold in here. Come warm me up."

One last look, and Carter jumped in feetfirst, bicycling his legs as he went down. He swam out and splashed a massive arc of water at her, just like he'd done that first night at Jeff's party.

"You didn't just do that," she teased him.

She splashed him back.

"Is that how it's going to be?" he said, splashing her again.

They splashed and splashed, dunked each other, kicked up the water, pushing and pulling and wrestling with each other, laughing the whole time, neither of them able to get enough of this freedom, this being alone together with nothing to do but play. Their slick skin slid under each other's hands as they grappled and kneaded and inevitably kissed each other.

Pulling back, Carter said, "So, you know that night at Jeff's house. The minute I saw you, I just knew. You were—I should have just admitted to myself from the start that I was totally—"

"Shut up and kiss me again," she said. "It's all over."

They kissed again, more deeply, bobbing in the water.

Something bumped against the boat. They couldn't see it—it was on the other side—but they heard the echoing against the fiberglass hull. A fish. A sea bass. A grouper. They'd been seeing them jumping all evening.

They smiled at each other, and then Jules wrapped her legs around Carter's waist and they went right on kissing. Carter's hands running up and down Jules's thighs, hers running up and down his back, finding their way under the waistband of his swim trunks, probing at the base of his spine.

A fish brushed against the back of Carter's leg. It tickled the sole of Jules's foot.

They laughed about this. There sure were a lot of them out here tonight.

"You're positive there's no sharks?" Jules said.

"No. No sharks. Promise."

And that was when whatever it was swimming around below them got ahold of Jules's ankle and yanked her out of Carter's arms.

58

Jules screamed. She kicked with all her might, but the thing tightened its grip. It wouldn't let go. This was no fish.

She went under. She kicked and kicked. She flailed her arms toward the surface, trying to pull herself away.

Then she was up again, briefly, gasping for breath, calling out, "Carter!"

And she was under again. The thing was crawling up her leg, clawing at her calf, grabbing at the waist of her bikini bottoms.

She was up again suddenly.

"Carter!" Where was he?

He was underwater, swimming straight down with

all his might. Blinking through the salt water, his eyes stinging fiercely, he could see murky shapes wrestling with each other just out of his reach. One of these was Jules. The other one was red. Was it human? Yes, it was.

The knowledge that this was Lilah crawling up Jules's body, pulling her down, sunk in peripherally as Carter pushed through the heavy water toward them. He had no time for dread. What was called for was action.

He grabbed at Lilah's arm, but it was too slippery to grip.

He grabbed at her shoulder—pushed at her, pulled at her—but this dragged Jules down, too.

They were—all three of them—submerged now.

Carter managed to tangle Lilah's hair in his fist. He yanked with all his strength and her head snapped back, but she didn't let go of Jules. He wrapped himself around the upper half of Lilah's body and twisted and turned, trying to shake her free.

She had to fend him off, at least, which gave Jules a brief advantage.

Peeling Lilah's fingers, Carter tried to pry them loose.

All the while, Jules was kicking, kicking, kicking. She kicked Carter in the head. She kicked Lilah everywhere.

Holding on tight, Carter twisted and yanked at Lilah's body. She had to use most of her strength to wrest herself away from him, and the concentration required to do this took her attention away from Jules.

One more kick. She was out of Lilah's grasp.

As Carter continued to wrestle with Lilah, Jules swam for the surface. Her heart beat in her ears. Her tear ducts felt like they were ready to explode.

Then she was up, gulping down air, paddling, swimming like she'd never swum before, toward the ladder hanging off the side of the boat.

It took Carter a moment to realize that Jules had shaken free. When he did, he pushed Lilah deeper into the water. He let go. He frog-kicked, using her body as ballast to propel himself toward the dark shadow that must have been the boat.

He reached the ladder a second after Jules did. They yanked themselves up.

"Pull the ladder up! Carter, quick!" Jules shouted.

But he couldn't do that. The ladder was bolted into the side of the boat.

And Lilah was already at the bottom rung.

59

When Lilah reached the top of the ladder and found Jules barring her way, kicking at her shoulders, trying to push her back and send her falling into the sea, she smirked. This girl was no threat to her—not now, now when she was so completely in her power. She was strong, too strong for Jules. A swipe of the arm, a twist of the wrist—that was all it took to gain the upper hand, to get Jules in a power hold, her arm torqued at the elbow, her whole body pulled down behind it.

Then up, off the ladder, and onto the stable footing of the deck. Lilah rammed her heel into Jules's neck, stunning her.

Jules's body curled into a fetal position. It was not

in her control. No matter how much she might want to defend herself and Carter, her body wanted only to protect itself. Her neck stung where Lilah had kicked her. Her trachea went numb. She could hardly breathe. At the very best she was about to be beat up. At the worst, Lilah would kill her, right here, right now. But no. Lilah stepped past her. Why?

She had no use for Jules. Not right this minute. Carter was the prize she wanted right now. He always had been; he always would be. Casually, confidently, she walked the length of the deck, picking up the harpoon gun she'd stashed against the gunwale early that morning while Carter and Jules were still back in Savannah eating Belgian waffles.

He was frantically digging in the compartment where the tools were kept, under the bench at the stern of the boat. There used to be weapons there—knives and lances and harpoons—but where were they? All he was finding was a tangled mess of ropes. And the more he dug, the more tangled they became. He wasn't watching his back. Yet again, he'd allowed Jules to be out there alone with no protection from him. Even as he kept digging, he knew he should have stood guard at the ladder instead of race for the toolbox.

Suddenly Lilah was on him, standing at his back, holding the barbed trident head of the loaded harpoon gun to his ear.

"Hi, Carter," she said. "I've missed you."

He turned slowly toward her. She was smiling.

"Where's Jules?" he barked.

She plumped her bottom lip out into a pout. "The first time we talk in two and a half months, and this is all you have to say to me? I'm disappointed. I'd have thought you'd be more excited to see me."

He was acutely aware of the harpoon aimed at his face. Instead of saying something that might inflame her, he let his facial expression do his talking. "What did you do to her?" he asked.

"She's fine." Lilah nodded toward the front of the boat. "She's over there. Resting."

Glancing, just briefly—he didn't want to take his eyes off Lilah long enough for her to pull something—he saw Jules's body curled on the deck.

"Is she hurt?"

"Maybe she's hurt. Probably. I mean, she's alive. I just kicked her a little. Why do you care so much?"

"Lilah . . ."

"No, you're right. You don't have to answer that. We both know you don't care about her. I know she's got you all turned around in your head, but really, I swear, you don't owe her anything. Don't you think it's time to remember who you are—who you really are—and what you really want?"

"What's that, Lilah?" Carter said sarcastically.

"What do I really want?"

She tipped her head skeptically. "You think I didn't hear you yesterday when my name slipped out while you were kissing her?"

Carter glanced at Jules again. She still wasn't moving.

"It's not too late. We can get through this just like we've always gotten through everything else. Forever, remember? That's what you promised me freshman year, and I know you still believe it. You just have to be brave enough to admit what you want. And then everything can go back to normal. Okay?"

Trapped, Carter waited to hear what she'd say next. But she didn't say anything. Instead, she fumbled with a snap on the diving belt around her waist. Keeping the harpoon gun trained on Carter's head, she pulled the knife out by its bright-yellow plastic handle and held it up for him to see.

"Come back to me, Carter. We both know that's what you really want to do."

She slowly crouched and laid the knife on the deck. Then she pulled herself back to a standing position, and being careful not to catch herself with the blade, she gripped the handle with her toe and pushed the knife toward Carter.

"You don't have to be afraid anymore. We can get rid of the whore together, right now."

"I promised Jules I'd never let you hurt her again. I'll take you down, Lilah. I swear I will."

Lilah stabbed the harpoon gun at him, one swift thrust that caught him on the arm, stinging and breaking the skin.

She smirked. "You must know by now that there's no way I'm going to let her have you," she said.

60

Jules was finally able to breathe again. She sat up and stretched her neck, gulping down air. When she saw Carter walking slowly in her direction, his expression—nervous, full of warning—filled her with dread.

It took her a second to realize that Lilah was still there, too, stagger-stepping forward, a few yards behind him, and it wasn't until Carter was almost on top of her and Lilah had stepped up out of the sunken compartment at the stern onto the high deck on which the mast was mounted that she saw the harpoon gun in the girl's hands.

She was talking. "See?" Lilah said. "I told you I didn't hurt her. Why would I hurt her when I can wait and watch you hurt her for me? It'll be so much more fun." Chattering on and on and on and on.

Standing up, Jules reached out toward Carter. If she could get close to him, maybe they could communicate somehow, send messages through their fingertips, strategize together with subtle nods and winks and flicks of their eyebrows. They could maybe gain the upper hand.

He shook his head, warning her off.

Lilah laughed. "You think it's that easy, Jules?" she said. "Your spell's been broken. He's realized his mistake. Right, Carter?" When Carter didn't respond, she shrieked at him, "Right, Carter?!"

He nodded in a distant way, as though the person he was had fled his body and it was now just a shell with nothing left inside.

Then he and Jules were standing, futilely, next to each other.

"You know what to do, Carter. Put it to her neck."

Carter looked at the knife in his hand. He hedged.

Rage flashed across Lilah's face. "Put it to her neck!"

He did as he was told. He raised the diving knife to Jules's neck and pointed the sharp blade toward her jugular vein.

Jules couldn't tell exactly how close the knife was to her tender skin. She couldn't feel the prick, but that might have been because of her surging emotions, crowding out all sensation. She concentrated on trying to pick up the signs from Carter, some psychic communication from him—a pulse in the tip of the fingers that held her elbow and braced her in place, a tingle in her ear as he telepathically gave her the go signal that would send the two of them rushing toward Lilah in one sudden and overpowering leap—but she received nothing.

As long as Lilah had her finger on the trigger of the harpoon gun, there wasn't much Carter could do but watch her edge closer and closer to the two of them, that psychotic grin trembling on her face, and hope he was ready when she made a mistake.

Lilah wouldn't shut up.

She'd take one step forward, then remember something, some sweet memory, or some insult from the past, and she'd pause to explain it away. To them? To herself? They couldn't really tell.

"Tell her, Carter. Explain to her. Tell her about all the promises you made me. How she was just a test to see how much you loved me. How you're going to come back to me. And we're going to UPenn and—"

Carter couldn't hold back. "Lilah! You didn't even get into UPenn. That's another one of your lies."

Tears were streaming down her face.

She took a step closer. "They're still considering my application," she said. "They know how important it is that we're together."

Carter let loose a cynical laugh. "You're living in

some fantasy world, Lilah. You can't admit the truth to yourself."

She took another step.

Carter waited, watched. He was tense and ready.

There were ropes coiled in piles along the side of the boat, each one connected to a different line, each one controlling a different part of the sails. Lilah didn't see them—she was focused on Carter—but she didn't trip, somehow.

"Tell her, Carter! Tell her! Now! Tell her now!"

"Don't you think you've made your point? I don't love—"

"Tell her! Tell her!" Lilah screamed.

She raised the harpoon gun to her eye and sighted him in it. Her trigger finger tensed. For the moment, anyway, there was nothing Carter could do.

"Jules," he said. "I . . ."

Jules could feel the knife pressed against her skin. It wavered there, and she sensed that Carter was trying to tell her something, but she didn't know what.

The words left his mouth slowly, with a certain amount of ironic defiance. "I love Lilah, Jules." He lessened the pressure of the knife on her neck.

Lilah's face pruned as the emotions surged through her. This was all she wanted. All she'd ever wanted. She took a step forward.

"Tell her again," she said through her tears. She

purred the words, like a child asking for a lullaby.

"Lilah," Carter said. "She heard me."

"I need to hear it again," Lilah said. Her tears overwhelmed her; they filled her words with water.

She took another step.

"I need to hear it! Never stop staying it, Carter."

Another step.

"Never, ever stop."

Another step. Her foot caught in a rope and she tripped slightly, taking her eyes off Carter and Jules for just a second. She kicked at the rope, trying to flip it off her ankle, but it wouldn't twist the right way. She shook her foot, raised it, and balanced on the other one.

Carter squeezed Jules's arm. This was their chance. He dropped the knife from her neck and the two of them scrambled forward toward Lilah just as she freed herself from the rope.

Swinging the harpoon gun in front of her, Lilah tried to regain control, but they were on top of her now.

Carter lunged at her trigger hand with the knife and she swung the harpoon gun like a bludgeon, slashing its sharp, hooked prongs at him.

A slice to his hand, cutting him open, sending the knife soaring out of his grip and off into the water.

She kept slicing. A slice to his forearm. A slice to his face, just missing his eye.

He felt the sting each time. He saw the blood. But

he managed somehow to press forward, to get in close enough to put his hands on the gun and yank at it, trying to twist it away from Lilah.

While Carter and Lilah tugged the gun back and forth, Jules grappled with Lilah's other arm, trying to hold her back as Carter struggled to disarm her.

Lilah was stronger than she looked. All those years of swimming and lifeguarding had turned her legs into sturdy, powerful trunks. Jules couldn't bring her down. Even one-handed, Lilah was able to push her off, fling her away toward the flimsy railing of the boat. Stunned, Jules lay there and watched as Lilah focused her violent energy on Carter.

It was almost as though the two of them were dancing. They stepped forward and back, each of them jockeying for position, their hands crawling up and down the barrel of the harpoon gun, turning it like a baton, each trying to get the other to let go.

And then as Jules got herself back to her feet and began to yank and twist at Lilah again, Carter finally got his hand on the trigger mechanism. He twisted the gun, trying to aim it at Lilah. He squeezed the trigger and the gun leaped back with a ferocious force.

The shot was wide. Trailing its line behind it, it went sailing over Lilah's shoulder, shooting straight up toward the mast, to which the boom had been raised and tied tight out of the way. It clipped one of the lines—the lanyard that happened to be holding the boom in place.

Set loose, the boom, in all its weight, fell with a terrible velocity. It swung down at a horizontal angle, slicing the air and cascading directly toward Carter and Lilah.

Carter was the first to see the boom descend. He recognized the grave danger it posed. He understood that it would strike them if they didn't dive out of the way immediately. And he knew he had to be decisive finally—if he didn't, not a single one of them would survive.

He dove for Jules and grabbed her by the waist. He pulled her overboard. The two of them fell to safety in the water.

A split second later they heard the *whoosh* and the *thud*—a horrible cracking sound that would haunt them forever—and Lilah tumbled off the boat behind them. The blunt impact of the boom had snapped her neck and crushed the temporal bone of her skull. She was dead by the time her body hit the water.

Carter and Jules treaded black water, staring dazed at the wide-open cloudless sky.

Lilah was there, too—she floated facedown, her arms and legs out wide like even in death she wanted to grab hold and squeeze tight the whole world. The blood leaked out of her, great gallons of it, mixing with the tidal waters of the bay, a great cloud of blood that swirled and spread around Carter and Jules.

61

Eventually, the Coast Guard arrived. They told the captain what happened—not all of it; there's no way they could explain all of it—but the essential facts. They didn't try to lie.

Huddled together under a thick felt blanket, they watched as Lilah's body was reeled out of the water. They saw it hanging limp from a sling at the end of a line as the uniformed men struggled to wrangle it onto the deck.

Jules touched Carter's hand, ever so lightly.

"Are you okay?" she asked.

He didn't answer. His eyes were glued to Lilah's body, her head bent down until her chin was in her neck, her arms caught in the sling, out wide like she was on a cross. He shivered, exhausted, chilled to the bone. He felt like he should cry, but he couldn't.

When he finally answered Jules's question, he said, "Not really." He didn't look at her.

They were unlatching the sling now. Lilah's body slumped to the deck.

Jules wanted to tell Carter that it would be okay, but she knew this wasn't true. She huddled close to him.

He covered her hand with his and held it between his two open palms.

"I guess now it's finally over," he said sadly. "Really and truly and forever. We're free now."

She touched his cheek, and he turned to her. She wordlessly tried to press her love into him, to let him know she was still there, to let him know she understood what the freedom they'd gained had cost him.

EPILOGUE
Six months later

It was bitter cold in Philadelphia the night of Valentine's Day. So cold that a winter weather advisory was in effect for the whole region. The UPenn campus closed early, sending students back to their dorms and faculty members to the warmth of their homes. News alerts advised people to stay inside and not to travel—it had snowed a little in the morning and the freezing temperatures could cause black ice to form on the roads.

Some listened to the warnings and made the best out of it. They canceled their special plans, made microwave popcorn with extra butter, curled up on the couch, and cued up a movie instead. Others ignored the risks and went ahead with their fancy dinner reservations, performances at the Kimmel Center, and candlelit walking tours through the city's historic district.

Carter wasn't about to alter course because of a little cold weather, either. He'd put so much effort into this date with Jules—two weeks of research to find the perfect French restaurant, tucked away in a refurbished space on Market Street; five days spent neck-deep in the work of John Keats, looking for the right love poem to give to her; and countless hours of shopping on Jewelers' Row, in search of something delicate that came in a blue velvet box, which he would tuck into his pocket and surprise her with before dessert.

Nothing short of the apocalypse was going to put a stop to their romantic evening.

Or at least, that's what he kept telling himself.

Jules was already twenty minutes late to dinner. Carter slumped forward in his chair and loosened his red tie, staring at the phone that was lying on his appetizer plate. He'd sent Jules a few text messages, asking her where she was, and she hadn't responded. He worried that she might have been in an accident—she'd been working at the Annenberg all day, helping stage design a student production of *The Playboy of the Western World*, so they agreed to meet up at the restaurant.

Carter pictured the twisted wreckage of the bus Jules planned on taking downtown, wrapped around a utility pole, no skid marks on the slick asphalt. Sparking electrical wires tangled around metal and splatters of blood on smashed windows. Exposed bones and mangled limbs.

And dead eyes that would forever haunt the living.

He could feel it happening again. The numbing sensation in his hands and the heavy weight on his chest. The dampness under his arms and the roiling in his stomach. He reached for his napkin and pressed it against his forehead, wiping away beads of sweat. He took a sip of water, his fingers barely able to grip the thin stem of the glass. When his waiter walked by, Carter could see the look of concern on the young man's face. If he didn't go outside and get his breathing under control, he could hyperventilate right now. The restaurant wasn't busy, so it wouldn't cause too much of a commotion, but Carter could still feel the humiliation burning his cheeks.

But before he could stumble toward the front door of the bistro, gasping for air, it opened and Jules walked in.

She was wearing a vintage black peacoat with brass buttons and a tweed pencil skirt that hit right at the top of her knee-high riding boots. Her dark hair hadn't been cut since graduation, so it flowed down almost to her waist. She only had on a hint of makeup—some mascara and burgundy lip stain. Carter wasn't sure if she ever looked this beautiful.

However, when she smiled at him, he was sure that he wanted to kill her.

Jules took off her coat and sat down across from him, pushing the sleeves of her sweater down to her wrists. "Sorry, sorry," she said, pretending not to notice the glare he was giving her. "There was a problem with the sets again. God, Jennifer is such a screwup. I can't believe Harold lets her anywhere near the painting supplies. It's like he's totally clueless to what a space cadet she is."

Carter clutched the napkin tightly, his knuckles turning white. He couldn't care less about the idiots in the drama department. She knew what would happen to him if she kept him waiting and it was clear from her usual, mindless chatter that she just didn't care.

"Anyway, I left as soon as I could." Jules picked up the menu and began studying it, like one of the scripts she had piled up in her room. "Got here in under ten minutes actually, since there was practically nobody on the road."

"Ten minutes? How'd you manage that on the bus?" Carter asked, his voice brimming with suspicion.

Jules sighed. "Craig gave me a ride."

The silence that loomed between them nearly choked the life out of Jules. She hid behind the menu for as long as she could, knowing this uncomfortably quiet moment was the precursor to one of Carter's ugly episodes. She inhaled deeply, preparing for the storm to break, wondering why she was still in this situation. The last few months with him had been pretty unbearable.

And then she remembered. All the nights Carter woke up screaming, terrified by visions of that gruesome day on the boat. All the days he spent locked in his room with the blinds drawn, before he'd seen Dr. Gallagher. If his father hadn't promised a sizable donation to the university, he would be on academic probation, due to three courses he flunked. Leaving him now would make her the biggest bitch in the world, wouldn't it?

"So how is Craig these days?" he said. "Are you two a thing now?"

Jules put her menu on the table and stared him down. "Stop it, Carter," she said firmly.

"What? I'm just asking, since you'd obviously rather spend Valentine's Day with him instead of me," he replied.

"That's not true and you know it," Jules said. "I was late and he offered to give me a lift over here so I wouldn't be any later."

"Really? Wow, he's such a nice guy," Carter said, feigning sincerity. "Why didn't you invite him to come along? I'm sure he could teach me a thing or two. You know, since I'm a shitty boyfriend and everything."

"You're not—look, I'm sorry I wasn't on time. You went through a lot of trouble to plan tonight. But there's no need to bring Craig into this, okay?" said Jules.

"Why not? He's the reason you were ignoring me."

"I wasn't ignoring you. I just didn't get a chance to

respond to the zillion texts you sent me," Jules snapped.

"Excuse me for being scared that you might be dead in a ditch somewhere," Carter whisper-yelled. "If I knew you were just fucking around with Craig, then I guess I would have relaxed and played Angry Birds."

Jules swiftly pushed back her chair, the feet screeching against the floor. "I'm going to the bathroom," she said through clenched teeth. "When I get back, you better do or say something to convince me not to walk out of here."

As Jules stalked off to the restroom, Carter's head bowed forward. He covered his face with his hands and cursed at himself for acting like an asshole. He hated when he did this to her. He hated how awful and helpless he made her feel. He hated just how familiar his words were, the sound of an unrelenting voice constantly echoing in his mind.

But did he hate it all enough to stop?

Carter stuffed his hand in his pocket, but not the one with the blue velvet box—the one with the small blue plastic bottle, filled with tiny yellow pills. His gaze drifted over to Jules's purse, which was hung on the back of her chair. He thought about how long she'd be in the bathroom. Two minutes? Maybe three?

He desperately tried to think of convincing things to do and say, just like Jules had asked him to, but instead he convinced himself that he needed to do something else. Something that he knew he could never take back.

He leaned over and quickly grabbed her bag by the strap, opening it and finding her phone in a side pouch. He plucked it out and swiped his fingers across the screen, accessing her text messages.

Twenty-three from him.

And one from Craig.

ACKNOWLEDGMENTS

Special thanks to Claudia Gabel, Katherine Tegen, Melissa Miller, Alexandra Arnold, Lauren Flower, Casey McIntyre, Onalee Smith, Kathryn Silsand, and Joel Tippie for their work on this book.

Read on for a sneak peek

at *Reckless Hearts*,

another sizzling

page-turner set in

Dream Point, Florida . . .

1

DP Movers—their slogan was "You point the way, Dream Point!"—had arrived this morning at eight thirty. For the past three hours, they'd been carting boxes of clothes and books and kitchen utensils, and mostly, the carved figurines and masks and exotic musical instruments Jake Gordon's mother had collected from all over the world, into the flatbed of their truck and stacking them up in tight systematic rows. The moving truck, a pale cavernous brick of sea-foam aluminum, was almost full now. Almost ready to haul the history of Jake's life across town to the north shore, where the fancy people in Dream Point lived in their elaborate mansions, bunkered between their security gates and their private beaches.

Watching the movers sweat in the crisp December air, Jake had a hard time getting his head around the fact that he would be one of those fancy people now. He didn't feel like he'd changed at all, but his mother, Janey, had married Cameron Pendergrass, maybe the fanciest of them all. He owned the Mariana Hospitality Group, a chain of hotels all over the world, including three massive, full-service island resorts, one in the Bahamas, one in Antigua, and one on some island in the South China Sea. He was easily the richest person in Dream Point.

As the stringy tattooed guys who looked like they shouldn't be anywhere near this strong carried the last of the boxes from the house, Jake sat in a wicker-backed kitchen chair, its legs sinking into the moist soil of the front yard. He stared out at Greenvale Street and tried to distract himself from thinking how completely his life would change by wondering what would happen to all the stuff they were leaving behind. The couch, the dining room table, the bed he'd slept in since he was six years old, even the chair he was sitting in now—they were ditching all of it. The white stucco bungalow that Jake had always known as home—new people would be living in it by New Year's.

And Elena Rios, his best friend and partner in skeptical endurance of the cliquey, shallow life at Chris Columbus High, who knew all his secrets, or all but one—she'd no longer be living right next door. She'd promised to hang out with him and watch the movers work this morning, and he'd dragged two wicker-backed chairs out onto the lawn, but the one next to him was still empty.

He'd texted her three times already, giving her status updates on the movers' progress, and all he'd heard back was one hard-to-interpret message saying, "THESE THINGS TAKE TIME ;D." Tilted on the uneven soil of the lawn, the chair looked sad and lonely beside him.

"Hey, yo," the crew captain called to him from the back of the truck, squinting under the dingy red Santa hat he'd draped over his head. "You wanna sign off on this, or what?" He wagged a tin clipboard at Jake as though he thought Jake should have been able to read his mind.

Jake wandered over to the truck. His mother had put him in charge. She had to be at Tiki Tiki Java, the coffeehouse she owned on Shore Drive, and Cameron, obviously, wasn't interested in spending his precious time coordinating with moving companies—he had employees for that. School was out for Christmas break, so it wasn't like Jake had anywhere better to be, anyway.

"Just the boxes, yeah?" the mover said. "That's some nice stuff in there. You're leaving all of it?"

"Yeah," Jake said.

"The TV? That speaker system? Shit ain't cheap."

"Salvation Army is coming to take it away."

"Oh?" The guy raised an eyebrow. He was trying too hard not to seem overly curious. "When's that?"

"This afternoon," Jake lied.

The guy ticked his cheek. He braced the clipboard

on his forearm and held the pen rubber-banded to it out to Jake. "You gotta push hard to get through all three layers," he said.

Jake signed the sheet and reminded the guy that his mother would be there to sign on the other side.

As the guy rounded up his three workers and closed the truck, Jake headed toward the house for one last look.

He checked his watch. It was almost noon. Still no sign of Elena.

She didn't usually flake like this, at least not with him. He knew she was elusive. She liked it that way. Enjoy being with me while I'm here and don't ask for more. That was her attitude. But Jake had always been the exception to this rule. He was the person she *didn't* hide from.

As he wandered the rooms of the house one last time, it took every ounce of his being to restrain himself from frantically bombarding Elena with the kind of needy, selfish where-are-you texts that he knew she hated getting from other people—her sister, her father, the couple of boys she'd briefly, disastrously dated.

He'd known her all his life. There was a photo of the two of them in their diapers sitting in the dirt under the swing set in Seminole Park, reaching out to fumble at each other's chubby hands. She'd been there for him when his parents' marriage finally broke up and his father moved permanently to the Keys. He'd been there for her throughout the long saga of her mother's death of ovarian cancer and the roller coaster of chemo and radiation therapy, of hope and despair and hope and despair that had consumed her life for a year and a half. He'd watched her grow from a sassy, string-bean tomboy to a dark-haired, dark-eyed, darkly intelligent young woman whose sense of the world was as off-kilter as his own.

He adored her.

The truth was, he loved her.

He'd known it forever. Since middle school, at least, when they'd both begun to wonder why the other kids in their class seemed to always, only want to talk about LeBron James and Miley Cyrus, when he'd begun to sense that Elena was the only person he knew who thought deeply about the world. She was curious, so curious that after she'd seen *Spirited Away*, the surreal, slightly spooky Miyazaki movie, she'd explored where it had come from and uncovered a whole world of Japanese anime. She didn't care if nobody else had heard of this stuff. It was interesting to her, and that was enough.

He loved that confidence he saw in her. He loved her compulsive joy, the goofy silliness she allowed herself to indulge in. And her fiery loyalty, the way she'd leap to the fight when she felt like he, or her sister, Nina, needed defending.

But it wasn't just that. Lately, it was physical, too.

5

Her olive skin. Her perfect toes. The way she wore her hair in that modified pixie cut, close and tight around the back, her curls swooping up over her forehead. The sweet curve of her hips and the faint strawberry mark that peeked out like a tattoo from the side of her bikini bottoms.

If she weren't his best friend, he would have admitted it long ago. Even though he was just moving across town, he felt he had to tell her now. At least then she'd know that all those songs he'd written for "Sarah," the "girlfriend" who "lived down the beach from his dad in the Keys," had really been about her.

If only she'd come out to say good-bye, he could say the lines he'd been rehearsing all week.

He sent her one last text. "THEY'RE DONE. GOTTA GO IN 10."

She responded immediately. "LOOK OUT THE WINDOW."

And there she was in the chair he'd put out for her, casual, in tight jean shorts crisply folded up just above her knees, sporting her favorite *Cowboy Bebop* T-shirt. She made a goofy face, crossing her eyes and sticking out her tongue, briefly, then returned to hunching over the open laptop balanced on her thighs just in time to stop it from falling off.

The future—the future he'd imagined, anyway— flashed in front of Jake. Him moseying out of the house, hands in his pockets, playing it cool. Just as he reaches her, Elena looks up from the computer and something in her eyes says she knows what he's about to say. That wry grin of hers, capable of communicating both her relish in experience and her ironic commentary on how silly life can be, breaks over her face. And before he can even say, "It's always been you. I can't hide it anymore," she's up on her tiptoes, her arms stretched out around his neck. A kiss that releases the years of longing between them into the world.

He could almost feel it electrifying his cells already.

The slow walk out of the house was the easy part, even if he could feel his hands nervously shaking in his pockets.

"Hey," he said, from doorway.

"Hey is for horses," she said with a wink. And there was that grin, but it didn't convey the revelation of longing he'd imagined. "Sorry it took me so long." She patted the six-year-old MacBook that, through the strategic placement of black electrical tape, she'd made look like a monster chomping down on the Apple logo. "Technology. I had to reboot this sucker like five times this morning."

"Shaun White's not what he used to be, huh?" Jake said. Shaun White was the name Elena had given the computer.

"Shaun White should have retired years ago."

"Maybe I can ask Cameron to buy you an upgrade," Jake said. He meant it, though the idea of actually asking Cameron for anything made him nervous. He'd never spent any time around super-rich people and he wasn't sure he understood the codes they lived by.

Elena shot him a look that said, *Yeah right*. "I'd never let you put yourself in that situation." She focused on the screen for a second and tapped the touch pad a few times. "I mean, he didn't even come help you pack up."

"He's a busy guy."

"I know. I'm just saying," she said, protectively defending him.

Elena locked eyes with him for a second, and as her face softened and seemed to reach out to him, he knew she'd seen through to the part of him that was scared about all the change that moving into Cameron's mansion on the beach would create in his life.

"Come look at what I made you," she said.

Jake sat in the chair next to her, conscious of her body heat, not getting too close with his elbow or knee for fear of touching her—if he touched her, he'd melt.

"Come on, Jaybird," she said. "You have to be able to see the screen." And she threw her arm over his shoulder and mussed his hair, like a buddy, like she was about to give him a noogie. "You ready?"

She adjusted the volume and clicked play on her video-editing program.

First came the music. "You've Got a Friend in Me" from *Toy Story*. Then the delicate, slightly nervous script she always used in her animations.

For Jaybird, it said.

Jake immediately felt the emotions swell in his chest.

The animated characters that always represented the two of them in Elena's animes—Electra, the tough girl with spiky hair of black flames, heavy kohl eyes, padded, studded leather armor, and jet-flight platform shoes; and Jaybird, tall and skinny with knob knees and a constant bewildered expression on his face—performed a choreographed dance to the music. A backbeat kicked in, and Electra grew larger and larger, her mouth opening until the darkness inside swallowed up the screen.

As Elena's voice rap-talked over the *Toy Story* song, stylized freeze-frame images of the two of them floated in and out of the frame—highlights from their years of friendship: the day they raced their bikes all the way to the Seminole monument in the middle of town and then climbed triumphantly to the top and sat on the Native American warrior's back; the time Jake's mom took the two of them to Disney World and they spent the whole day pretending they weren't having as much fun as they really were; the moment when Jake played his guitar in front of an audience for the first time and Elena was right there clapping from the front row. Image after image of the two of them sharing each other's lives.

The song, or poem, or rap, or whatever Elena was calling the spoken word she'd layered over the images explained what was happening in them. She talked about the day her mom died and the long walk Jake had taken with her, not speaking at all, because what was there to do but be there, a presence by her side, ready when she needed him. She talked about the day he found out his parents were splitting up, how they'd snuck into the recycling center on the west side of town after dark and let out all their rage by shattering bottles against the wall, bottle after bottle after bottle after bottle, until they were giddy, until they'd almost forgotten how sucky the day had been.

"Most boys only want one thing," she said at one point. "But Jaybird's different. Jaybird sees the all of me."

The anime ended with another scrawled fragment of text. *Jaybird, don't you ever change!*

Jake was devastated. Not because he was sad but because he was so deeply touched by her work. He stared at the screen, frozen on the final image of the two of them holding hands, and he couldn't help but wonder if she'd be saying all these things if she knew how much he wanted to be more than friends with her.

"It's just a rough cut, but . . . what do you think?" she said, the look on her face betraying a real and desperate need to know he thought it was good.

"I love it," Jake said, trying to twist his lips into an

earnest smile so she'd think he was telling the truth.

Her elegant eyebrows were arched in expectation, her whole face open, waiting.

"Should I post it to AnAmerica? You wouldn't mind?" AnAmerica was a web forum where Elena and other anime-obsessed kids from all over the country shared their animations with one another.

"Yeah. Yeah. Absolutely, you should post it. It's great."

But part of him was disappointed, too. No way could he confess his love to her now. Because what if she rejected him? What if she said, *Sorry, I love you, man, but I don't love you like* that? Better to be with her, even as friends, than to lose her friendship because he wanted more out of it than she did.

He rubbed his hands back and forth across his jeans, unsure what to do. "It's time," he said. He stood, dazed, and picked up his chair.

She flipped her lower lip down, trying to be cute as she made her sad face. When he didn't respond, she said, "Is everything okay?"

"Yeah. I've . . . I just have to lock up the house." He knew himself. He felt itchy. He had to get away. To go somewhere alone and lick his wounds. "And then I've got to go. I'm already late meeting Mom. Can you grab that chair?"

Leaving her computer on the lawn, she swung her chair above her head and carried it inside.

When it was time for them to say good-bye, he awkwardly held open his long arms for a hug. She fell into his chest, squeezing him tight, which was nice, but he couldn't bring himself to squeeze her back. He was afraid, if he did, that she'd see through him and learn his real feelings. Instead, he patted her chastely on the back.

"Don't forget us little people," she said.

"I won't. I'll see you soon," he said. "I'll call you every day. You'll see."

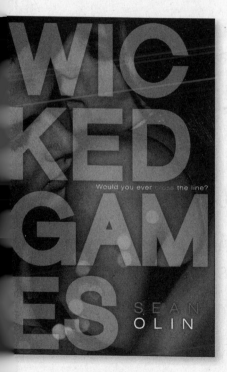